~ KENT DAVIS ~

A RIDDLE IN RUBY

GREENWILLOW BOOKS
An Imprint of HarperCollins*Publishers*

This book is a work of fiction. References to real people, events, establishments, organizations, or locales are intended only to provide a sense of authenticity, and are used to advance the fictional narrative. All other characters, and all incidents and dialogue, are drawn from the author's imagination and are not to be construed as real.

A Riddle in Ruby

Text copyright © 2015 by Kent Davis

All rights reserved. No part of this book may be used or reproduced in any manner whatsoever without written permission except in the case of brief quotations embodied in critical articles and reviews. Printed in the United States of America. For information address HarperCollins Children's Books, a division of HarperCollins Publishers, 195 Broadway, New York, NY 10007. www.harpercollinschildrens.com

The text of this book is set in 11.5-point Sabon MT.

Book design by Sylvie Le Floc'h

Library of Congress Cataloging-in-Publication Data

Davis, Kent, (date.)

A riddle in Ruby / by Kent Davis

    pages cm

Summary: "In an era called The Chemystral Age, magically augmented alchemy and chemistry have thrust an alternate version of eighteenth-century colonial America forward into industrialization. Thirteen-year-old Ruby is a smuggler's daughter and picklock prodigy navigating a world filled with cobalt gearbeasts, alchemical automatons, and devilish secret societies"—Provided by publisher.

ISBN 978-0-06-236834-8 (hardback.)

[1. Fantasy. 2. Adventure and adventurers—Fiction. 3. Alchemy—Fiction.] I. Title.

PZ7.1.D36Ri 2015   [Fic]—dc23   2015010296

15 16 17 18 19 CG/RRDH 10 9 8 7 6 5 4 3 2 1

Greenwillow Books

For Anna,
dearest of catalysts

CHAPTER I

*Sparking fire. The wheel. The written word. Each changed
the rules of our world forever. I have newly met a sister
to these titans. Her name is Chemystry.*
— Sir Francis Bacon, 1626,
Invisible College, London

❧BOSTON, BRADFORDUM COLONY—1718 ❧

Never pick a chemystral lock.

Ruby could have yelled those words from the
rooftops. But she wasn't on a rooftop. She was halfway
underneath a handcart stalled in the mad river of Stout
Street shoppers. A squat alloy trunk on sturdy iron
wheels, it was strong enough to turn a cannon blast,
and the doors on its rear were secured with a devilishly
complex lock.

All well and good; Ruby ate devilishly complex locks for breakfast. But this one was stocked with a reservoir of aqua fortis acid. The alchemists' apprentices called the stuff the Tinkers' handshake. At the slightest jiggle, the slightest misstep, acid would bubble out of the lock in a golden wave to devour careless thieves' hands and wrists down to the bone.

Never pick a chemystral lock.

Never, ever pick a chemystral lock on a busy Boston street, at high noon, on your back, with one hand, and blind.

Ruby stretched her arm up from under the cart, playing her fingers across the carved symbols on the rear doorplate until they found a keyhole.

With her thumb and forefinger she slipped her alloyed glass pick out of her sleeve. Any other implement— steel, iron, bronze—would have liquefied at first contact with the lock's deadly insides. Gwath Maxim Fourteen: "Always Use the Proper Tool."

The other proper tool, besides the pick, was what appeared to be her ruined foot. It was a horrible sight.

She and Gwath had beaten the old shoe within an inch of its life. It looked as if it had been crushed by a team of oxen, and the blood seeping from every corner would have turned her stomach if she had not known that it was nothing more than water, boiled ox hoof, and just the proper sprinkle of powdered rusted iron.

Gwath, playing the part of her master, drew all eyes to her crumpled paw like a mother bear, roaring at the two men at the front of the cart.

This final test was a true challenge, gruesome and grim, but Gwath would not have given it to her if he had not thought she could succeed.

She found the first of five tumblers and teased it open. It felt like old glue in there.

As if he had heard her thinking of him, Gwath launched into another tirade at the men.

She was good at locks. One day she might be great. But Gwath, he was a masterful sharper and in his element. He thundered: "Look at his foot. Look at it! It may well be ruined!" Ruby took the cue and wailed, lifting the injury from the ground. She took care to pitch her voice low. While her dark hair was pinned under the cap and her wiry frame showed them "apprentice boy," a girlish wail could give it all away.

"This is no fault of mine, sir," the Tinker said. "The boy should watch his step. This cart carries a delicate and precious package. We are anxiously expected, and we must, I fear, keep moving forward." Anger and fear fought for room in the twitchy little alchemyst's voice. Their magic—or science, call it what you will—had fueled the wonders of the Chemystral Age. But Tinkers still were men, and still they could be duped.

Gwath's voice shifted into a kind of gargle—part angry crow, part suffocating fish.

"The boy's fault? Your guard there moves like a drunken oliphant, and your cart has smashed my boy's precious foot to flinders. Look upon it!" Ruby flailed her leg about. "My lad is the assistant to the dancing master at my house. He is one of the most agile young men in Bradfordum Colony. He has played for the governor, even for the foreman of your own guild!"

She grinned.

Something twitched in the lock.

She froze.

She counted to five. Acid did not pour from the keyhole.

Careless. Cocksure. She grinned wider. She might be all of those, sure, but today was her day.

Gwath was too distracting. She blocked him out. Besides, they had practiced the sharp to death. Threats, allusions to powerful friends in the guild, expulsion and ruin for the man, prison and ruin for the guard, tra-la-la, thus was the sharper's task. Distract and worry, screen and sham. And all the while, in the shadows, the picker picked.

The second tumbler fell. Ruby wrapped calm around her like a cloak, and the words, the sounds of the busy street, even her sight, they all receded, leaving only the intricate tactile music of her hand, her pick, and their dangerous chemystral partner.

The third tumbler fell. Then the fourth. The path to glory.

"What have we here, then?"

A harder and leaner voice hauled her attention out of the lock and back to the street. On the other side of Gwath's thick, stockinged legs and gaily buckled shoes sat two pairs of pristine black boots with brilliantly white linen spats. Barnacles. It was Redcoats. The strong arm of the king.

Yet they, too, could see only her feet. She redoubled her efforts.

Gwath bent over her legs and squeezed her ankle twice, the signal for her to stop. Gwath Maxim Five was very clear: "Meddle Not With the Royal Military." But she was so close! The fifth tumbler had started to dance. A few more seconds and it would be open.

"His Majesty's Finest. You arrive in the very nick of time!" Gwath said. As he labored up to meet the soldiers, he pulled Ruby's leg once, hard. She slid toward him under the cart, her hand at least a foot away from the lock. It might as well have been ten thousand miles. She lay back onto the street with a moan, playing her part. Inside, she blazed with fury.

≈≈≈

An hour later Ruby waited in the deserted little walkway between Chubb's Dry Goods and Napper's Pub, just up the hill from Ruck's Wharf. She folded her apprentice clothes into the leather satchel, shoved the whole package into the nook in the wall, then replaced the loose board that covered it. She hitched up her patchwork pants and wrenched the floppy fisherman's cap down over her eyes. With a crane of the neck and a befuddled hunch of the shoulders she changed herself into Stonemason's Boy. Leaning into the shadows underneath the eaves, she waited, hucking pebbles at the wall, as a stonemason's boy might do. The morning had been an utter failure; and when would she have another chance at journeyman?

Gwath was coming up the hill from the wharf, framed by a leafless forest of masts. The one to the far right might be the *Thrift*. He had discarded the merchant's waistcoat and priggish wig for the chalky clothes of a stonemason, and his face was no longer flushed and unhealthy but seamed and leathered.

"Master," she said. He walked past her.

She followed him down the walkway into the sudden

chaos of Charter Street on a market morning. He bulled ahead with a stark look.

"Master?" she asked again. "What is it?"

"What do you see there?" He nodded at a chemystral meat cart, manned by a frantic little Irishman and fueled by an alchemycal cell hidden in its innards. The pastries turned around on a tinker's wheel, and a small silver flame cooked them from underneath.

"Pies! Pies!" the vendor called. "Meat pies for your sweet love! Bring her these home today and she'll forget where you were last night!" Two Puritan ladies ruffled like partridges as they passed the vendor, all pinched faces and whispered scandal.

Ruby answered Gwath. "A man who fears he has gone too far."

"Why?"

"He presses. Tattered coat, mismatched boots. He must have bought that cart on credit. I wager he's starting to cotton he won't pay the Tinkers back for that contraption in a lifetime of pies."

A dock worker, grunting under the weight of two

huge sacks, hands chapped and raw, shouldered his way past Gwath.

Gwath glanced at the teamster; then his eyes bored into Ruby. "Is that what we do?"

"Carry too much weight? Not I." She patted her stomach. "I almost never eat rice pudding, and with all manner of sweaty work on the *Thrift*—"

He flicked her on the head with his finger. "Do we blindly bull ahead, no matter the risk?"

She rolled her eyes. "Gwath Maxim Two: Use The World As It Is, Not As It Should Be. That hurt."

"Then dodge."

"You are too fast."

"Then keep your sass in the lockup."

She knew what this was about now. "I almost solved that lock! I did!"

He leaned in, jaw tense. "You almost solved us both into the governor's stockade! Your father would have been wroth, and the *Thrift* would have lost passengers while they tried to get us out. You have not spent time in a Boston jail. They are unfriendly."

"I will solve for nothing, ever, if you keep making a coward of me! I can handle myself."

Gwath raised up in the middle of the street to glance about. A large tinker's carriage lumbered around the corner and headed toward them. There was a gleam in his eye that she did not care for. To her credit, she sensed that he was going to reach for her. He was just too fast. He snagged a fistful of her shirt and wrenched her into the air with one hand. Over his shoulder the massive coach bore down on them. Gwath pulled her face close to his, and a forbidding challenge lurked there.

"You think you can handle yourself, monkey? Let us see."

The carriage was moving faster now. The crowd in the street parted before it like water, but the two of them stood dead in its path.

CHAPTER 2

What Fermat calls Alchemy is no boon to the virtuous. This "science" is a Wolf in the Sheep Pen. No good will come of it.
—Louis de Nogaret, Archbishop of Toulouse,
speech to the College of Cardinals, 1639

Cram loved every little thing about working for the Tinkers. Ever since he was old enough to hear words and shuck peas, his Mam had sung the praises of their chief, good old Francis Bacon. They say that he changed the world a hundred years ago, when he set snow on fire. Cram didn't know about that, but he did know one thing: A gutter punk like him could never have got what he got and did what he done and been what he now was in the bad old days of lords and ladies and by-your-leaves.

The coachman's seat sat high above the street, where every John and Judith could see your quality. The livery was flash. The deep blue sash on his shoulder marked him. Not just in Boston, but in Philadelphi and even as far south as Charles Towne, folk would know he was up to snuff. A man of the New World cut his own path and cared not a whit for the tired arguments of the Old. He couldn't give two snaps for what the priests and kneelers called the godlessness of the Tinkers' machines. The carriage had shining, sturdy wheels and a fresh load of chemystral flux to keep it moving, and best of all, it moved *itself*.

He turned the corner with a full head of steam and opened the wheel a bit more, laying into the horn again. The shops and people blurred into glimpses: a silver-nosed tinker; gearcraft harps in a window; a sign that boasted TINNE SALT—FRESH! Cram bared his teeth to the wind as the ironshod wheels clunked on the cobblestones of the narrowing street. On the left, a crowd of soot-covered grindshop serfs filled the walk, stumbling shoulder to shoulder out of a night smithy, blind and blinking in the sun. On the right, a parade of chem carts crept out into the way, hawking nitrate-singed meat and cut-rate mechanicals to the early-morning crowds. A donkey launched itself out of the way and galloped headfirst into a bakery.

Two figures stood unaware, square in the path of the hurtling carriage. A hulk of a fella was taking it to a sprat of a youngun. Cram grabbed a lever carved with the face of a screaming imp and leaned on the gas horn, but they didn't hear. The giant had lifted the young boy up by the collar with one arm and was shaking the feathers out of him, shouts drowned by the heavy clockwork of the carriage's gears.

Crowds left, market right, he could not turn.

Cram pulled on the imp whistle three times hard, and the boy looked up, eyes wide and squirmed more forcefully. The big man, though, stood planted in the street, yelling into the face of this boy, as Cram, his passenger, and eighty stone of metal and gears bore down on them.

Cram lunged for the floor of the bench and threw open the door to the tiny cabinet there. It was intricately carved and bore a red painted legend: "EMPLOY THEE ONLY IN DYRE AND SINGULAR CIRCUMSTANCE!" Inside was a red lever.

Cram pulled it.

CHAPTER 3

THROW DOWN THE PLOW.
TAKE UP THE FLASK.
A YOUNG MAN'S FUTURE
IS THE ALCHEMYST'S TASK.
—Poster searching for workers,
Tinkers' Compound, New Jamestown

Gwath was hurting her. He was shaking Ruby by the neck like a ferret shakes a field mouse and yelling at the top of his lungs.

"You daft boy! You left the mortar out, and now it's hard as stone," he bellowed. "The wall is ruined! The orphans will have no place to play!"

The carriage careened closer, moving far too fast.

She cursed. This was the test. This was it.

Atop the massive carriage a rat-faced young rascal in clothes too high for his pockmarked features reached down beside him, perhaps to hold on as he flattened two victims into griddle cakes.

Gwath turned to watch their oncoming doom, but Ruby couldn't. She closed her eyes.

FOOOMP.

The sound was one-half cannon and one-half geyser, and it blasted her eyes open. A cloud of soft blue mist billowed out of the carriage, eclipsing its lower half. The gas thickened in a heartbeat into what looked for all the world to be a giant pat of blue butter. The goo somehow held the wheels and axles motionless. The carriage hung, midroll, in the air for a moment, impossible, until the groaning mass of wood and metal cracked at the front axle, and the whole mess toppled onto its side in the street.

The street was silent. Then it erupted in bedlam. There was yelling. There was praying.

You could hop across the cobblestones between the front edge of the carriage and where she hung from

Gwath's hand. He gave her a look and dropped her on the cobblestones, where she lay in a heap.

The driver, a boy of her age and all eyebrows and corncob chin, was shouting at Gwath. He was struggling out of a contraption of straps and ribbons that was dangling him upside down from the coachman's bench.

Gwath pulled him out of the harness and back into the crowd, numbering his injuries, accusing the boy of incompetence, and spouting whatever nonsense might keep the crowd interested. Tra-la-la.

Nothing else had gone right. Instead of being docked in a concealing sea of market day shoppers, the carriage floated alone in a wide, empty circle, surrounded by curious eyes. The crash was too much of a novelty, and far too many were ignoring the dustup between Gwath and the driver. Ruby was the only other sight within the ring of the crowd. In moments some well-meaning soul would run to her aid. Nothing for it. She had to turn into the wind.

She pulled her cap down over her eyes. The Injured Stonemason's Boy limped over to the coach and scrambled up onto the top of the exposed side, opening the side door, obviously concerned for whatever passengers were still inside.

Ruby levered the door up and leaned down into the dark, well-appointed travelers' chamber. There was only one passenger, an older boy lying at ease in a jumble of cushions and curtains, with what appeared to be a blend of currant jelly and gooseberry tart stuck in his black hair and covering his face.

She flashed her fiercest smile, produced a knife out of her sleeve, and said, "Stand and deliver, sir. Your money or your life."

Normally the victims cringed and babbled, called for their coachman, who had usually just chased off after Gwath, and then obligingly produced their ready money and precious things.

This boy, however, stared at her, and he laughed.

Then he drew, very quickly, truly very quickly, a dueling sword out of his embroidered waistcoat. The blade was just long enough that the point pressed against a spot just under Ruby's left eye.

"You don't want to use that knife on me, boy," he said. "Now make your way. I have places to be and people to see, and your life is worth more than all the shillings you might loot from passersby." And then he winked at her. He *winked* at her, and his wrist flicked and Ruby felt a sting beneath her eye.

She reared back and vaulted down from the upended coach. She ran, bare feet slapping on the cobblestones, into the crowd, into an alley, and over a garden wall, hotfooting it into the maze of alleys and secret spaces that could hide her from anyone who might think to follow.

Just after midday, cleaned up and ready to return home, she emerged from Whistler's Alley onto the wharf. She once again wore the sensible frock her father insisted she wear on excursions into port. These days this felt more like a costume: the faded secondhand dress, the long sleeves to protect her tanned arms, the demure black braid, the pinching shoes.

As planned, Gwath was waiting for her on the back

stoop of the whale blubber works, working on a steaming meat pie.

He eyed her as she plopped down beside him. The bushy blond stonemason was gone, replaced by the dark olive skin and shaven skull of his true face. Gwath was a mystery. "No loot," she said.

He grunted. "No pie for you, then." He popped the last bite into his mouth and stood. "Keep working, and it will come. Come on. Thirteen summers doesn't mean your father won't worry if you ain't home by three bells."

They walked around the corner of the blubber works and into the early-afternoon lull of the wharf. The smell of salt and tarred wood welcomed her home.

"You think Skillet or my father found passengers for the southern leg?" A crowd of sailors rolling barrels up the gangway of a man-'o-war caught her eye.

Gwath said nothing. Indeed, he had stopped short, standing in the middle of the wharf, staring.

"Yes," Gwath replied.

She followed his gaze to the gangway of her father's ship, the *Thrift*, and saw two figures bargaining furiously with her father, hemmed in by a precarious tower of steamer trunks and a donkey covered in flour.

One was a rat-faced boy wearing a blue sash, with a bandage wrapped around his head. The other wore a tricorne and fashionable shoes, and sported a familiar rapier at his hip.

"Well, it certainly won't be a boring trip to Philadelphi," Ruby breathed, and she tucked herself behind Gwath as they hurried toward the other gangplank.

CHAPTER 4

It is the inner spirit that fuels chemystral science. Without that spirit, I shall fail at the simplest chemystral task.

If I have enough fuel? I can tear the world asunder or steal fire from the gods themselves.

—Robert Boyle, ed., FRS, *Principia Chymia*, 1666

❦LONDON, ENGLAND—ONE MONTH BEFORE ❧

The automaton was the spitting image of a mouse. It perched on the sign above the Clove and Camel and fixed its whirling eyes on a young lone figure hurrying into the venerable coffeehouse. This was nothing new. This particular mouse had stood vigil atop this particular sign for more than fifty years, since the night it was fabricated, the same night Grocers' Hall had burned to the ground in the Great London Fire of 1666. On a normal day it would have quick-burned a chemystral image of the visitor into the record in its tail, and that would have been that. The creature's masters had a long-standing interest in the inventors, tinkers, and alchemysts of the district, which was quickly becoming one of the greatest centers of tinkercraft in the world, and wanted their news updated daily.

Today was not a normal day, however. The tiny levers and interlocking gears inside the mouse had been delicately reconfigured. Its tiny chemystral brain ordered it to vacate its post and follow this visitor through the Clove and Camel. So it turned on its little carbon claws and skittered through a hole in the old brick wall to scamper unseen on beams above a group of men and women engaged in a debate over whether liquid silver could think for itself.

The visitor was simple to track as he hurried through the main common room and into the bustling kitchen. He retained his fashionable cloak and tricorne, as well as the richly embroidered waistcoat, sword, intricately carved sheath, and buckled shoes that would indicate a gentleman of some means to other passersby. He wore no wig and gathered his black hair in a queue. This data indicated a high likelihood that the visitor was under sixteen years of age. The mouse had no room in its bubbling brain for social analysis, but the visitor's silhouette in the guttering light had a certain *weight* that separated him from the shapes of the cooks, servers, and coffee hawks that he passed.

The visitor stopped on a small landing at the bottom of a flight of narrow stairs in the back of the kitchen. A stout, anonymous door barred the way forward, guarded by a stout, anonymous man. The mouse's chemystral cache recorded a sword and two clocklock pistols at the guard's hip.

The visitor began: "Thought, grant us grace."

The big man said, "Grace, protect us all." His eyes lingered on the dueling sword, and he snorted, "Your business here?"

"I am to see Lord Godfrey Boyle. I am expected." The visitor bowed deeply.

"Your scraping won't do you much good here. You are the sprat called Lord Athen?"

"I am."

"Welcome to Grocers' Hall. You are expected."

The man took a large silver key from the leather string around his neck and placed it in the sturdy, anonymous lock under the doorknob of the sturdy, anonymous door. The silver key, which was large and wide, appeared to have no chance whatsoever at fitting into the small, narrow keyhole. It did indeed fit, however. The key and the lock *adjusted* themselves, living metal flowing into agreement. The door swung open with a creak.

The figure—Lord Athen—hurried through the door. As the guard turned his back and began to close the door, the little mouse jumped through the air, landed with a very soft clink, and scurried between the man's legs.

On the other side was another landing graced with a little iron table. The table supported two or three artifacts that looked like oil lamps, if oil lamps were also made of gray, dappled metal topped with some kind of smoky crystal instead of glass. As the door closed and light disappeared, Lord Athen picked up a lamp by its base and turned a small wheel. The growing light revealed a delicate nose and a resolute chin. It also filled the landing and a stairway below it with unwavering pale blue illumination.

The stairs were much older than the polished cherry floors of the coffeehouse. Furrows made by the feet of generations of travelers had cut into the stone of the steps, and the ancient walls wept moisture. At the bottom waited an even more stout, but emphatically unanonymous door. It was bronze, triple braced, and covered in signs and equations that would deflect a warship's broadside with the indifference of a mountain. It had no keyhole and no handle. Lord Athen hesitated, then removed his sword from its sheath. He searched the door for a moment and then pressed the hilt into a small hole in the upper right of the portal. The mouse registered a small click. The bronze door swung open silently.

Beyond was a large circular room with a very old mosaic on its floor. It was not a picture of a knight slaying a dragon. Nor was it a scene of grand armies or ancient kings and queens. It was of a pepper mill, and it seemed very well taken care of.

Eight corridors flared off from the circular room, and Lord Athen walked to the one opposite the bronze door. The other corridors opened onto high-ceilinged laboratories, and the mouse glimpsed beakers, forges, scales, burners, and innumerable gears. This corridor ended at a plain stained wooden door, upon which Lord Athen knocked.

A voice from behind the door called, "Enter."

Beyond the door was another circular room, made from ancient brick. Floor-to-ceiling bookshelves covered every wall. An older man in plain breeches and waistcoat, an open collar, and rolled-up sleeves stood with his back to the door at a long table, also filled with books, burners, and an ivory scale.

The mouse hid under a bust of Zosimos of Panopolis, a classical scholar of chemystral science, of whose rich role in alchemycal history it was completely unaware.

The boy scuffed his heel against the stone floor and looked about. "So this is where you spend your days now that the hierophants have shown you the door."

Snapping his book shut with a clap, the old man

turned to face the visitor. He had a rough egg of a face, with a fringe of white hair. "The work we do here is essential. You know this."

"I know no such thing," Athen replied. "Though I am certain the wardens of the Royal Society would be most intrigued to discover unlicensed, unsupervised alchemy not a quarter mile from the palace."

"We have maintained balance for hundreds of years."

The man leaned back against the table, popped open a small crystal bottle of oil, and began rubbing it into his hands, which were stained and burned along the fingers and palms.

"Your tinker's claws betray you, Lord Godfrey," Athen said. "How long until you are found by the Reeve?"

Lord Godfrey Boyle, high alchemyst of the Worshipful Order of Grocers, ignored the question. "And yours?" He nodded at Athen's gloves and asked, "Why the finery?"

Athen answered, "Delicate skin requires protection, you know."

The man sniffed. It was eloquent.

"You sent word that I should prepare for a trip, did you not?"

They stared at each other. The mouse was not uneasy, but only because it had no social sensibility or access to human feeling. At this particular juncture, it could be considered lucky.

Lord Godfrey broke the silence. "Yes. I require you to travel to the colonies in the Americas."

"The Americas? It is a land of wood, mud, and odiferous mountain men. I shall be bored past all endurance."

"Nevertheless, I require you to travel there. You will seek out two individuals and escort them to the safety of the house of the Bluestockings."

Athen snorted. "The Bluestockings?"

"They have more power than you know, they are part of our order, and they will be your only allies in the colonies. You will find these two individuals, and you will escort them to safety. For many years they have hidden a secret of great value to us, and it may have been discovered."

Athen raised an eyebrow. "What secret?"

Boyle ignored the question. He handed Athen a letter, camel and pepper mill on the waxen seal. "See that you use this wisely."

The boy examined the letter. "Why not one of your students?"

"I need courage and loyalty, and you have those, despite your flaws," Godfrey said.

"Ah! Danger then? Perhaps it will not be so tedious a journey after all."

"Enough!" He reddened. "This is no jest. Great danger will follow you."

Athen looked aside. "You are concerned for my welfare? I am touched."

The old man turned back to his book. "Your welfare is immaterial. You will sacrifice it for your duty and your mission, if necessary. Your ship leaves at first light. Say your good-byes and be on it."

The mouse's sensitive visual mechanisms barely detected the flicker on Athen's face, masked by a bow. "I am a Boyle, and my duty is my life. Good-bye, Father."

CHAPTER 5

Your spine is tin, and your fire is false. They will never master the heart of a true Frenchman.

—Halvard de Anjou, *Bastionado*

Ruby turned the weathered page, and for the thirty-first time, the brave Leftenant Capliche shot the dastardly Duc de Nantes in the foot, and for the thirty-first time the villain fell over the edge of the lighthouse, to drop for the thirty-first time into the icy waters and hungry rocks below. France was saved from the chemystral hordes. Well, until five years later.

The *Thrift*'s second mate, Pol the Gizzard, had told

her the true story on a late watch one night. The Duc had actually escaped into the mists. Five years later he and some of his tinker friends had used chemystry to smash the entire royal palace right into the ground, flat as a two-penny coin, all in the name of liberty. Anyone who practiced alchemy and tinkercraft (and fortune-smellers and weed doctors and anyone else the mob wanted to be rid of) were hunted and driven from France by the church and those few nobles who escaped flattening. Many refugees, including Pol's parents, found their way to Philadelphi, where they were taken in by William Penn and the colonial government.

It was still a good book.

But Ruby snapped it shut and almost threw it across the tiny cubby. She was thoroughly, painfully, unimaginably bored. She should be climbing yardarms, cutting turnips in the galley, throwing turnips at Skillet from the forecastle. She was doing none of those things. Instead, she was hiding from a rich boy and his noxious servant.

She grabbed the dog-eared copy of *Bastionado* and

curled up with a huff against the wall once again, to open her only book in the wide-open world to page 1. "Julien Capliche woke to see his father's farm ablaze in the valley. The alchemysts had returned. He pelted down the slope, but he knew . . ."

She was not reading. She was reciting. She knew it by heart. Ruby scrunched up her eyes and rapped her head against the wall, keeping time with the clack of wooden spoons creeping in from the galley. The smuggler's cabinet built into the hold of the old Portuguese corvette was little more than a windowless box with a hidden door, but it was her refuge, her place. Now, though, it had turned into a cell for true, and she was driving herself mad with dreams of fresh sea air and the sun.

The narrow slot in the back wall of the hidey-hole snapped open. The back of Gwath's breeches shuttered into view, followed by his calloused foot and his toes, which grasped a folded slip of paper between them. The cook often served the entire crew with his back to the galley wall, all the while speaking in images to Ruby, drawing and folding up the notes with his feet.

She opened the paper in the dim blue glow of the tinker's lamp she had nicked their last stay in Charles Towne. She rolled her eyes. A brilliant caricature of her father and his ridiculous hat stared off the edge of the paper, looking deep into the distance through an oversize chemystral monocle. He was looking for her, and not casually. It was too late to go back to her cabin. She tore up the paper and ate it, just to make sure, and then quickly stowed the lamp and her book in the compartment under the false floor. The *Thrift* had more secret nooks and crannies within crannies than a weed doctor's traveling cabinet.

She opened the view slot on the wall opposite the galley. No one was on the other side. She pressed her fingers to the proper spots, and a knee-level panel opened silently. Slipping into the hold, she closed the door behind her and barely had enough time to place herself in glum style under a sunbeam on a pile of sailcloth before her father's immaculate boots dropped into view through the hole leading to the deck.

Captain Wayland Teach was a big man, and he levered himself to the floor of the hold like a careful pumpkin.

Ruby looked up from the needlepoint she had rescued in the nick of time from the front pocket of her dress. Her father lifted up the eyepatch he wore over his left eye, which was just as good as his right.

"Arr. There ya be, me lassie," he growled, fully Brownbeard style. She hated it.

"Arrrrrrrr," he rolled at her, raising his bushy eyebrows. "I looked for ya in your cabin, and you wasn't harbored there, so I set sail down here, and here ya arrrrre, as fresh a young lady as ever I set me eyes on."

"How can I help you, Father?" she asked, picking at the needlepoint.

"We have passengers. I thought mayhap ye might wish to make pleasant conversation and to provide cultured diversion for our guests."

She was fair certain that real pirates didn't say "mayhap." "Are not the daring stories of Blackbeard's brother food enough for any man?" she asked brightly.

He plucked at the worn lace cuff peeking from the ragged leather overcoat he wore on even the hottest days of summer. He was angry. "Aye, but ye cannot season every night's beef with gunpowder and deadly storms," he rumbled. "A young lady's company can brighten the cabin of the meanest scalawag."

The *Thrift* was a small ship, and there was little privacy anywhere. They might be overheard by their two passengers, and Ruby took advantage of that fact not for the first time.

"I fear I have a touch of seasickness, and I may not be fit company."

"Arr, well, mayhap the night breeze will bring you some relief." He leaned in, looming, and stared at her hard.

"Do your job, Ruby," he growled, no trace of pirate in his voice. "This young prig is bored out of his skull, and my yarns fell on tin ears last night. Dinner was a disaster, and after was worse. Skillet and Mawk did 'I'll Kill You for That Whiskey,' but he loathed it, and Remy Flatfoot could not even get him to crack a smile."

"Really?"

"He slipped on a bucket, some pudding, his own feet. They even brought out one of the goats. Nothing."

"What is that to me?" she whispered right back. "They'll be in Philadelphi in three more days, and we'll have our money. Why do you want me to—"

"This is important," he pleaded. "There were no goods to be had in Boston and no goods in two ports before that. Our purse is light, and we need this lad to enjoy his stay with us so he will recommend us up the ladder. Please, girl."

"What ladder?"

"He is close with the Tinkers, and from England as well. If we can tap into those markets—"

"Then we shall have more fire, ice, and noxious gas on the *Thrift*? Or even better, stuffy lords and ladies full of their own noxious gases? No, thank you."

"It puts bread in our bellies and keeps us afloat. They pay far more for a ferry with a jolly pirate crew than just a ferry. They want to take their passage with a hint of mystery and adventure and add on the best grub in the colonies."

"Father, they laugh at you. We are no pirates, and this is beneath you."

He looked at her sidewise. "It keeps us safe."

She gritted her teeth. "But what is the point of harmless thievery? Safe pirating?"

His face was bleak under the thistle of his beard. "When you pass Gwath's test, you can do as you like. But for now you are my daughter, Aruba Teach, and you will do as I say."

"I cannot."

"Why?"

She could not tell him of the failed carriage robbery. Not now. The whole ship was in danger because of her. If only there had been some way to deny them passage. If the boy did not see her, he could not recognize her, and if he could not recognize her, then they would not be taken by the constables at the next port. She could do no more than frown and shrug.

He crooked his mouth. "We are who we say we are, girl. A man is the stories he tells himself. And so is a woman. You need to find a way to make this right."

She nodded.

His face split into the huge, false grin she hated so much, the grin for money.

Brownbeard's pirate drawl returned. "So glad you're feelin' better, my lass! See you tonight!" He flashed his blacked-out tooth at her and clambered back up the stairs into the afternoon light.

Curled on the sailcloth, Ruby ripped the needlepoint out, piece by piece, imagining each was a hair in her father's scraggly, desperate beard.

Ruby tried to lose herself in her pudding. At the top edge of her vision, the Hand, wrapped in an immaculate gray glove, lifted her father's best wineglass from the threadbare tablecloth. She spooned the perfectly sweet pudding into her mouth. Even in moments as raw as these, Gwath's Passenger Pudding was not a concoction to pass over lightly.

Dinner was almost over, and Ruby had managed the entire evening without once meeting the boy's eyes.

"Has she lived long on your ship, Captain?" the Voice asked.

"Why, yes, ever since she was born." She could see her father smile in her mind. "Haven't you, Aruba?" She nodded, looking for deeper holes in the pudding. The cut under her eye burned.

"She is not usually this reserved." She could hear the demand in his voice. He drummed his fingers on the carved plank lying across his bed, which was also his seat in the tiny cabin.

Silence. She took another bite.

The *Thrift* listed to starboard. The boy in the corner clutched at his belly, which grumbled loudly.

The Voice chuckled, and the embroidered waistcoat twisted toward the servant. "You have a complex relationship with the seas, do you not, Cram?"

"Not really, sir." Even the boy's voice sounded ratty. "It's fair simple. I was reared to live on the land. My mam raised us on sawdust and cobblestone soup. Begging your pardon, sir."

"Not at all, Cram. I like a bit of straight talk from my man. I appreciate your crew as well, Captain. They are quite the jolly brotherhood."

"We aim to please, my lord. If I may ask, Lord Boyle, how did you come upon our vessel? We are used to entertaining men and women of quality, but I did not think our reputation had spread to the Continent."

"Nothing so exciting, I am afraid. I have urgent business in Philadelphi, and yours was the first ship sailing."

"I see," the captain said.

"Captain Teach, if you do not mind my question, I would inquire after the presence of a young girl on your vessel. It seems a singular practice."

"He is my father, sir. All I have in the world." She couldn't help herself. She chewed fiercely and forced her eyes to follow the line of a small tear in the tablecloth.

"I meant no offense, Miss Aruba," the Voice replied, "and I would cast no aspersions on your noble father. However, hired men are not family, and this is a rascally crew, if I do not mistake my eyes."

Her father laughed his Brownbeard laugh. "My men owe me a blood debt, young sir. Loyal to the core, they are, and think of Aruba as sister or niece, I daresay."

"But aren't there traditions among sailors that warn against this type of thing? Hexes and curses and what have you? This wine is excellent." He was certainly full of himself.

"Thankee, sir. It should be. It was waylaid on its path to a Castilian viceroy in Cartagena!" he rumbled.

Thankee?

"Indeed? Cram, please make sure to check my valuables in the cargo hold. We don't want anything waylaid."

Ruby caught the faintest whiff of sarcasm in the boy's voice. She dug her fingers into the edge of the folding seat where she was sitting, fighting to keep her eyes on the pudding.

"Waylaid? Oh, no, Lord Athen, those days are long behind us," her father reassured. "This crew battled its fair share in the teeth of the warring sea, but that was years ago. Now we carry travelers, not sixteen-pounders."

She wanted to scream. How easily he lied. She shoveled another spoonful into her mouth. She had spent thirteen years on this ship, and Wayland Teach had been repeating this tired old spiel for at least as long. He only seemed a pirate. They were smugglers, no more. Sneak into port with a hold of tobacco or rum. Do their business. Move along to the next port with the next shipment.

"And what of your famous brother, Captain? What is it like to be the brother of Blackbeard the Pirate?"

Teach puffed up, ready to launch into his favorite lie, the one with the walrus and the powder keg. The hooks that held the makeshift table into the wall groaned as he planted his hands, leaning across it. "Well, sir," he said.

"It is a hard thing, sir, to be brother to a legend." It rumbled out of Ruby from somewhere deep. "To be Blackbeard's brother is to fly ahead of a firestorm with an iron anchor cutting into the sea floor below ye! Nowhere to turn, demons and krakens to port, the crown and all the iron angels of the Royal Society to starboard! Why, there was one time—"

"Ruby."

"Paw, I must tell the story of the walrus! This beastie, you see, had tusks the size of birch trees, and—"

"Aruba." Sometimes the captain's voice could sear.

The door to the cabin burst open. Skillet's slight frame blocked very little of the wind and rain that rushed past him. Hunched under an oilskin slicker, Gwath appeared a moment later.

The little man raised his voice above the howl of the gale behind him, "Mawk needs you at the helm, Captain!" he yelled. "It's coming on out here!"

"So be it!" Teach roared. "Stow the chow and finery, Skillet. Lord Athen, I trust we'll continue another time. Gwath, help the gentleman and his man to their cabin. Aruba, bide here, lass."

The stuffy little room burst into action. Skillet and Gwath scurried in to break down the table, and her father danced around them and out into the blow without a second word. She kept her head down and pretended to help clear the table as Gwath ushered Lord Athen and Rodent Boy (what kind of name was Cram?) out the door.

Her only company the wind and the rain, she breathed and straightened, shaking the tension out of her shoulders. Another storm weathered. The *Thrift* rolled hard, and Ruby braced herself against the wall.

One of the table legs rolled onto her foot. She grabbed

it to stow it, but her hand closed on leather, not wood. It was the scabbard of a sword, with a bronze-capped hilt. It wasn't her father's sword. He carried a cutlass.

Then the door opened. She might have turned away, but it happened too fast. She took a step back, and cold brine splashed her face. The cut under her eye burned from the salt. Lord Athen was there, staring at her. He had swung into the room, one gloved hand on the doorframe, the other outstretched. "Quick, boy, hand me that." She held it out instinctively, and he grabbed it and launched himself into the storm. It was only after she closed the door after him that Ruby realized what he had said.

CHAPTER 6

The gale had come and gone like a fierce cat, tossing the vessel back and forth on the waves but losing interest after a few hours and bounding off to pounce on some other ship.

The narrow passage into the lower level of the *Thrift* was quiet in the aftermath of the storm. Most of the crew were dead to the world in their hammocks in the hold after the night's exertions. This hallway led down only to the galley and the two small passenger cabins. The waning moon cast little light down through the hatch above.

A panel in the wall at the bottom of the stairs disappeared soundlessly, and Ruby eased her head into the gloom. She pulled herself into the hallway and closed the panel behind her. On bare feet in her work shift, dusty from the crawl through the hidden passage, she crept to the door of Lord Athen's cabin.

She put her ear against it, listening for breathing, or muttering, or she didn't know what. The servant boy, Cram, was bunked with the crew. Ruby thought for a moment about opening the door and going in there and . . . what? Knock him on the head? Truss him up like a prize calf and have Gwath throw him overboard? Neither would probably go over well with her father.

Something about this Athen just set her teeth on edge. Why didn't he reveal her secret? What did he want from her? What was in all that luggage? Clothing? Could any boy be so vain?

She turned on cat feet and crept to the galley door.

The storm latch was set, but latches had never been a problem for Ruby. She slid the thin blade of her knife through the gap between the frame and the door to pop it open without a sound.

She floated into the room and secured the door. Gwath was there, up to his armpits in a pot of stew.

"Gwath," she whispered.

"I'm busy," he said.

Gwath fished around at the bottom of the stewpot, shoulder deep in the rich red mixture of garlic, beans, spices, tomatoes, tubers, and who knew what else that made up his specialty, Goats in the Bilge. No one knew the list of ingredients, and Gwath would never let anyone in the galley when he cooked it.

"That is scalding! Are you all right?"

"Do I seem to be in pain?"

He didn't. She leaned back against the wall next to the stove, close enough to whisper.

"Out," he whispered.

"I need your help."

Gwath remained silent, sniffing at the bubbling

surface of the stew and looking as if he'd lost his favorite spoon at the bottom of the pot.

"Gwath."

"Busy."

"Listen, last night right before the storm there was—

"Pirate Queen," he warned.

Ruby bit her lip. He never called her that unless he was sore with her. She changed strategy. "Why do you have your arms in the Goat?"

"You have to massage it. Otherwise it won't set right." His brows narrowed, "Give me a moment. Can't rush a good stew." He sniffed at the pot, grimaced, and hoisted one muscled arm out of the brew. It was completely dry.

Gwath Maxim One: "Gwath Is a Mystery. Do Not Try to Solve Him."

He teased a leaf out of the leather pouch he always wore around his neck and crushed it, plunging the bits deep into the depths of the concoction. He took one more sniff, nodded, and then pulled both arms out of the pot dry as a sun-baked shore.

"How did you do that?" she breathed.

"What?" he said, grabbing a wooden bowl from the stack in the corner. He ladled out a steaming bowl of the Goat and passed it to her. She took it, but she knew he was trying to distract her.

"We don't have time to stuff our faces, you mound of meat," she said.

"Eat. Maxim Thirty-two: 'Food Feeds the Wise, and Hunger Makes for a Fool's Errand.'"

She snorted and flopped down on the ground but still tucked in with a vengeance.

"This is good, but I'm not going to sigh like some alderman's doxy and forget my own name," she said around a mouthful of stew. "You just pulled your hands out of something scalding, and they're dry. How did you do that?"

He ladled another bowl for himself and sat down on the floor of the galley. He smacked his lips and sucked down some of the Goat.

"I'll answer your question if you answer mine," he offered.

"Fine," Ruby said, and then regretted it. "Make it quick."

"Did the young sir recognize you?"

Ruby hissed, "Yes! How did you know?" The big man opened his mouth. "Don't answer. That's not my question." She shoveled another bite into her mouth. "We need to deal with this! I could be on wanted posters from Plymouth to Charles Towne. If that happens, I'll be restricted to the *Thrift* 'for my own safety.' My father will keep me tied to his apron strings until I'm seventy-seven."

"Your trouble, not mine. I'm not the one the young man recognized." Gwath chuckled.

"If I go down to the bottom, I'm dragging you with me," she said, only half joking. "I want some more stew."

"Help yourself. What should we do? Trap him in his cabin? Thump him on the head with a caulking mallet?"

"Yes!" she whispered. "No. I don't know." She picked up the ladle and stirred.

"Little one, I see two choices. One? Talk to the boy and charm him silent. Two? Hope that he sticks to his present course and keeps mum."

She blew out her breath. "A tall hope, at best." She fingered the slice below her eye. "And he will not be coaxed."

Gwath shrugged. "Maybe take a little gander at choice three. What if I put something in his food?"

Ruby stopped stirring. "What do you mean?"

"Nothing serious, just something that might keep him ill for a few days until we get him into port and off the ship. Or perhaps Mawk bumps into the boy when he is on deck. Oops! Over the railing!"

"We are not killers."

"Oh, really?"

Ruby did not answer. The big man finished off his bowl. He was hairless and thick muscled, wrapped in shapeless clothing, breeches and tunic made from castoff sailcloth. He had always been on her father's ship and in her life. He had taught her to sneak and hide, to pick locks and mask her appearance, to move through crowds like the wind through marsh grass.

She knew nothing else of him. Not one but a thousand questions ran through her mind. Where did Gwath come from? Did he have any family? Why did he stay on the ship? Why did he teach her sneakery? Why did the crew step lively at his every word or gesture? How had he met her father? Captain Teach had a hundred stories about each of his crew, every one more outlandish than the next. But he never talked about Gwath.

The cook fingered the stone hoop in his ear and stood eye to eye with her.

"Queen Ruby." The way he said it was different from before. He sounded reserved, almost formal. "You sense that there is something important about this decision. This will not be the last time. Keeping the secret of all that you are, of all that you may become, is crucial."

"The secret of all that I am?" she said.

He opened his mouth.

A clanging stopped him. The alarm bell! Skillet was calling all hands on deck, hammering on the bell like there was no tomorrow.

The sound of sailors thumping out of hammocks and feet running on wood shattered the silence of the early morning. Gwath hesitated.

Ruby turned back to him. "What? What were you going to say?"

The cook unlatched the galley door and grinned as if the moment before had all been a joke. "Another time," he said. "You must go to your cabin. Alarums wait for no one."

Indeed, as Gwath moved past her to lash down the lid of the stewpot, Mawk and Jerky hustled with grim faces into the galley to help secure the rest of the gear. The moment was gone.

Skillet wasn't ringing the pattern for a reef or an iceberg or for another storm on the horizon. He was ringing to quarters. Something was coming.

She did not go to her cabin. She found her father at the stern with Skillet. The little man had relinquished his place at the wheel and was grimly sharpening the edges of his namesake, a heavy cast-iron pan that he wielded two-handed. Her father told a story about his killing a Portuguese admiral with that thing. Ruby had only seen him cook bacon in it.

Wayland Teach was looking astern through his eyepiece, a marvel of tinkercraft. There was some sort of watery stuff inside, and the green metal housing heated and pulsed when you held it up to your eye. It could see twice as far as the finest spyglass.

He was uncharacteristically silent.

He stood there for a long while, and the deck was still. Skillet's whetstone kept time with the wind. The entire crew was shoulder to shoulder on the main deck, staring up at them, bristling with the oddest collection of weaponry Ruby had ever seen. Gwath was there, with a pair of wicked-looking kitchen cleavers, Mawk had what looked to be a sharpened parasol, Pol the Gizzard had a sledgehammer studded with stones, and Frog Jerky wielded a huge haunch of swine. They looked comfortable, alert, and twelve times more dangerous than the band of harmless and good-natured scalawags that she had thought manned her father's ship. Lord Athen and Cram were standing to one side, the serving boy taking long, loving looks at the lifeboat. Athen sketched a bow to her across the deck.

Big Shem and Little Shem, the carpenters, were pulling apart a barrel on the starboard side and assembling a hidden machine from its insides. Ruby leaned over and asked Skillet, "Is that a cannon?"

He winked.

Captain Teach cursed under his breath and dropped the eyepiece. The crew watched as he cleared his throat. "They may have found us, men," he said, and there was no trace of pirate in his tone. "It's flying Royal Navy colors, a black kraken of metal and chem. A tinker ship coming after us at full tilt, fair dancing across the waves."

Skillet's whetstone stopped. No one spoke.

Lord Athen called from his place by the rail, "Captain, I think they may seek me." Cram looked at the lordling as if he'd just grown another head. The crew craned their necks around to stare as if it were a lawn tennis match. The waves and wind dominated the conversation.

"Why would you say that, young sir?" Her father's tone somehow genially cut glass.

"Well, Captain, I did say I was in a touch of a hurry to reach Philadelphi."

"Indeed, sir, but you did not deign to tell us that the undue haste was in anticipation of hot pursuit by the king of England's Admiralty." The glass cutter was no longer genial.

"I was unsure of the response to my exit from London. It was possible I left unnoticed."

"Possible, but not likely, given the two thousand tons of doom bearing down on the *Thrift* that will catch us within the hour. Can you tell me why I shouldn't just lower sail, let them approach us, and turn you over?"

"Perhaps they are searching for you?"

"Explain yourself."

Athen reached down to his belt.

Twenty dangerous men raised knives, pans, tools, sharpened umbrellas, and a heavy hog's leg.

Athen raised a letter, sealed with wax.

"I had thought to give you this when we arrived in Philadelphi. I do not know the entirety of its contents, but I was told to give it to you if circumstances warranted."

"Pol," Teach snapped, and the skinny mate shouldered the sledge, snatched the letter from the gentleman's hand,

and hurried it up to the captain. The captain handed the eyepiece to Skillet, broke the seal, and read it. He became very still.

"Your letter is persuasive, sir."

Athen bowed. "I am glad it proved effective."

"Oh, indeed," Teach replied. "Effective enough to compel me and my family to unprecedented action. I warn you, however. We compel effectively but not happily."

Lord Athen's lips curved into a thin smile. "I have never been taught that a tool should feel anything toward its master."

A deaf man could have heard a pin drop. In fact, Mawk dropped his teeth. The wooden ones, right out of his open gums. They clattered onto the deck in the silence.

Teach fingered his cutlass. "Perhaps, boy, if we all see the end of this day, I might offer you a moment of instruction in the manipulation of tools."

"I am at your service, Captain."

"Do we run or fight, Captain?" Skillet rasped from

the wheel. "They'll be on us in two snaps." The speck to the east was growing with alarming speed.

Teach looked at Ruby for a moment, face unreadable. "Neither," he said. "We keep on as usual. I won't throw away thirteen years of hiding in plain sight for a hunch. Crew, about your business. Lord Athen, a word."

As the crew sprang into action, Teach turned to his daughter.

Ruby interrupted before he could speak. "What is happening?" she demanded.

"Ruby, listen to me."

"I won't until you tell me—

"There's no time, poppet." He put a hand on her shoulder, pulling his beard on with the other. "An enemy may be upon us."

"What did we do to make England angry?"

He ignored the question. "You need to go down to your hidey-hole that you think I don't know about and wall yourself in."

Athen had taken the steps to the forecastle two at a time, and Teach handed him the letter.

"Captain, I fear they may be accompanied by members of the Reeve," Athen said.

Teach looked to the heavens, as if for guidance.

"Who?" Ruby asked.

"Special agents of the crown, my dear. They are . . . formidable." Teach turned to Athen. "You, sir, and your servant, please accompany my daughter. She is taking you to a safe place. Be silent as a tomb and open for no one, even for me. Only come out if you hear Skillet ring that the coast is clear." He crushed her in a bear hug. She found herself clinging to him as well. "Bring your knives. You may have need of them."

CHAPTER 7

. . . a Glorious Revolution, indeed. Change one king for another king, and give me Charles or James, Mary or Lizzie. But mark me, this new king with his Tinker lords? They care no more for plain folk than for the dung on their carboshaeth shoe. My man and me? We're headed for Sweden.

—Overheard on Victory Night,1689,
outside the House of Progress (formerly the Palace of Whitehall)

Ruby, Athen, and Cram were sitting knees to nose, shoulder to shoulder in the tiny space. The lanky serving boy had taken off his hat and was hunched over into a ball, but the top of his skull still touched the boards above them. Ruby had taken the tinker's lamp out of the panel so that they could see. Athen clutched a small bag of flasks and vials he had saved from his trunks before the crew sent them over the side. He had put on a good show, but as he watched them sink below the waves, he'd looked as if someone had just drowned his favorite pony. Gwath was crouching, staring in through the opening of the hole.

"Stay quiet," Gwath said.

Ruby began to speak, but Lord Athen interrupted. "We will. Thank you for your help, sir."

"You can thank me by helping to keep this one safe," he responded, nodding at Ruby.

"I can take care of myself, Gwath," she sputtered. "Besides, it will only be a few hours. You'll pull the wool over those jolly jacks' eyes, and then we'll be on our merry way." She reached down and grabbed his hand. She didn't want to let go.

He smiled, pressed her hand, and then pulled his back out of the opening. "Keep an eye out for fair winds. And don't forget to check your pockets," he said, and closed the hidden panel. It was pitch black.

Ruby turned the small wheel at the base of the lamp, and they were lit by low, molten blue.

"Tinker's lamp, hmm? Well, you are full of surprises, Aruba Teach," Athen said in a low voice. He had eased himself around so that his shoulders were against the back wall. The sword scabbard lay across his lap. He was at ease and attentive, as Ruby imagined a theater patron might look before the curtain on opening night. "You know, you could trade two of those little lights for the wages of half this flea-bitten crew? No fuel, lasts two lifetimes. From whence did you acquire that?"

"That is my business," she said. "And they are not flea-bitten."

"And this is the famous hidey-hole? I had imagined something more spacious."

She had thought that it was her place, the refuge only she and Gwath had known about. Apparently her father had known about it, too.

Ruby sidestepped. "What about you? Awfully late in presenting that letter to my father, weren't you?"

"That was a different matter."

"Different, how?"

"Milord, miss, please," Cram hissed from behind Athen. "The cook said we needed to be quiet, and I do think that—"

A loud banging penetrated the wood and filled the little room.

"What is that?" Athen asked.

Ruby tried to control her breathing. "That's a hammer on a nail." She put her hand on the door and felt the quick, steady vibrations pass through it. Bam. Bam. Bam.

"Oi!" she yelled. "Gwath? Big Shem? Little Shem? What are you doing?" She pushed, but the door wouldn't budge. They were walling it up. "Gwath!" Athen shushed her. The hammering went on, quicker now, and she pushed harder. "Oi! Stop!"

Athen grabbed her wrist and pulled her arm away from the hidden door. She tried to free herself, but he was stronger than her. She kicked at him hard, in the chest. He grunted and then pushed back, banging her shoulders against the bulkhead with both hands.

"Stop it!" he hissed. "They are doing this for us so we cannot be found!"

Hitting the wall had knocked the breath out of her. Athen was hunched over the bag and breathing heavily, watching her in the half-light. She realized that her knife was in her hand.

"I am sorry," he whispered, holding his hand up in surrender, "but we need to be silent. We need to assume the worst."

The worst? What did that mean? Who was this? Who was following him?

Athen then reached behind him and grabbed the little barrel he had brought from the hold. He popped the lid, and the heavy, tarry smell of oakum filled the little room. Ruby was even more confused. The gooey, dark substance was caulk for the joints of the ship. Big and Little Shem would scour the deep places of the *Thrift* with it, filling in and spreading it into the cracks, so that the joints would keep watertight. But there was no chance of a leak here, and while the stuff didn't exactly stink, in such a small area the smell was powerful. Lord Athen gave Cram a wide little knife and held one out to Ruby. She looked a question at him but then sighed and took it. He tapped his nose and then grinned. He motioned for them to cover the walls and ceiling, and he went to work on the cracks of the doorway. Cram tasted the knife, made a face, and got to work. She did the same.

The hammering continued for a few more minutes, then stopped abruptly.

When there were streaks of oakum all over the door, as well as the walls and ceiling, Athen motioned for them to stop. Ruby leaned her head back against the bulkhead, dizzy from the fumes. She rolled over and opened the slot to the galley to let some fresh air in. Athen immediately closed it and covered it with the tarry glue.

They waited.

Voices and activity buzzed like a hive of far-off bees. After a few minutes the bees subsided, but the *Thrift* jolted, and they braced themselves against the bulkheads. The impact was brief but felt like a giant had reached down and nudged their little ship to the side with a flick of its massive finger.

Athen leaned over and turned down the wheel of the tinker's lamp.

Darkness and oakum seeped into her head.

Shortly thereafter, after two more muffled thumps,

feet came onto the deck. Then there was talk. The sounds were far off, like termites, and Ruby wondered in the fumy darkness if she was a termite. At rest in a tiny corner of the *Thrift*, taking a break after a hard day of chewing before making her way down the beam roadways back to her termite family, who would be waiting at home with Gwath's Sawdust Pudding and her father's tales of termite pirates from the olden days.

Voices tugged her out of her oakum dream. She couldn't make out who was speaking but thought one voice might be her father's deep rumble. Muted conversation became sharp words. She pressed her ear to the stained wall to try to hear a little bit better but only got a sticky ear for the trouble. The argument deepened and quickened.

A pistol shot rang out.

She pulled her head back and reached out instinctively to grab Athen's gloved fingers. After the first shot, a wave of sound crashed down upon their heads: the clash of blades, the pop of muskets and pistols, the cries of men. There were other, deeper roars that sounded like metal lions. Ruby stared up through the darkness, willing herself up through the deck so that she could see, so that she could help.

She had no idea how long it lasted, though she suspected it wasn't all that long, but the battle slowed and then stopped. The wall of sound faded away, replaced by a strange, tense quiet, punctuated by flurries of running, a musket, a yell, the clash of swords, back to silence.

Then something landed in the hold outside the boarded-up door. Something metal, like a sledgehammer dropped from a height onto the planks. There was a whirring, slower, and then more quickly, into a steady ticking, like the sound of a music box. But this was deeper. Tock, tock, tocktock, tocktock, tocktocktocktock. Athen let go of her hand in the dark and drew his sword. She reached into the scabbards Gwath had sewn into her dress and pulled out her two knives. They were fine ones, blister steel, that Skillet had given her special from his trip back to England, and they sometimes gave her courage. Not today.

The whirring and tocking had stabilized into a

rhythm, and then there was a metallic sound, like shaking out an iron sail. Ruby's hands hurt from gripping her knives. She found herself staring at the door, even in the pitch-darkness. On the other side, whatever was out there was moving around the hold. The underlying tocktocktock of clockwork gears was peppered with a rhythmic clacking that she knew her ancient ancestors would recognize as claws. There was another sound, like a harsh wind forced through a teakettle. The thing was sniffing. Smelling. Hunting.

Minutes went by as the creature searched the room. It stopped right outside the door. It sniffed more persistently, and it growled a jangling snarl. A man asked something in a low voice, but it was lost under the tocking of the thing's innards. A metal claw slowly rasped down the walled-up portal like a file, mere inches from her face.

Ruby bit her lip so hard it bled.

CHAPTER 8

Them smelly little jangling demons, puttin' me right out of business, they are. They ain't purr, they ain't yowl proper, and they just gives me the woolies. 'Tain't even real cats!

—Maisie Fallows, ratcatcher

Athen put his hand on Ruby's shoulder. In the tense quiet of the hidey-hole, she thought that even the sound of his glove on her dress might call the attention of the beast outside. She couldn't chide him, or move, or even breathe. There would be fangs. Many fangs. And claws. And she had to stop imagining what it might look like, because the imagining was making her want to scream.

The ship had been seized, and some sort of monster

prowled outside the secret door. The monster's keeper, who had a rough voice with no good in it, was also in the hold, and the only thing standing between them and savaging and chomping was a few new boards, a flimsy secret panel, and a pail full of oakum. Clever on Athen's part. If not for that, they surely would have been already discovered.

Ruby cocked her head. It couldn't smell them because of the oakum. Which Athen had brought into the hidey-hole. So he knew this beast might be here!

If she dared move, she would have struck him. If she dared speak, she would have lit into him like a raging bosun. If she dared breathe, she would, well, she would breathe him to melting with the devil's breath of Gwath's Goat, and that would set him straight.

But she could do none of that.

So she sat.

It felt like a very long time.

All at once there was sound. A muffled voice called down into the hold. A jumble of scrambling, gears, clumping, and whuffling sounded as the searchers, one metal and one not, climbed out of the hold and then were gone.

Silence. She dared not move. If she were searching a ship, she would play savvy and wait out the final stowaways, silently leashing her snuffling monster until some stupid innocent popped her head out of the hold like the youngest of chipmunks. Ruby would not have her little furry head popped off from lack of caution. Gwath and her father had taught her better.

Sometime later they were jolted about. Cram stifled a whimper. She reached across Athen and squeezed his shoulder. He started, and it sounded as if he had banged his head on the ceiling. She listened to the waves and took in the motion of the *Thrift*. They were moving, but slowly. Perhaps the business had been dealt with, and the Royal Navy had gone on its way, taking its ship, noise, guns, and monsters far away from here. But she didn't believe herself.

There was a soft breeze that smelled of mint. Athen's lips were right up on her ear.

"How do we get out?" he whispered, light as a june bug on a leaf.

She thought a moment. Then she leaned over and whispered, just as lightly into his ear, "I have no idea."

It was quiet again for a good while.

She felt him lean away, and he whispered something to Cram that she couldn't hear. Then Cram whispered, in a voice more raspy foghorn than careful whisper, "Well, sir, she have to know how!"

The muffled thump that came after must have been Athen's glove over Cram's mouth.

And then no one came.

It had been hours at least since the last sounds of the monster and its master had dissolved. Now there was only the steady motion of the waves, the occasional creak of the *Thrift*'s beams, and a faint growling that must have been Cram's stomach.

She scooted closer to the door panel. Athen held on to her arm for a moment, but she grabbed at his wrist once, firmly, and he relented. She suspected he wanted out as badly as she.

Ruby pushed hard on the panel. It didn't budge. She pushed again. It didn't even wiggle. She couldn't breathe.

She didn't know why, but she hit the panel, hard. It made a thump. Athen quickly pulled her back, but not before she had hit it even harder. She started beating her feet against the wall until Athen and Cram lay on her feet and hands. She eventually stopped struggling and lay there in the dark.

She might, she thought, be going a little mad.

She tried to calm herself by taking deep, quiet breaths. Athen risked a very low light from her tinker's lamp, which he gave her to hold.

In the half-light he rummaged around in his bag, and he pulled out a little wooden box and a vial. The vial glittered. He knelt in front of the door and took something out of the box. When he held it next to the vial, there was a small pop, then a sizzle, like pork in a frying pan, followed closely by a smell like fresh mushrooms. He eased the neck of the vial around the edges of the door, leaving green foam behind it. When he sat back on his knees, he was breathing heavily.

Ruby's only experience with chemystry up close was watching the weed doctors and fakers in city squares trick people out of their coins. She had not seen much real chem done, but this sure looked like it.

After a few moments the smell of mushrooms became less intense, and she felt a breeze from somewhere. Athen pointed a question at her knife. She handed it to him, and he slid it into the foam across the top of the portal. He tipped the hilt up, and the whole thing tilted toward them like a puzzle piece.

Clever.

She uncurled her screaming legs and was first out of the hole, slipping past as the other two grabbed at her.

The cargo hold had been ransacked, but it didn't look as if anything had been taken. She ignored the boys as she scrambled silently up a stack of boxes and pulled herself like a monkey up over the lip of the hole in the deck.

If anyone had been on the deck, he would have seen her pop up quite like a chipmunk and squint into the sun, but there was no one. Not a single living person, and no dead bodies, either. A terrible picture flashed in her mind of her father with a ball of shot in his head or Gwath skewered right through, but the main deck of the ship was empty of life. The foredeck, too.

A quick, silent search of the stern cabins rendered the same result. They were all gone. Skillet, Frog Jerky, Pol, Big Shem: There was no trace of them. But the ship was moving.

Her chest was tight as she ran back into the sun.

The two boys were just pulling themselves out of the hold as she sprinted up to the foredeck to look out into the water ahead. The Royal Navy ship was nowhere to be seen. From horizon to horizon there was only water and sky save one little boat right in front of the *Thrift*. A long gray rope was tied fast around the waist of the figurehead. Other lines of the same gray hawsers were knotted around supports to the left and right sides of the foredeck. It was springy at first touch but left a slick film on her fingers that felt nothing like rope. All the lines were fixed to the rear of the little boat below. The tug, for indeed, it was somehow towing the *Thrift*, was tiny. It was fit for no more than five crew, she guessed, and was powered by a tinker's wheel that ran the width of the stern.

She ducked down behind the rail. Athen crept up beside her. "That tiny water bug has no business pulling a ship that weighs ten times as much. It must be hauling some powerful tinkercraft," he said.

"Who are these people?" she asked.

His eyes clouded.

"Where is my father?" Ruby pressed.

Athen said, "I do not know. I am deeply sorry if I brought this upon you."

"You are deeply sorry? What do we do now? Who is on that boat?"

He looked away, then met her eyes. "I do not know. I wish I could tell you more, but I cannot."

She wanted to scream. She wished that he had never come on this ship. She ran to her cabin and shut the door with her back against it. It smelled of salt and cedar, and she rubbed at her face to keep the tears from coming.

Her best friend was missing or dead. Her father was missing or dead.

She pulled off her work shift, covered in oakum, dust, and filth, and threw it on the floor. The cabin was ransacked. She pulled on a pair of old breeches and a shirt and then curled up against the built-in cabinet of her bed. On the floor, next to her crumpled dress, was a folded-up piece of parchment.

Right before nailing them in, Gwath had said, "Check your pockets."

Her pulse was racing.

She opened it.

CHAPTER 9

CHATSBOTTOM: *A proper servant should be seen and not heard. My man, Farnsworth? Haven't seen him for a fortnight.*

THUNDERFATCH: *I hear he gets on quite well with the Mrs., and I seen him climbing out of her chamber window....*

CHATSBOTTOM: *Thunderfatch!*

— Marion Coatesworth-Hay, *The Tinker's Dram*, Act II, sc. iii

"You and me need to have a sit down, my lord." Cram huddled under the rail between a staved-in barrel and a pile of tangled rope.

The gentleman kept his eyes on the tugboat below and did not respond.

"Lord Athen, m'lord, if I might have a moment of your time?" Aristocrats cottoned to the grovel. They lapped it up the way cats did milk, and Cram was happy to lay on the cream when his skin was hung out to dry.

"It will have to wait." Athen worked his way, frog style, back down the deck. Cram hoped that the boy's greatcoat might tangle his feet and pitch him to the deck. No such luck. For all his pride and distance, the dandy moved like a dancer. Then he vaulted over the railing and landed surefooted on the main deck, ten feet below.

Cram duckwalked after him. He tangled his legs over the rail, though, and flailed into a heap at Lord Athen's feet.

Athen headed for the hallway to the cabins. Cram grunted his way up to standing and called after him, "Oi. Stop."

Athen turned. "No time for this, Cram. We need to get the girl and create a stratagem."

"I know what to do. They's Tinkers, ain't they?" He squared his shoulders. "I worked for the Tinkers back in Boston. They're an odd lot, but they take care of their own. I'm one a their own, though low in the pecking order. Driving a coach and driving a tugboat seem savvy. I can talk to 'em."

Athen's clear gray eyes narrowed. "And what would you talk to 'em about, Cram?"

"Well, their betters are certain lookin' for you, but maybe we can work out an arrangement with them, of the currency variety, if you catch my wind."

"I catch your wind wherever you stand, Cram."

That was the straw that broke it. "I just spent the better part of a day cramped and in the terror dark with you, *m'lord*." Cram took a step forward. "Order me around like the king of Timbuktu when there's a ship of men at your back, but right now I don't see no others, and I outweigh you by two stone. Let's amble down Cram Street, or maybe I just throw you overboard, make my deal, and then yell for 'em to fish ya out."

Cram did not see the hand darting to the hilt of the sword or the steel flashing from the scabbard. What he did see was the blade just below his chin. The point was pressing a mite too firm against his Adam's apple.

At the other end of the sword, the china of the boy's face had changed to granite. "Two stone won't do you much good if it's dead weight, Cram. Now.

We have business to attend to at speed, and you and I don't know each other very well. We have been thrown together by Providence, and perhaps we should clarify our relationship. For my part, I am heir to a very large fortune and will reward your service well when we find our way to safety. Is that clear?"

"Very clear, milord."

"If I fall here, however, be assured that my family will seek out anyone involved with inexhaustible zeal, and they are not forgiving souls, as I am. They are suspicious and mean-spirited, and they love me very much. Also clear?"

Cram swallowed, carefully. "Like a mountain lake."

"I doubt you have spent time in the mountains."

"There is some truth to what you say."

"For your part, I must now determine whether you are a scalawag, and need to be dealt with permanently and posthaste, or a coward, whom I have inspired to unswerving loyalty via the avenue of my generosity and merciful behavior."

There was a pause.

The pressure on the blade increased ever so slightly.

"Coward, sir." Cram assured him. "Most definitely coward."

"Capital." Athen smiled with what might have been relief. "You fold shirts with a rare excellence. I would hate to lose you." He turned to hurry down the hallway.

"Sir, may I ask—"

"Not at this time."

"Very good, sir."

CHAPTER 10

The finest tonic is a letter from home.
—Israel Cestus, captain, Her Majesty's Ship *Disbelief,* 1708–1714

Ruby was stumped. Her father had considered this of utmost importance. Otherwise, he would not have sneaked the letter into her dress and given Athen the-devil-knows-what scrap of paper.

Letter of Grocery and Recipe Transfer

His Excellency
Lord Godfrey Boyle, Baron, Sc.D.
Lord High Pieman, in and over His Majesty's Royal

High Society for Improvement of Crusts and Fillings

These are to certify that the bearer of these known as Emory Athen Boyle, Esq., initiate into the arts of bakery and cutlery, acts under my Authority to travel to the New World, specifically the colonies of Bradfordum and Pennswood.

I do by virtue of the Power & Authority to me given conformable to His Majesty's pleasure expressed to me by the Right Honourable and Most Noble His Grace the Duke of P. and by the Right Honourable F. B. Authorize and Empower the said initiate maker of pastries and sundry sweets to command the assistance of any other practitioners of the noble and ancient baking arts that he may encounter in his travels.

Given under my Hand & seal of Arms
at Oven House this 6th day of Sep.
1718 in the 4th Year of His Majesty's Reign
Lord Godfrey Boyle, Sc.D.

A baker? The boy was many things—polite, mysterious, graceful, clever, arrogant—but she doubted he had ever gotten his hands dirty in his life, let alone elbow deep in a bowl of dough. And what debt would her father have to pay to some aristocratic loaf baron? It had to be a code of some sort, but she had no idea how to even begin deciphering it.

Secrets. Athen had too many of them, and he even owned one of hers, though a botched robbery was a far sight from kidnapping and murder. She stopped herself from thinking about that. "Master the Wave in Front of You." Gwath Maxim Fifteen.

She sat on her ruined bunk and took stock. Whatever beasts and men had been on the ship had torn its insides out. They were looking for something, or someone, with a vengeance. Her room was carpeted with ripped clothing, broken boards, and smashed furniture. Some of the *Thrift*'s walls had even been broken apart, and there were dark red stains in spots. Time for that later.

Her father's monocle was tucked in a pouch in the secret panel under her bed. Had he known all of her hidey-holes? A new wave of fear washed over her. If he had hidden it there, he had been planning on something that might take him away. Her mother's button was still there as well, looped on the piece of rawhide Skillet had given her. He had put it on hide the fourth time she had broken its delicate chain. Her father would not talk about the button, except to say that it was her mother's. It had a faint ivory finish, never scratched, and was unbreakable. You could drop a barrel of anvils on it, and it would come out unmarked. There were no paintings of her mother on the ship. She had left when Ruby was very young, and Ruby did not remember her.

She squashed that feeling down, too. No time for woolgathering.

She pulled the loop over her neck and a dress on over the shirt and breeches. She slipped her knives into the hidden sheaths sewn into the lining.

She tucked the letter into the waist of the breeches. She stowed the tinker's lamp and the eyepiece into a carpenter's bag from the mates' cabin across the hall and slung it across her shoulders as she stood.

The door hung on one hinge, but it opened all right, and she stepped out into the hallway. Athen was there, Cram behind him. She didn't want to go back into her room. It would have been going back to something lost. She had left.

Lord Athen spoke first. "War council?"

Cram cringed. "Milord, perhaps the young miss

wishes to wait here while we, er, manage things?"

"She is made of sterner stuff than you might think, Cram, and we will need all of our assets in the coming fracas."

"Aye, sir." Cram nodded sagely. "And, um, what is 'fracas'?"

"A fight," Ruby put in. "We have to hurry before we come to ground wherever they are taking us. We need to find out where they spirited my father, and whoever is at the wheel of that scow may know."

"A scow is—"

"The tugboat, Cram."

"Thank you, miss."

Cram shuffled his feet.

"Spirited?"

"Kidnapped."

"Ah."

Fat Maggie had seen better days. The wooden figurehead at the prow of the vessel was a wide sea wench of the old Portuguese style, and all the crew had loved everything about her, including her girth. Ruby was sad to see her shoulder and part of her chest sheared clean away. A wayward warning shot or some strange chemystral engine? In any case, Fat Mags easily hid the three of them behind her ample waist as they spied on the small boat at the other end of the gooey gray tow ropes.

It was tiny. In length you could have lined up five front to back and not matched the *Thrift*. It was very wide, though, and had a large, active, and churning paddle wheel at its rear. There was no sail, not even a mast. No colors, though on top of the little freestanding cabin at its prow was an empty flagpole. Whoever was piloting it was brilliant, towing the *Thrift* like this on the open sea.

Athen held out the monocle to Ruby. "Just to the right of the wheelhouse."

She took it and moved to the rail, focusing on the little boat. The green metal warmed under her fingers, and the chem sloshed around inside it, and the picture cleared. The tug was a length of the *Thrift* away, and everything was big as life.

She was, however, looking at the waterfall rolling from

the paddle wheel. She panned past the windowless wooden planks of the back of the wheelhouse, and indeed, the edge of a foot was sticking out of the doorway. "Bare feet and dingy trousers mean a sailor, not a soldier," she said.

"From the size of that thing, no more than two or three others." Athen mused aloud. "We've lost the greater part of the day, and we have one foot and a glimpse of trouser to show for it."

Ruby nodded. "Time is pressing. Who knows if we strike land tomorrow or if that ship's momma comes back to cuddle?"

Lord Athen ran his hand along the gray hawser. "This rope has good purchase. It might be possible to climb across to get a better look."

"Begging your pardon, milord, but you'd be plucked like washing on a line if that fella or fellas pokes his head out the door to take a breath of fresh air," Cram said.

"He's right," Ruby said, and began winding a piece of twine from the deck into her hair to make a pigtail.

"So what would you have us do?" Athen demanded. "Just sit here and wait until we reach our destination, whatsoever it may be? If they find us, Cram, I assure you it will not go well."

"What about the money? Like I said, no disrespect, sir, but a few shillings here, a few pounds there . . ."

"Do I need to remind you of our previous conversation?"

Cram casually brushed the front of his neck. "No, indeed. Just trying to help, sir."

"If I don't go down that rope, and maybe you two as well, we're prisoners. Is there any other option?"

Ruby finished her other pigtail. "I have one," she said, and climbed up on the railing, holding on to the blown-off edge of Fat Maggie's shoulder. The churning frenzy of the ocean waited far below.

Athen, eyes wide, looked up at her. "What are you doing?"

"Help!" she screamed over the water as loud as she could. "Heeeeeeeelllp!"

"Ruby, stop!" Athen grabbed at her leg, but she kicked back and caught him a good one in the forehead. Mostly unintentionally.

She heard him sprawl back to the deck, and she muttered in a low voice, "Don't. You'll ruin the sharp. I'm the only one they can see, and I'm a terrified girl in desperate need of saving."

She yelled again, "Help me!"

Sound carries well over water. A grizzled old sailor stuck his head out of the wheelhouse and looked back at her. His eyes turned into saucers when he saw a young girl in pigtails trapped against the very front of the empty ship that they'd been towing through the empty ocean for the better part of two days. This was what Gwath meant when he said to her once, "You show the target a scene so ridiculous that it must be true."

The sailor's head ducked back inside the wheelhouse as if his gray hair had been set afire, and then another head popped out: a bigger, younger one. The head had a haystack of blond hair and perched atop the shoulders of a huge cat of a man. He looked up at her across the span of water, and he began to laugh. He laughed for a good long time.

Ruby began to think that perhaps she might have

made a mistake. She threw in another "Heeeelp!" and a little scream for good measure.

He cupped one scarred hand to his mouth. "Ahoy, *Thrift!*" he bellowed. "Bide your time and we'll find a way to get you down."

And then he waggled his finger at her like a sweet old schoolmaster. "We've been looking for you, Ruby Teach!"

CHAPTER II

We are the seekers in the night,
We forge on when all are spent,
We harry the guilty and punish the wicked,
We are England's arm,
We are England's bones,
We are England's hammer.
There is no rest, there is no pain, there is no barrier
Until our shores are safe.

Oath of the Reeve

The man stood in the aft of the little tug and bobbed up and down with ease, like a bug on a branch. His breeches and coat were dark, lightweight wool, and his face was cheerfully empty. He reminded Ruby somehow of Gwath.

"Heeeelp!" She tried to regain the initiative. This man knew her, but she had never seen him before. Why was he looking for her?

"You are safe!" he called.

"But where is the crew?" Ruby called back. Gwath had called the scams and con games they ran sharps, and Sweet and Fearful was one of her best. Marks saw a harmless girl, paralyzed with fear, and they would run down the alley to her aid; Gwath would clean up from there. It helped that she truly was terrified. She wailed, "They've all disappeared. I fear what may happen to me!"

"Now, now, Miss Teach. I have informed you that we shall find a way to get you down from the *Thrift*, and that is exactly what we shall do. Please allow me and my companion some little time to hatch a stratagem."

"Can't you just reel us in? Where is the crew? Who are you?" She knew full well the answer to the first question but thought that might unstopper a talkative man in the direction of the second and third.

"Point the first. I imagine you know that we can't get too close to the *Thrift*. She is heavier than we are, and Squires in the wheelhouse is having a tricky enough time bringing her in on the open sea without having her crush our tinker's wheel here to bits." He brushed his thick fingers over the paddles as they dived past him into the waves. "Point the second. Perhaps we can speak of the crew when we have you close and safe. As for me, my name is Wisdom Rool. I am special envoy to Parliament and first captain of the Reeve of England. Delighted to make your acquaintance." He sketched her a bow across the water and then turned and disappeared into the wheelhouse.

As soon as he was inside, Ruby jumped to the deck.

"Just what do you think you're doing?" Athen hissed, crouched out of sight under the railing. "You have compromised our tactical advantage at the very least."

Cram was less diplomatic. "That was dead stupid, girl."

"Do you have a better plan?" Ruby attacked. "They could be towing us who knows where, to a base with more men, or farther from my father and the crew."

"And that other ship might be hightailing it back at any moment," Cram said.

"If it is, we are lost already," Ruby cut in. "Let's get back to the wave in front of us." She turned to Athen. "Can you and your man help me with yon great stack of pork?"

The dandy leaned in. "Our alliance has never been in question for my part. You, if I recall, were the one who kicked me in the face."

Ruby reddened. "I asked you a question."

Somehow Athen bowed from his knees. "I am, of course, at your service, milady."

She turned to Cram. "And you?"

Cram frowned even deeper. "Mam always said the only way to snuff a real fire was to throw family at it until it goes out. The more family you got, the more it spreads out the burnin'." He tapped his nose and gave her a look that he must have thought looked wise.

"I'll take that as an aye," Ruby said. "Keep an ear out for a change in the wind. I'll try to call out anything I can to help."

As she scrambled back up to Fat Maggie, Wisdom Rool called out from below. He had returned to the stern. "Miss Teach! Welcome back. I had begun to think I might need to navigate this crevasse without your pleasant company!" His speech was fine, but there was no feeling behind it. It gave her the itches. He was kneeling down at a heavy metal box and was sorting through its contents. His waistcoat and shoes were off, and he was down to vest, shirt, and breeches. He wore strange stockings that exposed his big, knobby toes.

Ruby went fishing. "Have you a plan? Will you be sending your men aboard somehow, or help us down?"

Wisdom Rool smiled as he pulled a thick glove out of the box. It fitted over his massive hand halfway up the forearm and looked metallic. For a moment Ruby thought it might be a gauntlet of iron or steel, like those knights wore in olden times, but the way it flattened to his skin and rippled in the sunlight made her think of cloth or snakeskin rather than metal.

"Alas, I have no squadron of bravos, Miss Teach. They have left me behind with only a skeleton crew. We are a complement of two, Squires and I, and he needs must stay at the wheel. I am but a boarding party of one. I trust that you have not prepared an ambuscade for me?" He smiled. Ruby clenched her teeth. "I hope you have no hidden compatriots ready to fall on poor me at a moment's notice?"

"Course not." Ruby's lie sounded weak to her own seasoned ears. "It's just me up here."

"I am glad to hear it," Rool said. "That way our relations can continue to be cordial. Otherwise, things might go another way, which neither you nor I might prefer." He pulled the other glove on, and it fitted as tightly as the first. He stood and rolled his shoulders around, then tucked a large bag into his belt.

"What are you doing?" Ruby asked.

"Why, I'm coming up there to see you, Miss Teach, so that I can help you down here to safety," he said. "And if you will not come down, I shall pop you in this sack like so much market day baggage."

Then he jumped into the air. At first Ruby thought the man had gone mad and was throwing himself into the deep. But he caught himself on the thick, greasy rope, and he hung there easy as you please. Then he began to climb. He swung himself forward and up, muscles bunching under the thin wool of his vest. His other mitt followed the first, and he pulled himself hand over hand up toward Ruby. He was moving quickly, far too quickly, with no sign of effort, legs dangling over the hungry waves.

Ruby muttered over her shoulder, "Ready for it? He is coming quick!"

There was no response.

"What was that, Miss Teach?" Rool interjected as if he were at a garden party. He was halfway across the gap now and if anything was gaining speed.

She risked a glance behind her. Cram was standing there wide-eyed with a boat hook dangling from his hands. Fear had stuck him to the deck. When Ruby gave him the stinkeye to get him to move, he shook his head vigorously and even took a step backward. Lord Athen was nowhere to be seen.

Ruby cursed under her breath. A life on the *Thrift* had taught her some phrases that might light a parson's wig afire. She used them all in rapid succession. She shifted her feet backward along Fat Maggie's rail toward the deck.

"Careful there," Wisdom Rool counseled, hanging by his hands not two man-lengths from the railing. "Without

gloves like these the basaltic cables can be quite slippery."
This close she could see that it was not just his hands that
were scarred but his face, feet, and neck, too. Every inch
of his skin was covered with ropy trails that looked like
some devil's mad quilt.

Ruby reached the edge of the figurehead, without
slipping, thank you, and clambered down to the deck.
Neither Cram nor Athen was anywhere to be seen.
Cowards, both of them. She turned back to the prow to
see Rool loose one hand and swing himself like a jungle
beast to grasp on to the railing right next to Fat Maggie's
belly.

Nothing for it, Ruby thought. Head straight for the
storm. She pulled her knife from under her dress and
rushed forward to slash down at Wisdom Rool's glove
just as he was swinging his other from the hawser. She hit
something, she was sure of it, though he made no sound.
His hand disappeared from the railing.

The other hand did not land on the railing.

Just like that, the man called Wisdom Rool was no
longer hanging from anything. She rushed to the edge

to try to spot him in the water, but she did not need to look far.

He was hanging there, halfway down the hull of the *Thrift*, feet dangling above the water below. The tinker gloves were pressed flat against the hull, and he was clinging with them like some kind of huge fly. He looked up at her, and he smiled.

He levered one hand loose, the thick muscles on his back shifted, and he threw the hand higher. Somehow it stuck to the hull. This way he began pulling himself upward. Ruby whirled to see Athen framed in the opening to the hold. She would have flayed him alive if she had not been so happy to see him.

She waved him over, holding a finger to her lips. His eyes widened, and he hurried quietly up the stairs. He had gone back for his cloak. Ridiculous. She pushed him in the shoulder and almost knocked him from the forecastle. She reached out, horrified, but he caught himself with one hand on the railing and one to her wrist. He had small hands, but an iron grip inside those gloves.

He stared at her for a moment, hard. She shrugged

an apology and pointed at the place where Rool had gone over the side. He hadn't come up yet, but she knew it was only a matter of time. Athen scanned the deck for Cram and grimaced when he saw the servant had run. There would be many reckonings if they all made it through this. Ruby pulled her other knife from its hiding place. She had never fought anyone before, but Gwath had taught her what to do. She hoped she wouldn't crack.

Athen's eyes were all wild, and he grinned at her. He drew his sword. It made a small, leathery scrape as it came out of his scabbard. In *Bastionado* swords hissed and sang. The blade widened into a heavier diamond-shaped cross-section at the hilt. Ruby hoped he knew how to use it. He wound his other hand deep into his cloak and nodded at her.

They crept to the railing, the sound of the waves accompanying their progress. Athen mouthed counting to three, and they both popped their heads over the edge.

Rool was not there.

"Rudimentary," rumbled a voice from the other side of Fat Maggie. Ruby whirled. Rool was crouching on the railing as if it were his favorite rocking chair. "Why would I climb back up to have you stab me once again, Miss Teach? That was inhospitable." He assessed Athen. "Will you introduce me to your friend? No? That is a fine blade, young man. I would suggest you sheathe it before one or more of us are harmed. I am unarmed, as you see." He spread his hands wide. The gauntlets up close seemed to be covered with a fine layer of scales. Blood trickled from the right one down his arm. "I fear that a friendly solution is past us, but we can still have a result where no one is irredeemably damaged."

"Your words are wind, sir," Athen responded. He took a small step to the right, point aimed at the much larger man's right eye. "You are hardly unarmed. I know a Reeve when I see one."

"And I know what I see, as well, *sir*"—Rool laughed— "though Miss Teach may not."

Sometimes things happen very quickly.

Athen uncoiled like a spring and lunged forward, point dropping, to try to take Wisdom Rool in the chest. Feet balled beneath him, the big man could not have dodged to the left or right. He tried to do neither. Instead, he jumped upward, tucked his legs in a somersault over Lord Athen's outstretched blade and landed upright behind him. Rool spun and clubbed Athen brutally between the shoulder blades with one gauntleted fist and aside the head with the other. Athen crumpled to the deck insensate.

The scarred man turned to Ruby as she ran toward him, knives ready, yelling with either fury or fear, she did not know which. He brushed her aside with one massive hand, and she flew through the air to crash against the outer rail near Athen. The bulkhead gave her a nasty knock on the head as she landed, and she struggled to stay conscious. Little purple halos surrounded everything. Bells were ringing somewhere. She looked up, and Wisdom Rool was standing over her. He was saying something, but she couldn't hear it. She was at the bottom of the sea. He laughed, and then he pulled the sack from his belt. She scraped her feet against the deck with what little strength she had left and pushed herself backward.

Rool opened the sack. Suddenly his eyes widened in suspicion. He whirled, but it was too late. A man rushed toward him, someone Ruby had feared she would never see again. Gwath was brandishing, of all things, a heavy iron stewpot. He swung the pot around like a Titan, and it slammed squarely into Rool's chest. Rool flew into the air, over Ruby, and over the rail. Gwath sprang forward to peer over the railing.

Now where has he been hiding? she wondered as she drifted off to sleep.

CHAPTER 12

I, Tom Givens, foreman at the Benzene Yards, have for some time been troubled with a Wracking Cough. Upon the prescription of one Doctor Argosy, 8 Seraphim Court, Shambles, I have begun each morning with a Heaping Spoonful of Mercury. Since then, I find myself Light at Heart and Steady in my Chest. I do heartily recommend his services to all who may labour under the same Distemper.
—Advertisement, *The Onlooker,* September 22, 1718

Ruby woke. Above her were the points of a thousand knives. She raised up on an elbow, but the starlight and the moon cut into her eyes in earnest and a band of fire tightened around her head. She lay back, shut her lids against the annoyingly cheerful heavens, and attempted to get her bearings.

The rough, soft pillow cradling her throbbing head smelled of sawdust from the carpenter's shop. They had bags of the stuff down there. She knew the feel of the *Thrift*'s deck against her hands the way other children knew sums or Bible passages. She breathed in the sea, wrapped herself in the bass creak of the masts, and relaxed into the timbers. She was still home at least.

The moments before her blackout danced away from her stumbling thoughts. There had been a fight. Athen hurt. Rool had thrown her. She had smashed her head against the rail. Then what? The terrifying man flew through the air over the rail. And Gwath. Gwath had been there! The whole series of events flew back into her mind, and she forced her eyes open, propping herself up on her elbow, steeling herself against the pain.

"Gwath?" she rasped. Thunder in her skull. Her throat was dry.

Someone groaned behind her. She turned slowly, wincing, to see Athen, propped up against a sack of cornmeal. He looked like a sack of flesh himself, a broken marionette flopped there in the moonlight.

"What happened?" he muttered, reaching up to rub his temples but stopping with a hiss. "Where is Rool?

Did you fight him? Are we captives?"

A small part of her thanked him for even thinking that she might have been able to hold off that force of nature. The larger part of her, however, focused on the small piece of parchment she found tucked under the bag of sawdust.

It was one of Gwath's drawings, sketched lines that suggested shape, rather than defined it. Two figures stood back to back on a ship, weapons drawn, and one cowered in the hold. Circling the ship was a shark, covered with ropy scars. A shadowy squid stalked the shark. Rool was alive, and Gwath was hiding, hoping to flush him out.

"Miss Teach?" Athen pressed.

"It was Gwath."

"The cook? Where is he?"

"I don't know." Where had he come from? Why had he hidden himself from her?

"Where did you go?" Ruby asked.

"To the hold, to get my cloak."

She gave him a look.

"You would be surprised what a skilled duelist can accomplish with a cloak in the off hand."

"I will be sure to keep an eye out when I meet a skilled duelist," she snapped.

Athen tightened his lips and did not respond.

"We should get out of the open," she whispered. "This feels too exposed."

He tensed. "You think that—"

"I am not sure, but I would just as soon not have some demon man drop out of the rigging on me like a sack of coal."

He cast a glance over his shoulder and levered himself slowly up to standing. "Come on." She grabbed the hand he offered and pulled herself up next to him.

Athen was not a brute of a boy, perhaps a head taller than she. But he had fought beside her, against a terrible opponent. He had a weight about him. He carved space somehow. He was more *here* than anyone she had known, even Gwath or her father. And there was something else, too, right now, prowling about behind the stars reflected in his eyes—

Wait.

Ruby pushed Athen away to get a better look at the lights in the distance.

"Those are not stars." She pointed at the base of the horizon.

"Ruby—" Athen turned to her. "Wait, what?" He followed her arm and stared at the cluster of sparkles, wavering in the mist. "That is a city."

They had turned up a wide river. Ruby checked the shoreline, casting about for a landmark. She recognized nothing. She felt a little dizzy. "Yes, and even though this tug is slow, I'd say we'll be there by morning. Come on." She pulled his arm toward the hold.

She hurt all over. She pushed the pain and the moment from her mind, and they tottered toward the steps of the deck, clinging to each other like an old couple she had seen once on the courthouse steps in Charles Towne.

Athen stopped for a moment at the top of the stairs. He stared down at the deck, avoiding her eyes. "I didn't know he would be so fast."

Ruby nodded and clapped him on the back. "Now we do know." It sounded hollow. She couldn't think of anything else to say.

CHAPTER 13

- *Butter of antimony*
- *Prussic acid—do NOT jostle. Remember last time.*
- *Reverberatory furnace (two)*
- *Slaked lime (one bucket)*
- *Tin salt (as much as you can carry)*
  —Shopping list, Aubrey Smallows, apprentice Tinker

The corner was cozy. Better yet, it had the advantages of cornerhood. The walls pressing into Cram's shoulders were solid and fixed, and the wood of the deck was equally solid on his bum and his feet. He snuck a look up to make certain that the ceiling hadn't sprouted spikes or that there wasn't some wild-eyed bogeyman staring down at him. It seemed trustworthy for now.

But Cram was coming to believe that objects were

not necessarily what they appeared to be on this mad vessel. First, the crew of genial boobs and pirate shams had snapped into a band of hard-bitten toughs when they kenned the crown was coming for them. Then the hold had opened its secret doors and cabinets to hide them from the boarding party of sea demons that were after his new master. What could a young man trust if he couldn't trust the seat under his, er, seat?

Cram had fled the deck. He was not proud of it, but it had been the savvy thing to do. That mad girl had rallied them to battle against whatever force of nature that man Rool was. Cram had been ready to do his part: a knock on the noggin from behind, a well-placed trip to tip the balance of a fencing match. He was ready to scuffle his share. But when Lord Athen turned tail like a flushed rabbit, he could see the tale of the ticket. It was every boy for himself, and Mam always said the last to run is the first to get nicked. Quick and quiet, he had tucked down the stairs, shot the latch on the door (not his proudest moment), barred it for good measure, and hunkered down behind a barrel in the deepest shadows of the unlit galley.

That was when it all turned ipsy-dipsy.

He had slunk behind the barrel to shield himself better from the doorway, in case the wild man might open it, but before he could catch his breath, the barrel wood under his hands had wriggled. Shifted, slightly, and then it hadn't even felt like wood anymore. It had been more like skin. Or something in between. Wood skin. Then just skin, and there had been a big man in the dark in front of him, who'd pinned him by the throat with one hand and whispered thunderously into his ear, "Where is Ruby Teach?"

Cram had entertained, for the tiniest of moments, lying to this barrel shade, this kitchen monster, but the strength in the beast's hands had wrung all thoughts but self-preservation out of his head. "Up top," he had squeaked, and as quick as a stoat after a mouse the hands were off him and the door tore open. The light had framed, just for a moment, the bizarre picture of the back of a huge naked man holding an iron stewpot. Then he'd disappeared up the steps.

That had been hours ago, and the rest of the galley had remained reassuringly solid. Cram, however, was not a trusting soul. He had grown up in a neighborhood somewhat south of trust. So he had rebarred the door, hunkered down in his corner, and waited.

The sounds of a ruckus had filtered from above a few moments after the barrel man had bounded up the stairs, but after that it had remained eerily quiet.

Until the door rattled. Cram jumped and cursed under his breath. The demon had come back for him. It had finished off his companions and most like was still hungry. Both of the others didn't have much meat on them, so it had come back for the main course.

The manly thing to do would be to grab a chair or a weapon, rip open the door, and sell his life as dearly as he could.

He put his hands over his eyes and tried to keep as still and quiet as possible.

"Cram!" The voice was familiar and urgent. "Let us in! We know you're in there! We've searched the rest of the ship." It surely sounded like his master. Of course, what was a human shape to one that had so recently mastered the art of barrels?

"Don't think you are pulling it over my eyes, demon!" he shot at the barred door through clenched teeth. "If you hain't already broke through the door, there must be some kind of prevention on you, like them bloodsuckers my mam told me about. If you need permissions to come in, you ain't getting them from me!"

"Cram, it is Ruby and Athen!" The beast's voice had switched to the girl's. Clever. "We need to get in there and out of the open!" It was very talented. It even captured that hint of frustration or scorn that was part of most of her conversations with him.

He inched closer to the door and said clearly, "Not for a thousand pounds or all the tea in Araby will I open this door. There's monsters and huge naked men about, and you're most like one or t'other."

The beast switched back to his master's voice. "Cram, you must recognize us. How can we prove it to you, so that you might unbar the door?" It was a coiled, controlled anger, as when you might speak to a child who was doing wrong, but who would just do worse if you got angry with it. It reminded him of Mam.

The memory weakened him. "All right, but you only get one chance. I and my master, whose voice you now wear, recently had a sit-down regarding my long-term contract with him. I declared myself at said time as a certain type of man. What did I call myself?"

"A coward."

"Untrue."

"What do you mean, 'untrue'? It was only a few hours ago! I remember it clear as noontime sun!"

"Clearly you do not remember correctly. My master came to me in fear and appealed for my aid in counseling his afraidness."

"I did no such thing!"

"I am sorry to say that that is how I remember it." Cram folded his arms.

The voice oozed menace through the cracks in the frame. "You open this door, Cram, or you will soon be utterly alone on this ship."

"Better alone and alive." Cram leaned back against the wall.

"We will simply break it down."

"See, your true colors are shining through."

There was a silence on the other side of the door.

"You know that you'll never get off this ship alive without the other two of us." It was the sneaky voice, the girl's again. "Also, if you let us in, I'll show you where my father keeps his secret stash of rum."

He pulled the bolt and cracked open the door.

A small, bony, incredibly sharp foot lashed through the opening and cracked against his shin. He howled, and two bodies tumbled through the door in the dim half-light. One replaced the bolt, and the other kept kicking him.

"Ow! Ow! Stop it!" he said, trying to fend off the little lightning strikes aimed at both his shins.

"It is us, you muttonhead!" the smaller figure whispered. "Ruby and Lord Athen." The kicks were painful, but not nearly as strong as the terrifying strength of the previous monster.

"All right, all right. We'll see if you don't turn yourselves into muskets or barrels or worse," he whispered. "Please stop the kicking." The two figures calmed a bit, and the one that looked like Ruby took a tinker's lamp out of a bag and turned up the light. They were a mess, a mass of cuts and bruises.

They stared at one another.

Cram spoke first. "What about that rum then?"

The girl looked him up and down. "I lied," she said.

Perhaps it was them after all.

CHAPTER 14

Laugh at the Rain.
Laugh at the Reaper.
Run from the Reeve.
                    —Old Irish saying

Ruby crept from below like a ghost in mist. The full moon had cooperated and snuck behind a bank of clouds like a coconspirator. There were shadows and dark corners everywhere. It was the kind of night Skillet had called just enough light to make trouble.

She slipped from the shadow of the mast to an island of rope in the central deck, to the shelter under the forecastle stairs. Now that they were moving, now that they were in action, she let all the worries fall away. She ran her thumb over where she had carved her name in the underside of the third step. The *Thrift* was her place. No jumped-up, scarred-up constable would find her if she didn't want to be found.

Once Cram had opened the door, they held a quick council. Gwath's strange power. His hunt for Rool. The nearby city. They settled on a desperate plan, but they had all agreed it was their only chance.

So she sneaked up to Fat Maggie. The dim line of the hawser rolled down to the tug, and a little island of light spilled out of the wheelhouse. The city twinkled beyond, perhaps a few miles away. By morning at the latest, the tug would bring them into dock, and the ship would be flooded with soldiers and sailors and chemystral monsters. They were truly flushed rabbits, and the hunters were closing.

She threw one of the wood nails she had brought with her, and it made a solid clack on the wall next to the stairs. At the signal Athen and Cram sneaked out of the door to the lifeboat hanging from hooks on the port side. Ruby scanned the rear deck and the water below for sinister shadows as the two began to lower the little vessel over the side. This was a game of cats and mice. She understood mice more deeply at that moment than ever in her life. Whether or not the cats are fighting, the mouse just wants to go on its way.

Behind her, down on the deck, Cram muffled a curse. It carried like a gunshot in the ocean air. She whirled to see what had happened, and Wisdom Rool was there before her.

"You're quite the little sneaker, Ruby Teach," Rool said. He was dripping water head to toe, and one arm was lashed to his shoulder with a sling of torn sail.

Ruby backed against Fat Maggie.

"Quiet now. Your two compatriots have just discovered that there is a fist-size hole in that lifeboat, and the prissy one at least will deduce that the thing will begin sinking the moment it hits the water." He closed in a step, looming over her. "You and I have unfinished business. Now, duty still requires that I offer you the opportunity to surrender and avoid any unpleasant actions, which may, perhaps, descend upon you and your allies. What say you?"

The man was a demon. Terror clawed up her legs and fixed its claws around her throat. She couldn't speak. She needed to summon a ruse, to pretend, to make it all better and trick him into letting them go.

Nothing came.

She fumbled under her dress, drawing her knives.

Rool laughed. "I was hoping you would say that." His good right hand snaked forward, knocked one knife to the deck, and then flashed to the other hand, where he bent her wrist. She heard a pop. She gasped. He snatched the knife from the air as it fell toward the deck.

She tried to seize the moment and darted past him, but his foot lashed out and took her ankle from under her. She fell to the deck, and the first knife skittered over the edge.

Rool unlimbered the sack with his wounded arm and let it hang open. He was not a demon. He was a demonic ratcatcher, and she was as helpless as a rodent in a trap.

The moon came out, time slowed, and she wondered

if Wisdom Rool was the last thing she would see for quite some time. Staring up at his empty eyes, she was perfectly positioned to see the shape of Gwath drop like vengeance toward him from the rigging, high above.

She was also perfectly positioned to see Rool spin and plant her knife squarely in Gwath's chest before he slammed into the deck next to her.

"Now that was just lucky," Rool said as he crouched in a ready stance with her knife poised to slash in once again. "This gentleman and I have been dancing all over, around, above, and below the ship for hours, and you have finally helped me uncover him."

Gwath moaned beside her and pushed himself up to one knee, breathing heavily.

Rool smiled. "Run along now, or stay if you wish. He and I also have unfinished business. Talk some sense into your friends. This won't take long."

She turned to Gwath. He was bent over, fists bunched in his trousers. "Go," he said. There was blood on his lips.

Ruby ran.

≈ ≈ ≈

Cram was standing with his back wedged against a pylon, inching out the two ropes. They passed up through suspended pulleys over the side to the lifeboat below.

"It's Rool!" Ruby breathed, and the boy cursed.

"Grab a line, Ferret." He nodded to the two hawsers. He was struggling to hang on to both of them. Without thinking Ruby grabbed at one, and Cram let it go. As soon as she had all of the weight, pain flowered up her arm from her injured wrist. She gasped and tried to hold on, but the rope burned her other hand as it sped past her palm.

Cram yelped in pain and held on for a moment, but then both ropes were free, and there was a splash below. The ropes passed up through the pulleys and then spiraled down to the water.

"Like party ribbons," Cram said as they both peered over the side. The shape in the dark that was Athen waved to them from below.

Cram kicked a rope ladder over the side and started down. Ruby grabbed at him with her good hand. She couldn't think straight. "The boat . . . it's not—"

Cram waved her off. "The master fixed it, popped some tinker goo in there. Won't last long, he says. Come on!" He started down the ladder.

She tried. She threw her leg over the rail and held on with her good hand, but the rope was wet. Her foot slipped out, and she barely kept on the ladder with the other foot. She was splayed out like a cooked fish on the rail.

"Wait!" Ruby whispered.

Cram looked up.

"I—I can't. My wrist." It was already beginning to swell.

The boy blinked, and she thought he might keep going, leaving her to die or worse. He cursed under his breath and climbed back up to her.

"Come on then, Ferret." She wrapped her arms around his shoulders. His odor of cheese and turnips was the best thing she'd ever smelled. She held on tight with her good hand and the elbow of the other arm.

They both landed in freezing ankle-deep water in

the bottom of the boat. "What happened? Can we go?" Athen asked.

Her wrist was ice and fire, and the monster behind too terrifying. "Go! He's dead. Go!" she whispered, and the others grabbed oars from the oarlocks and began to row away from the *Thrift* into the night.

CHAPTER 15

At tea, treat your guests with Honor and Warmth. No matter your skills with a flask, Surly Hosting always leads to a Tarnished Reputation.
　　　　　—Bethilda Fwallop, *A Young Tinker's Guide to Polite Society*

The mouse's single remaining chemystral eye recorded a scene far distant from London's Clove and Camel coffeehouse. Its olfactory sensors had scented over three thousand miles since it had hitched a stealthy ride on Lord Athen's boot.

The past seventy-four hours, five minutes, and twelve seconds had pushed its ingenuity and survival protocols to their limits. The boarding of the *Thrift* by a horde of thundering boots created an ever-shifting maze of huge soles stomping down from above, punctuated by the bodies of men crashing to the deck. Lord Athen had disappeared, and its secondary target, Captain Wayland Teach, hurtled about the pitched battle with unsettling speed and violence. The fat man was a mobile cyclone.

Trapped on a piece of exposed rigging, one eye clawed out, hiding scripts depleted, the mouse had almost been ready for scrap when an island of safety passed below it. The little mechanical did not hesitate and jumped silently into the shelter of cut-rate pirate finery.

It was not a moment too soon. Captain Teach, half a bloody cutlass in one hand, chair leg club in the other, suddenly relented. He delivered his broken sword to the captain of the huge ship that had grappled onto the *Thrift*.

The mouse's view dropped precariously toward the deck and then righted itself as Teach bowed. The Royal Navy captain, a younger man with a set of rich red muttonchops, returned a bow of his own.

"You have us, sir. We surrender."

"I accept your surrender, Captain. We will take your vessel as a prize. Please coordinate the movement of your crew and passengers over to the *Grail*. Mr. Flanders here will situate them."

"Very well, sir."

Without ready access to the metals that powered it, the mouse went into fuel conservation mode. It captured one frozen image per minute. The following days were a hurried picture book of metal corridors, a spartan cabin, a porthole view of a city at night, more metal corridors, and then a posh stateroom. Captain Teach spent almost the entire time by himself, often on the ample feather bed, where he restlessly failed to sleep.

From the depths of the dark corner, the old man asked, "What stands out to you?"

The apprentice, well past boyhood but still not yet a man, froze the flickering story in the looking glass and made certain that the calipers were secure on the mouse automaton he had liberated from a garbage bin. He stared for a long while at the picture on the screen.

"The captain surrendered too soon," he said. "They were holding and could have repelled boarders."

"Did he seem incompetent?"

"Far from it. I have never seen a braver showing. If his cutlass had not broken . . ."

"Then why surrender?"

The apprentice turned to the screen and then back to the corner where the old man crouched in the overstuffed chair like a spider. "I do not know."

"Good. Neither do I. But if we watch further, perhaps we shall discover it together."

The apprentice measured out more of the silver gray powder into the hole in the mouse's back. The mechanical jerked once, and the screen flared to life again.

The mouse's iris (singular) opened as a new stimulus jolted it out of hibernation. It was still perched in the hat, which hung from a hat rack in the corner of the room.

The heavy door opened, revealing a tall man flanked by two much larger men. The mouse immediately filed the two big ones, despite their spotless naval uniforms, into that area of its chemystral brain labeled "Thugs." They remained in the hallway as the third stepped into the room and closed the door behind him.

It was the captain of the massive tinker ship that had taken the *Thrift*. He was young, but his weathered skin and ropy build told the story of a hard life at sea. His splendid red muttonchops flared below the line of his jaw like dual rudders. A scar peeked out from behind the left one. He was accompanied by a gearbeast crafted from red iron. It had been modeled after an Irish wolfhound and sat poised at his hip. It snuffled through its iron nose. The mouse's eye became very still.

The younger captain removed his hat and tucked it under his arm. "Captain Teach?" he said. Teach had taken up residence in the window seat, leg tucked under him in a pose out of place for such a big man. He was staring out the window but turned and stood after a moment.

"Sir, you have me at a disadvantage."

"Ah, my apologies. I am Captain MacDevitt of His Majesty's Ship *Grail*. At your service."

"And I am at yours, for accepting our surrender. It is not an easy thing to curb one's men when there is blood on the decks."

MacDevitt's eyes flickered about the room. "I trust your quarters are suitable?"

"Indeed, Captain. Will you sit?" Teach motioned to the glass-topped table and the two comfortable chairs in the corner of the room.

"I thank you for your offer, Captain, but I am not a man who spends much time at rest."

"Well, I am." Teach flopped into a chair. "I find that sitting improves one's humors, especially when one is carrying around one's own personal ballast." He patted his not-inconsiderate belly. "Now, how may I help you, Captain?"

"Before we begin, I wonder if you might like some refreshment." He called to the closed door, "Gregor?" One of the two big men ambled into the room, a tea tray in his massive hands.

"You grow your stewards large in His Majesty's service," Teach commented.

"Indeed. Gregor and Big Bill are two of my best."

"Big Bill is the other one?"

"No. That is Saul. You haven't met Big Bill yet."

"Ah. So Big Bill is even bigger than . . ."

"Yes."

"Ah."

The two men sipped their tea.

"How are my men?" Teach asked.

MacDevitt smiled. "They are well. They have quarters befitting their rank, and I have had my people see to the wounded. Some cuts. Your bosun, Skillet, refused to surrender when you ordered your men to stand down, so he is a bit more banged up but will recover. They have asked several times after you. Their respect for you is obvious. You are lucky to command such men."

"We have been together a long while," Teach said.

They sipped more tea.

"This is quite a vessel you command," Teach ventured.

"She is a fine ship."

Teach laughed. "More than fine. I have never seen anything like her."

MacDevitt smiled. "I will not disagree with you."

Sipping.

Teach put his cup down on its porcelain saucer. "Have we finished with the pleasantries?"

MacDevitt sighed. "Yes, Captain Teach. I believe we have." He replaced his teacup on the table. The gearbeast snuffled and began pacing. "I am intrigued by your passenger manifests, logs, and other papers."

"What in particular intrigues you about them?"

"We could not find any such item on the entirety of the ship."

"I am sorry to hear that."

"Were you carrying any passengers on this trip?"

"No."

The mouse's eye, which had been following the conversation between the two men, must have been overridden by its danger fail-safes. It was now focused almost completely on the red iron gearbeast's increasingly agitated snufflings around the room.

"Captain Teach, I must tell you I have heard you were a marshmallow of a man, a show captain, a jumped-up carriage driver who would roll over at the slightest pressure. You seem nothing of the kind."

"Thank you?"

"Do you know that I am a student of history?"

"Indeed? In what area?"

"My position on this ship allows me to spend a good portion of my shore leave neck deep in the Invisible College Archives, reading accounts of exploits that are kept secret from most eyes."

"Ha."

"You chuckle, sir?"

"I mean no offense, Captain MacDevitt. My laughter is to marvel at the vagaries of chance, that is all."

"Chance that your captor may be in a position to understand your true identity?"

"We are a band of jumped-up minstrels, sir. We pretend to pirate. We chuckle and scrape. We offer an entertaining myth, so that those with too much money may travel from place to place with a sense of adventure."

"You are not, then, the captain of an infamous crew of scalawags, thought lost on the seas of time?"

"I cannot say."

"Sir, I must tell you that I am pressed by circumstance toward dishonorable action. If you do not answer my questions, I shall be forced to have Big Bill ask them for me."

"I understand your position, sir. I have old acquaintance with the Big Bills of the world, though I am somewhat out of practice. I am certain we will get on splendidly."

"Very well. My apologies for what is to come. Gentlemen? If you would be so kind—"

Snuffling and growling overwhelmed the conversation, as the face and metal jaws of the gearbeast moved toward the camera of the mouse's eye at breakneck speed. There was wild movement, violent shaking, the scream of sheared metal, and then darkness.

"That is the last of it." The apprentice teased the disconnected mouse tail out of the horn silver vat and replaced it in the padded case with the other parts of the rodent automaton.

He then began to break down the connection between

the vat and the clever tinker's lamp that had allowed them to watch the projections of the little artifact's last moments.

The old man, swathed in blankets even though the heat in the room was stifling, stared at an orrery on a side table next to his overstuffed chair. The planets swung round one another.

The round room had no windows. It was tall, at least three stories high, and floor-to-ceiling shelves covered the walls, filled with apparatuses, devices, and books. There were many, many books. It was the most complete library on the continent, though perhaps only four or five people living knew that it existed.

Finally he rasped, "What do we know?"

The apprentice placed the sensitive connectors in a rack on the wall. He straightened his uniform jacket.

"Very well, Master Fermat—"

"Do not call me Master," the old man interrupted.

"As you wish, Professor," the boy began again.

"Or Professor either," the old man reinterrupted. "It has been forty years since I taught at university, and

I relish every moment I am free from the gabbling and preening of entitled fops. If you insist on giving me formal titles, I shall call you Midshipman Collins, and then where shall we be?"

"But you teach me, do you not, Ma—Pro—do you not?"

The old man's silver eyes gleamed. "Do I?"

"You do."

"So. What do we know?"

The apprentice spoke slowly, as if examining each word before it came out. "I discovered the remains of a chemystral artifice in a bin at the naval yard. Its rodent appearance suggests that it was a surveillance device of some kind."

"Why?"

The apprentice chewed his lip. It was a bad habit that he might have attempted to break if he had known he had it. "It requires a large investment of resources and expertise to disguise a chemystral recording device in a mobile platform with some capacity for independent reason."

"Plus it is sneaky."

The apprentice chewed harder. "I'm sorry?"

"Mice. They are sneaky. You will discover that metal, wood, and chem, much like flesh, acquire the nature of living things after which they are modeled."

Eventually the apprentice said, "Why?"

"We do not know," the old man said.

The apprentice rolled his eyes.

"What else do we know?" the old man asked.

The apprentice ticked off numbers on his hands, which were formally clasped behind his back. "One, that this Captain Teach is resigned to his fate. Two, that his true nature is different from the one he delivers in public. Three, that he holds information desired by the Royal Navy and, perhaps, Royal Society."

"Why do you say that?"

"MacDevitt, who has captured him, is the captain of the *Grail*, which is a chemystral and martial collaboration between His Majesty's Navy and the Tinkers, who are controlled from Invisible College by the Royal Society. It rests in a secure dock in the Benzene Yards, which is the headquarters of the Tinkers in the colonies."

"Continue."

"Four, that he has been tortured before."

"I would have liked to have had a glimpse of that Big Bill."

"Yes, sir."

"Do not call me sir, either."

The apprentice chewed his lip. "Affirmative."

"What else?"

After quite a long pause the apprentice said, "Nothing."

"You have questions."

"I do."

"What are they?"

The apprentice began to pace.

"Remain still. Pacing shows a lack of discipline."

The apprentice stopped, though he still moved his toes in his boots.

"Your questions? I don't have all day, boy, and you are due back at your post."

The apprentice straightened. "One. Teach claims there were no passenger lists on his passenger ship. But ships of that class almost always carry logs of some type. Why would he hide them or destroy them unless there were passengers?"

"Interesting. What else?"

"Why was MacDevitt so interested in the passengers unless they were searching for them in the first place?"

"Indeed."

"If the finest ship in His Majesty's Navy and its elite crew were hard-pressed to subdue a ship full of mismatched scalawags, who are these scalawags?"

"One more, I think."

The apprentice straightened a button on his frayed but spotless uniform jacket.

"Who and where are these most important missing passengers? And why is the combined power of military and chemystral England searching for them?"

CHAPTER 16

RULES
1. *All iron to be checked at the door.*
2. *All flasks to be checked at the door.*
3. *Civil discourse at all tymes.*
4. *Any body scraps or scuffles, yew shall exit the back way.*
5. *We take pounds sterling, manufactory marks, or horn silver.*
6. *England, Frenches, or Other Continentals are*
   UNWELCOME. Yew shall exit the back way.

       Posted at the Alembic Coffeehouse, UnderTown

It was Philadelphi. Of course it was. A tinker tug *would* be towing the *Thrift* toward the city that had become the center of the colonies. It was almost too cruel that they had been headed there to begin with. As Cram and Athen rowed the leaking lifeboat up the river toward the steamy, glistening shoreline, Ruby cradled her wrist and tried to keep what they were fleeing out of her head. So she filled it with old, familiar landmarks.

To the south squatted the ever-expanding maze of the Benzene Yards. Even in the dark of the earliest morning, the great wheels, towers, chutes, and steam stacks were lit orange and purple from odd angles, shimmering in the heat of the great chemystral furnaces, pulsing from fairyland to nightmare and back. To the north, its dark mass blocking out the sky, loomed the Great Keep of the Rupert's Bay Company, with its fancy shops and fancier folk.

They were headed for the center, the valley between those two mountains on the shore of the Delaware River. The heart of Philadelphi, called the Shambles, was a bubbling cauldron of hard work and hard times.

There were two cities, one stacked on top of the other one. The old town was built on the earth of the shore, and the other hung above it, resting on an artificial shelf built by the Tinkers. The whole thing looked like the mouth of some gigantic beast sticking up out of the river, and their little rowboat was headed straight down its gullet.

There had been little time to talk as they fled the

Thrift. Cram and Athen had both set to their oars as if the devil himself were chasing them, and perhaps he was. Ruby had sat in the prow of the boat, ankles slowly going numb in the frigid standing water. Whatever Athen had done to seal the hole had worked. She had poked at the spongy mass stopping it up until he had whispered at her to stop it.

It did not feel sturdy. She thought about just reaching for the stopped-up hole, ripping up a handful of the stuff, and sending them all down into the dark water. That was what she had done to Gwath, however you wanted to paint it. She had spent the first minutes of their flight staring over her shoulder at the receding mass of the *Thrift*, desperate to sight a big, friendly shape diving over the side and then strongly pulling for the boat triumphant and spent from whatever savage duel he had undergone to guard their escape.

That did not happen.

Indeed, the tug continued toward the Benzene Yards docks as if nothing at all strange had occurred. Not being chased was welcome but confusing. Why was there no alarm? Why did Rool not descend on them like a tidal wave? But he did not.

After that there was only the pain in her wrist, the haggard breathing of the two young men, and the hole in her heart.

Cram finally broke the silence. "Where we goin'?" he asked through gritted teeth. He had begun grunting with each pull, though to his credit he had not slowed.

The sun would be rising soon. Athen, just as winded, covered in sweat, was waiting for her to answer. They would soon be in and among the ships, where too many might note the passage of an odd boat. Her instincts clicked. She needed to curl up in a quiet dark place. She needed to go to ground. In the back of her head Gwath told her to blend in.

"Slow down," Ruby muttered.

"What?" Athen looked up. "Ruby—"

"Slow down," she chattered through chilled teeth. Cold was creeping up through her legs. "We look like we are running. This needs to be an early-morning delivery. We're three errand makers who just got up. We have to blend in. Sleepy, slow, and forgettable."

Cram almost stopped rowing altogether. "As your ladyship wishes," he gasped. They moved slowly into the landscape.

According to her father, the docks had once been a single level, close to the water, but UpTown had changed that. A little girl sat on the edge of the overhang high above, legs sticking out into the air. She was blond and was wearing a pretty little frilly dress. At this distance Ruby couldn't see what it was, but she was eating something, probably something sweet, and she was tossing pebbles over the edge into the water below. It had to be a hundred feet to the water, but the girl didn't seem the least bit concerned and was kicking her legs with that slow consistency that indicated the deepest of pleasures. A pebble splooshed into the water, and the girl noticed them. Ruby waved. She waved back, tossed another stone into the drink, and started kicking her legs again. She obviously had much more important things to think about.

They crawled past the new docks that had grown

up underneath the edge of Uptown, rowing between the massive stone and carbon pillars that supported the platform of streets, houses, and money above their heads.

The air under the overhang was reassuringly thick, like bean and bacon soup with the spicy tang of metal. Ruby breathed deep. Athen coughed and scrunched his lips. Cram perked up like a hungry puppy.

They pulled the boat up on the gravel shore in a deserted shadow between two of the house-thick pillars.

"Where are the clear skies and coonskin caps?" Athen pulled his clinking bag out of the boat. "Where are the beasts of the wild? I thought this was the land of fresh air and indomitable spirit?" He reached over to help her out of the boat as Cram stowed the oars.

"Tinkers and Rupert's Bay needed to build close to the shore and their manufactories. And then there are the Algonkin in the woods. They couldn't build inland and stay close, so they built straight up. They put another town on top of the old one, like a layer cake."

"Amazing," Athen said.

"Isn't it? All you Euros, you have no idea what's

happening over here." She reached down into the lifeboat and ripped the gray, gooey seal off the hole in the bottom like a scab.

Athen grabbed her arm. "What are you doing?"

Cram said, "I think she be sinking the evidence, sir. We don't want no one picking up our trail." Athen nodded.

Ruby turned to Athen. "Give me your cloak."

He hesitated, "I need it, Miss Teach."

"For what purpose, to protect me?" The boy nodded. "If I need someone to crumple at the feet of a brigand, I know where to turn." Cram coughed. Athen blushed in the dim.

He threw it at her. She reached out her hand and grabbed it out of the air. It would have been impressive, but she used the hand with the bad wrist. The cloak dropped to the ground and lay there. The other two looked at her, and no one bent down to help. After a moment she picked it up with her good hand and wrapped it about her face.

"Welcome to Philadelphi," Ruby said. They pushed

the boat back into the river. It sank into the dark. "Come on," she said, and started down the strand. "It's not far." Thankfully they did not argue.

Ruby had faint memories of sun on the cobblestones in New Market, which is what the neighborhood had been called before they put a roof on it.

Now it was the Shambles. Away from the harbor opening, it was always just past dusk. The constant half-light came from cheap, smoky chem pots hanging from pillars or pipes on the main streets. In the alleys, well, you took to the alleys at your own risk. They were clogged with pipes and steam holes and refuse and chem waste. The pots hung farther apart, and danger lurked in the dark. If you brought your own light or weren't from the neighborhood? Well, the runagates and bullyboys would thank you kindly for pointing yourself out to them and offering them the bounty of your purse. If you were lucky, that was all they took.

The lifeblood of the docks and the Benzene Yards lived in the Shambles, crowded together, scrapping and fighting. People here lived on top of one another in makeshift shacks at the end of blind alleys or in camps on old rooftops with the Lid (that's what they called the roof) as a ceiling. Two, three, four families in flats built for one. Boardinghouses for thirty in mansions abandoned by the high folk who now lived Up There.

Very fine neighborhoods had been covered by the Lid. Instead of relocating, some of the most influential families had been allowed to stay, and their big houses went all the way up, through attics and storerooms dug right into the Lid.

Above the Lid were salons, bedrooms, dining rooms, and great halls, and below was everything that made all that possible. Down here the kitchens cooked, the shoes were shined, and the gears were greased. In a way, Ruby thought, it was like other cities, just more so: a few folk that sat in the wheelhouse, and a whole mess of people down below, rowing as fast as they could.

She cut right and led them between two swanky town houses into an ill-lit alley. Haphazardly placed chem pots hung from support pillars or the corner of a fence.

On this particular block the people had abandoned their houses and gone who-knows-where or had just closed up below and built anew on top of the Lid. But they had closed them up tight with solder and chem, with bars on the windows and stout locks on the doors. It was still deserted.

Ruby led them to a gap in a high brick wall. A wheelless carriage was the only occupant of the back lot on the other side of the crack, and an empty town house loomed, waiting for them.

"Welcome to our home," she said as she slipped through the gap.

CHAPTER 17

Gray lung, black scale, pickle, and sweat,
Lost them fingers to the saw today,
Save your pennies and duck your head,
So your boys and girls climb UpTown way!
— UnderTown drinking song

The next morning Ruby struggled up to the roof and shouldered the trapdoor open with her good arm. Cram was there in the dim half-light of UnderTown, pushing against the sky of stone hanging above his head. He looked a bit like a dignified monkey poking at the lid of a trap. The canopy of rock spread from horizon to horizon, except for back toward the harbor, where the pink edge of dawn crept through.

"What is it?" He kept probing at the ceiling with a pointer he had found in the music room.

Ruby sat straight in the great chair she and Gwath had dragged up when they first found the abandoned town house years ago. "It's called the Lid. It is the roof the Tinkers put on top of this city, so they could build a better city on top of it." She reached out her arm. "Hold this steady, will you, please?"

She held out a brace, pieces of a picture frame she had found in the dining room. He abandoned his poking and eyed the two spars of wood next to her wrist. He was not her favorite at the moment, but asking a favor of Athen would be worse. He grabbed the sticks like oars.

"Ow!" she said. "Gently, you oaf."

He grinned. "Mam says never look the other way when a jug of rye drops off the back of a wagon."

"Just hold it. Like that." She began carefully wrapping the napkins around the frame, immobilizing her wrist.

He was looking up at the Lid again. "It's tinkercraft, you say?"

"Yes."

He whistled. "Foreman Jecked never made nothin' this big." He squinted into the distance over the railing on the rooftop. "How far does it go?"

"Two miles in, to the banks of the Schuylkill River. Grab this bit here. Good." She pulled the other loose end around her wrist and looped it around with the bit the boy was holding. "They say it was like God ripped a curtain of rock out of the ground and pulled it over the town like a good-night blanket. The strain of pulling it up wrecked two Tinker grandmasters for good and all—they burned from the inside, like quick pitch—and almost killed the eight teams of foremen that grew the pillars up to meet it on its way to the Delaware."

Cram whistled again and stared into the distance. "Never thought I would see nothing like this. You want me to hold that bandage for yuh, Ferret?"

"I have it. Do not call me that."

Cram grinned. "What, Ferret?"

She pulled the knot closed with her teeth. "If you want to slander me, why not Kitty Cat or Ladybird or Countess?

He snickered. "'Cause you ain't a kitty cat or a ladybird or a countess."

"What about Rabbit?" Athen popped his head through the trapdoor in the roof.

The air felt prickly, or tight, or something. Ruby pulled herself into motion.

"Because I run and hide in the bushes? I like that." She moved past the trap and knelt next to the chimney, pulling at a loose stone with her good hand.

"I was trying to say 'agile' or 'stealthy,' but suit yourself." Athen sort of flowed up through the trap and lounged in the chair. Cram clammed up and was staring at his shoes.

"As requested, the door below is as secure as my modest talents can make it."

"You shook up a jar and sprayed goo on it?"

"Something like that. I jammed it by filling the lock with sawdust and then hardened the mass with a thickener."

"Exciting." The stone dropped with a thump to the roof. "Why didn't you change it into a mirror of liquid gold or set a lightning trap?" Ruby fished about inside the hole and produced a bundle of lumps.

"*Primus*, because I have not the skill or the inner fuel to create such a thing but, *secundus,* because it was not necessary. When I am sewing, I use a needle, not a cannon."

"Right now I could fancy a cannon to address your *secundus*."

"The practice of chemystry is not all sprays of fire and ripping up battlements from the unsuspecting earth. Much of it is simply understanding the properties of the world around us and employing them creatively."

"Have you ever thought about teaching school?" Ruby asked as she unrolled her bundle of tools, checking through the small array of picks and wires and stranger things—bulbs, levers, and oils.

"No, no, I have not," Athen said, softening. "Why do you ask?"

"You remind me of this governess I had once. She was truly gifted at boring me to tears."

"My apologies. Sometimes I have trouble remembering that the simple lose interest when their betters speak of things they cannot understand."

"Betters?"

Athen smiled. "Did I stir up your humors? Have I your attention now?"

"Oh, indeed."

"Good." Athen perched on the edge of Ruby's chair and began unloading his pockets with the things he had saved from his chest. "A council regarding our options?"

"Fair," Ruby said. The sooner they could get her father back, the sooner she could rid herself of these chowderheads. "There is a man I know—"

"This is an affinital." Athen started to speak at the same time, holding up a small square of red clay.

"I was talking," Ruby said.

"Were you?" Athen eased back into the chair. "My apologies. Please proceed. I will offer my plan after."

"All right." Ruby felt flustered. "There is a man I know who has the ear of the city. His name is Fen. He runs a tavern not far from here, and if anyone can, he will be able to help us find my father."

"That is all?" Athen said after a moment.

"Yes. Well, it won't be as simple as that," Ruby sputtered. "He is a wily—"

"Excellent." Athen cut her off. "As I was saying, this is an affinital—"

"Do not interrupt me."

"I am sorry. I thought you were finished. Please continue. He is wily?"

"Yes, a wily one, and well, that's all."

They stared at each other for a moment.

"Well, thank you." Athen leaned forward with the square of clay. "This is an affinital. It is an alchemycal method of communicating with others, and now that we are in the city and closer to its mate, this one should function."

"That looks like a lump of clay to me, sir," Cram offered.

"Yes, Cram, but it has a unique makeup. It is half of a whole piece of clay. For lack of a simpler way of explaining it"—he nodded to Ruby, and she rolled her eyes—"the clay is still connected to its sister earth. This can speak to its sister."

"You can talk to that and someone answers on the other end?" Cram's eyes widened. He leaned in to address the lump. "Hello?"

Athen pulled the cube away. "In a manner of speaking. May I have my bag, please?" Cram handed it over. "Please observe."

Athen produced a small iron apparatus, which held a saucer-size plate over a small burner. Once the flame was going, he teased a small dollop of what looked like runny lard out of an ampule and dabbed it onto the clay, which he then put on the saucer.

They began to melt.

"Amazing." Ruby shook her head with wonder. "It communicates to me that it is a gooey cake on a tea plate."

"Wait," Athen said, and then he produced a grease pencil and a few pieces of parchment, which he set on a flat section of the roof. By this point the clay and the slime had melted, filling the saucer with orange soup. He carefully painted the substance onto the entirety of the pen with a fine brush. "There is a stand somewhere in this city, holding a pencil like this, covered with the affinital clay, just like this one. When I move the pencil, the other one will move with it in tandem, inscribing the message onto the other paper. Then, I hope, there will be a response."

Ruby snorted. "Well, get to it."

Athen thought for a moment, then wrote in a brisk, concise hand: A. BOYLE, IN CITY.

They waited two minutes before Athen's hand moved. The handwriting seemed different.

HAVE YOU DISCOVERED THE QUARRY?

Athen responded: YES. SMALL PACKAGE IN POCKET, LARGE ONE STOLEN.

There was a short wait.

WE HEARD. PITY. DELIVER SMALL PACKAGE TO SMOKEHOUSE, ARCHER FARM, DREGS. WITH HASTE. TAKE PRECAUTIONS. YOU ARE HUNTED.

Athen thought for a moment.

PLACEMENT OF LARGE PACKAGE?

The response was quick: CROWNED. PACKAGE CAGED. PRIORITY SMALL PACKAGE DELIVERY TO SMOKEHOUSE. THAT IS ALL.—HEARTH

"'Small package.' That would be me, yes?" Ruby said.

"And 'large package' your father. Correct." He looked up at her, his eyes wary.

Ruby could not speak for a moment. "You did not just happen to be on our ship! You came looking for us. And they came looking for you."

He flattened his lips. "We should be going to the safe house, the smoker. I will need your help in locating it. We need to protect your secret."

"What secret?"

Athen shook his head. "I don't know."

"You led them to us!" Ruby yelled at him.

"I did not know they were following me!"

"You led them to us!" She struck the stone with each word. "And now my father is taken, as are the rest of my family, and Gwath is dead." Saying it out loud made it real, and her chest hurt and her throat burned.

"You ain't knowin' that, Ferret." Cram cut in, trying to keep the peace.

She grabbed her picks and headed for the door. She did not need these people. They were the cause of the problem.

"It is not safe for you out there," Athen called.

"Safer than it will be with you." As she passed through the trap, something glass broke on the edge. It was one of Athen's flasks. Thick tendrils of green stuff shot across the opening and splattered across her back. Ruby ran. She ducked down the stairs and out the third-story window, then down the rope ladder.

They were calling for her and hurrying after, but she was too quiet and too fast. "You are as much a failure at holding on to me as you are keeping me safe," she whispered to the shadows.

And then she was gone.

CHAPTER 18

Bravos, Cudgeliers, and Crumps, Enter Here. Bottleheads, Clapperdogeons, Spungers, and Trugs, Round Back. Lily Whites Need Not Apply.
—Employment notice, Spruce Street Hooligans

The door to the Smelted Grouse did not budge. Ruby cursed under her breath and pulled the collar of the worn coat up to meet the bottom of the cap she had scrounged from a line in an alley. She had been hoping for something more, well, anonymous, but all she had been able to find was a patchwork covering that must have belonged to a junior pastor or a failed mushroom broker. It was the smelly green-brown of something you'd find on the bottom of your boot. At least it helped her fit in in the neighborhood. She checked over her shoulder again.

It was very early in the morning. The street was dark here in the deep shadows where the Lid angled down to meet the ground, but she felt exposed.

It had been a difficult night.

Word had spread that the crown was after her. Posters with her picture were up all over the Shambles, and no one would take her in. At least they had not tried to turn her in for themselves. Fernanda Gaioso, who led the Spruce Street Hooligans, would not even see her. Abigail Whelk took her in the front door of her crawfish shack and then shuttled her out the back just as quickly. Kevin the Walrus at least offered to smuggle her up to Acadia and out of England's reach, but she refused.

She could not, would not leave this city. Not while her father and her crew might be here. They were in danger, and it was up to her to save them. So here she was, at the Smelted Grouse, a run-down tavern that both Gwath and her father had counseled she never go to alone or out of disguise.

She rapped lightly on the door, and there was still no answer. The shift change was nigh, and workers coming to and from the Benzene Yards would soon fill the street. She hitched up her breeches and made her way down the alley to the back door, past the clunking clockwork still that bulged out of the wall like a metal pimple. She knocked lightly on the back door as well. This one was stout metal, where the front door was worn wood. No response.

Ruby dug deeply and with palpable interest into her left nasal cavity. She was known in this part of the Shambles as Robby Thatch, a homeless waif and ne'er-do-well, and Robby had an unfortunate preoccupation with the internal contents of his nose. She craned her neck over her left and right shoulders, to be certain there were no passersby.

She placed the bag on the worn wooden step in front of the door and pulled her ring of slim picks from the coat's inner pocket. She knelt and peered into the intricate lock for a moment, then eased two strong slivers of wire into the square keyhole. The lock was one of the newer tinker-forged ones with all the tiny fiddly bits.

It took her fifteen seconds.

It had been a bit challenging with her wrist, but the brace helped. After oiling the handle, she eased it down and pushed the door open silently.

She glided in, closed the door behind her, and turned to come face-to-face with something unexpected, the barrel of a very large blunderbuss. Ruby dropped her bag, raising her hands in the air.

"Robby Thatch," the man at the happier end of the blunderbuss rasped. "I did not know you was back in town."

Ruby took a step to the side. The barrel followed her, but at least she had a better view of Grundwidge Fen. He was a small man, about Ruby's height, but almost square, and had embraced the Tinker's way more than most in the Shambles. He was smiling now, and his iron teeth glimmered in the shadows. "Why did you wander in to my back room, Robby? I do wonder that."

"Hello, Mr. Fen," Ruby said.

"Do not 'Hello, Mister Fen' me, young Robby, until

you tell me where your partner is. I do not want some giant African pounding in my portal when he gets it into his thick head that you might have been less than sneaky."

Grundwidge Fen knew Ruby as a sneak thief and errand boy, who often made a team with Jim Stout, a big escaped slave. They had used Fen several times as a fence, as he was the only one in UnderTown who would buy the clockwork keepsakes or alchemycal reagents that they had fleeced from Tinkers. He was obsessive, cheap, and paranoid, but he was smitten with all things chemystral. He also knew more about both Up- and UnderTown than three friendlier, saner fences.

She kicked at a split knot in the scrap wood floor. "Jim is dead," she said. "And I am in a pile of trouble, Mister Fen. It does not get much more simple."

Fen fiddled with the brass and quartz monocle he wore over his rheumy right eye. "So you are not come to rob old Fen?"

"No, sir." She groveled. Robby Thatch was a fine groveler. "I need to know some things, and the Deep Well of Fen is known throughout the Shambles as the Man

Who Knows Things." Robby had also been known to flatter.

The little penguin flapped his arms around the stock of his gun. "But why not come in the front door or knock?"

She blushed. It was only mostly fakery. "The street ain't no place for a boy like me right now." Fen frowned, and Ruby rushed on before he had a chance to interrupt. "I have money."

Grundwidge Fen clicked his tongue behind his iron molars and smiled. "Well, then, young master, sit down if you please. We shall jabber, and you may even have some pie."

The pie was good. Ruby did not realize how hungry she was until she bit into it. The pigeon was soft and gooey and there were roast vegetables and it was warm. She had been living for days on salt pork and whatever else they had scrounged from the ruined corners of the *Thrift*.

She popped the last piece of pie into her mouth, sad to say good-bye to such a wonder of sage, juice, and smoky goodness. Ruby licked her fingers. "This was delicious," she said. "Thank you."

Fen perched on a high stool with his blunderbuss, legs splayed and slippers flopped. The wall behind him was covered with little shelves and cubbyholes, one full of square cobalt gears, the next with a scattering of wooden hammers and awls, an antimony butter churn, and a host of stranger pots and urns, racks and chests, spilling harsh odors and granules that glinted in the half-light. It was a floor-to-ceiling catalog of Philadelphi's history. Fen had been one of the first settlers to set foot on the shore of the Delaware, and no one knew how old he was.

He was just sitting there on his stool, looking at her: a staring, gun-toting sloth.

Ruby giggled, and then she clapped her hand over her mouth. Why did she do that?

That was funny, too, so she chuckled again. She pointed at Fen, who had climbed a ladder to drag a coil of rope off the top shelf. He staggered back from the weight and fell out of Ruby's vision behind a work cabinet with a thump and a squeak.

When Ruby finally stopped laughing and rubbed the tears from her eyes, Grundwidge Fen was advancing on her with the heavy rope.

Ruby jumped up and danced out of his way. Or she wanted to, but really all her legs did was sort of twitch and flop around like fish dying in the bottom of a boat.

Fen clicked his tongue behind his iron smile and began winding the rope around her waist and shoulders, tying her to the chair.

"Pie." She finally got the word from her brain to her mouth, which no longer seemed to care what she wanted it to do.

She could not see Fen behind her because she could not move her head. He tittered. "Yes, young Ruby. That pigeon pie has a very special set of seasonings, and this one rises very early every morning to prepare it for unruly folks who might come into Fen's place and stir up some trouble."

"R-Robby," she managed to get out.

Fen poked his head back into her field of vision and squinted at her through the brass monocle. "Oh, forgive me, young master. Robby. Of course. Robby." From the way he said her name, she knew that she was cooked as sure as that pie.

Her ropes secure, the little man hopped up onto the stool at his workbench and began dissecting some mechanism that kept flaring in and out of Ruby's focus. She realized that it was the room and everything in it that was wavering, and she threw all her considerable will into getting a final word out.

"Why?"

Fen glanced up from the disassembled wreckage on his worktable, as if to swat at a fly. "Because, young Robby Ruby, people are looking for you. People more important than you. And your sweet pa is caught, and his not-so-sweet past is coming home to roost. He cannot touch me, and Grundwidge Fen knows which way the wind blows." He went back to his work. "Go to sleep. I know not what the future holds for you, but I am certain that whatever it may be, you will need your rest." Grundwidge Fen and his chemystral workshop faded into darkness.

She slept.

≈ ≈ ≈

She woke.

She did not open her eyes. Gwath had taught her better than that.

She was no longer in the chair. The rough, splintered wood of Fen's floor was harsh against her face, and new, tighter bonds gripped her chest and wrists. Ruby inhaled slowly and caught the unmistakable odor of bootblack, masking a subtler hint of sweat and bad cologne. The creaking of the floorboards told a story of at least five standing around her. It could only be English naval officers.

She chanced opening her bottom eye, the one nearest the floor. There were two sets of boots that she could see without moving her head.

Behind her, a man said, "Fen, this had best not be a jape."

"Of course not, leftenant!" Grundwidge Fen replied, "Fen is the soul of honor. This scrofulous waif is the Teach girl. I am certain."

"Fair enough. But if this is not the girl we want, you

will not spend a tenth of that reward before the Reeve finds you, whatever forsaken rock you hide under."

Fen gasped.

The leftenant continued. "I trust I need not sing the praises of the Reeve to you, sir?"

"No! Of course not!" Grundwidge Fen groveled. "His Majesty's most fierce and loyal agents need no compliments in this wee shack. Nor do I wish to have anything to do with, er—" He began to stammer. "That is to say, I have no wish to be *observed* by the forces of— ha, my meaning is that I am only guilty of other, er, my words do not indicate—oh, dear." He inhaled like a forge bellows. "Leftenant Potts, please leave my words from any official report you may—"

The leftenant interrupted. "Mister Collins, if you would collect this package? It is time we were on our way."

"Yes, sir," replied a younger, lighter voice, and solid, gentle hands lifted her underneath her shoulders and hauled her up. There was a whiff of sulfur. She made sure to hang limp and heavy. She caught a glimpse of a sharp nose and an overlarge forehead as she rolled her head around. This midshipman who held her, Collins, was very tall but slim. She shifted her weight as he stepped forward, overbalancing him. He cursed under his breath and almost dropped her. She had one leg free, and if she could disengage the other—

"She is heavier than she looks. Billings, Chaw, help me here." The hands that grabbed her from behind were big, rough, and hard as horn. She smelled salt. Seamen's paws, she was certain.

"Here, put her in this. Less commotion in the street." That was the one Fen had called the leftenant. Ruby risked opening her eyes a slit further. Two big men had her in the air above a large burlap sack, held by a blond, flat-faced thug stuffed into a naval lieutenant's uniform.

Something snapped inside her. Ruby struggled in her captors' arms. Surprise got her almost free, but the men were too strong, and they regained their grip.

"Careful, boys," the leftenant said. "Rool said this one was a wildcat."

Rool! Ruby redoubled her efforts. One of the men twisted her arm, and the skin burned.

She poked one with bulldog jowls in the eye. "Gah! Into the sack with her," he grunted, and they wrestled her legs into the burlap. It was a large one, like a seaman's duffel. A seaman who did not bathe. As they got her waist and shoulders into the sack, she realized what it truly was: a shroud. They used shrouds to bury bodies at sea. And indeed, over her shoulder, the other seaman produced the tough needle and the rawhide used to sew the shroud closed.

She almost made it out of the sack then, but the bulldog, a big, strong man with loose skin, wrestled her down onto the floor. The one with the needle knelt next to them. "Don't move, girl," he counseled through bushy eyebrows with the calm of a massive milk cow. "You don't want to get stuck."

"My goodness!" someone said.

The voice rang from the far side of the room, the door back into the common area. Everyone froze. A young woman stood in the doorway, in the ugliest flounciest dress Ruby had ever seen. It was a nightmare of lace, gingham, and forty other fabrics, and it looked as though it went on forever. A serving man stood next to her, holding the oversize train and a parasol. He could have been Cram's brother, though he sported a dead caterpillar of a mustache. Stranger still, the beautiful girl trapped in the horrible dress bore a striking resemblance to Lord Athen. Ruby squinted. Cheekbones, gray eyes, that nick in the ear. An exact resemblance to Lord Athen.

Things happened quickly after that.

CHAPTER 19

*Some Gentlemen, that I've showed this Piece of Art, count it not
fair Play, but I'm not in the least of their Opinion.*
—Ezekiel Pelham, *Arts Martial and Practice*

Grundwidge Fen was the first to speak. "Miss," he crooned, "this establishment is closed for business. Please return during normal business hours."

"I merely require refreshment and direction, my good man," Athen said, playing the haughty heiress. He was pitch perfect. The gestures, the tone, and the *feel* of "girl" were all there. The insufferable boy had a future on the stage if he ever could lower himself to it.

"My man and I have wandered astray, and I wish to return to— Is that a boy in a sack?" The lady and her serving man, who was most definitely Cram, never mind the mustache, advanced into the room to get a better look. Bulldog pushed Ruby's head further down with his massive hand.

Fen glanced around him at the upset worktable, the man with the bleeding eye, the young "boy" most of the way into a bag. "We do not have tea brewing at this time. This establishment is closed. The stairs to UpTown are ten blocks down, at the end of the alley."

The lady persisted. "No tea? But certainly—"

"This is the king's business, girl." Leftenant Potts threatened. "Turn around and walk away, or if you like, we will escort you and your man here bodily into the street."

Athen purred, "Not a true gentleman, I see." The lady turned to her servant. "I fear we must depart, Cramwich, lest these king's men do us violence."

"Ah, weeel, moi laydee." His butler's accent would have slain an actual duchess on contact. "Ahee surpose we muhst mahk our departivo."

Athen stared at Cram. "Indeed. My parasol, if you please."

Cram hesitated and tugged at a large, purple, inappropriate scarf tied around his neck. "Thy parasol, moi lahdee?"

"Yes, Cramwich. My parasol."

Cram smiled weakly and slid a step to the side. "Howeverward, the clouds outward produce no rain. Indeed, the Lid covers the street. Perhaps thy need it not."

Athen tapped his foot. In a delicate ladies' shoe.

Cram sighed, "Very well, mah lahdee. Eef thy insist."

The bulldog sailor looked at the cow sailor. The cow shrugged.

The servant presented the little umbrella with a flourish. Like lightning, Athen tore his dueling sword from the concealment of the parasol. He wrapped his wrist three times in the long train of the dress and leveled the point at the eye of the leftenant.

"You will stand aside and give us that boy or we shall take him." Athen's voice had dropped lower.

Potts barked laughter. "Miss, your governess needs to spend more time with you on sums. I count two of you and we number six."

"Five." Fen cleared his throat. "I urge you to take this matter into the street, away from the many delicate mechanisms that—"

"We are six," Potts repeated, "and I will warn you that indeed, I am not a gentleman, and neither I nor my men have any hesitation toward applying violence to servants or to young ladies who have the gumption to draw steel on me and mine."

Athen did not move. "Duly noted. You are a pig who beats women and has no interest in a fair fight."

Potts laughed. "At least we are on familiar terms." He drew his sword. "Mister Collins, Mister Pratt, boys."

Cram grabbed the closest weapon, which happened to be a feather pen.

He put the pen back and instead grabbed a heavy metal butter churn.

The tall one in the back, Collins, had drawn his blade and edged toward the back door, next to a shelf stacked with powders and oils, set to guard the exit. Pratt, round like a puffer fish and twice as creepy, stood fast next to the leftenant. He opened his mouth to start a jape of his own. It became a howl of pain as Athen lunged forward and pierced him through the leg.

Athen ripped his blade out of the middy's leg just in time to parry two cuts from Leftenant Potts, whose eyes widened in surprise. Athen whirled to the right, dress billowing, and enveloped Bulldog's long knife in the folds of the rest of the gown. With a twitch of his wrist, the knife clattered to the floor. So that was why he was always going on about his cloak.

Behind Ruby, Cram screamed like a banshee and leaped forward with the butter churn over his head, and Cow stood still in shock. Cram, misjudging his leap, bounced off the man's thick chest like it was taut sailcloth. He landed where he began, took stock of his situation, and screamed his battle cry again. Cow shrugged and circled his massive fists like a street fighter.

Grundwidge Fen scuttled up his ladder in the corner of the room, as if trying to put distance between him and a rising flood. Midshipman Collins was rummaging in one of the shelves.

Pratt, stuttering with pain, grabbed at Ruby's foot, gripping the knife from the floor in his other hand. Ruby kicked at it with her sacked-up legs and scrambled back like a crippled inchworm.

Her head bumped hard on a wall. Pratt slashed out, and she barely twisted away. She bunched up her knees and kicked at his face. She missed, hitting his shoulder. He gathered himself for another stab. Nowhere to go.

Just then a delicate shoe came out of nowhere and slammed down hard on Pratt's knife hand.

Athen, pressed by two opponents, had backed across the floor and was now standing on the midshipman's wrist. The knife skittered across the planks. Leftenant Potts was bleeding from a number of cuts, and Bulldog was pierced in the shoulder.

The big sailor pulled a press gun out of his belt and slammed the heel of his hand down on the contact, firing a ball deep into Athen's waist. Now Athen yelled, something between a gasp and a scream, and tottered.

Bulldog dropped the spent firearm, picked up the discarded knife, and closed in.

Cram, openmouthed and with a strength Ruby did not believe from his skinny frame, hurled the metal churn across the room.

It completely missed Bulldog but slammed into the shoulder of Leftenant Potts, plowing him into the far wall of the workshop. Athen reversed the hilt of the dueling sword and slammed it into Bulldog's wrist, knocking the knife from his hand.

The big sailor lunged forward and wrapped Athen in a crushing bear hug, pulling him up into the air. Pratt was now free, and Ruby kicked at him again. This time she landed both feet straight in his face, and something crunched. He rolled away, moaning.

Athen, sword useless in the clutches of the sailor, reared his smooth, pale forehead back. Then he slammed it full into Bulldog's face. The sailor dropped Athen and staggered back. Athen dropped to one knee. There was a bloom of red dyeing the lace at the hip of the dress. Cram, making threatening motions with his hands, backed over to them. Cow had not seemed inclined to violence in the first place and did not pursue.

Wounded, they stared at their opponents across the dismantled workshop.

When she read *Bastionado*, Ruby had always imagined swordplay as a thrilling dance, filled with grace and daring.

This was not a dance. It was a chicken coop on fire.

Cram helped her out of the sack. She thought she should say "thank you" or "my hero" or something similar to Athen, but all that came out was "pretty dress."

Through gasps, Athen managed, "This old thing?"

Across the room, Leftenant Potts raised two clocklock pistols and yelled, "Show them your iron!" The sailors leveled long guns, and the midshipman on the floor cradled another press gun.

Potts grinned at Athen over the barrel of his pistol. "You dance prettily in that dress, girl. Can you twirl around a pistol ball?" He rolled his left shoulder, where a nasty cut was bleeding freely. Terror gripped Ruby. It was Potts's blood on Athen's sword, and now Athen was going to die. Just like Gwath. Potts motioned with one of his pistols toward the blade. "Now put that pigsticker down, and call off your man there"—he nodded at Cram, who had recovered his churn—"and we can come to an understanding."

Athen stepped in front of Ruby and Cram. "I think not, sir. I estimate that you will cut at least two of us down as soon as we lower our weapons."

Ruby whispered, "What are you doing?"

Athen did not have time to answer, however, as Potts grinned. "I am dearly glad that this is your position." He cocked his weapon. Ruby leaped forward, too late, to drag Athen down.

She saw the tall midshipman, Collins, forgotten in the corner, pull two bottles from a shelf, strike the necks together, and then point them at Potts.

FLEFFLEEFFLEFFLEFFLE.

Black stuff jetted out of the two bottles. Quicker than lightning, a wave of black foam filled the room, taller than a man and thicker, an impossible supply out of those two tiny flasks. It completely enveloped

Potts, Bulldog, Cow, Pratt, and the back door.

All was silent.

After a moment a muffled shot sounded, as from far away.

Nothing came out of the chemystral chunk.

Fen's head and shoulders stuck out between the top of the mass and the ceiling, and he was staring bug-eyed at Collins.

"Compelling chemystry, young sir!" he breathed.

The midshipman, Collins, turned to the shelf again, grabbed two heaping handfuls of red dust from a bin, and tossed them at the wall next to him. The dust clung there, shining as if it were wet, and then changed to a darker scarlet. A tiny glimmer flashed in the center of the circle, then grew. Ruby gasped. The flash was light from the street outside, and a great hole was appearing. No, the wall was crumbling, falling to the planks below like heavy Christmas snow.

Wild eyed and sheathed in sweat, the boy turned to them. "We cannot leave through the front. There are more out there. They will shoot us, and I can do no more tinkercraft. The reeve, Wisdom Rool, is coming. I am a friend. Follow me." He jumped through the now man-size opening in the wall.

They looked at one another. It was Cram who said, "Come on then," and they limped through the hole into the street beyond.

In the quiet that remained, his head protruding from the great black blob that filled the room, Grundwidge Fen said, "Oh, dear. This will be troublesome for me."

CHAPTER 20

Quintessence is not endless. Many young chemystral scientists have Burned themselves Dry in their enthusiasm to accomplish Great Works. The wise student nurtures the candle before assaying the bonfire.

—Robert Boyle, FRS, ed., *Principia Chymia*, 1666

They went to ground in the abandoned remains of a boathouse, tucked into the angle between the street and the Lid, where the city's great roof came out of the earth.

They had stumbled through the hole in the wall of the Smelted Grouse and scrambled into the brief shelter of a narrow alley. From there it had become clear that Ruby was still half drugged, Athen was gravely wounded, and the midshipman, Collins, was caught somewhere between passing out and paralysis. So it had been Cram who led them sneaking away from the early-morning traffic into a building in a dark, quiet corner of UnderTown.

They were alive, for certain, but it was all torn sails and tangled knots. Her crafty trip to Fen's had failed. The daring rescue had almost killed them all. And now they had a companion she knew nothing about, except that he could make wood melt and was dressed in the uniform of the ones who had taken the only family she had known.

They hustled from the front room, a kind of office, into a warehouse, much larger and higher than the first. Half-completed barges and rowboats lined both walls, looming in the shadows. Light from a long-abandoned tinker's lamp cut down from a hook in the ceiling and illuminated an overturned hull on the factory floor.

Athen lay facedown on it atop a man's weight of Switz lace and ugly fabric. They tore the back of the dress open so he was bared to the waist. It was a bloody mess. On the right just above the hip there was a rough hole about the size of a thumb. Athen's pale back shuddered with breath.

The young naval officer rummaged in Athen's bag, muttering, with Cram looking over his shoulder.

"Give me that!" Ruby snarled, just as he said, "Luck. I think this is one." She snatched the bag out of his grasp, leaving him holding a little bottle up to the light. The ampule was full of bright green, translucent liquid.

She put herself between him and Athen.

"What are you doing?" She wanted to intimidate him, but her voice came out more panicked than threatening.

"Helping your friend. I need to pour this mixture—it is a chemystral aid—into the wound."

She balled her fist. "Back up, middy. Just because you pretended to help us does not mean that we trust you and will let you pour some devil potion into our friend." She looked between the two. "Cram."

The servant boy did not move.

"Cram!"

"He says there be metal still in the wound. The potion is some tinkercraft that will dissolve any little metal hangers and seal the hole up."

"Then Athen needs a physicker to help him, not some

pimply mariner who was just pointing a gun at us."

"I never actually—

"Ruby." The whisper came from behind her. Athen was looking at her out of one eye in a stark white face. He mumbled something inaudible. She knelt next to him.

He took a shallow breath and looked her deep in the eye. "Don't be a mule," he said. "Wound needs to close. My ampule. He could have betrayed us. Let him help." There was something else in the way he was looking at her. Something big.

She stood. "What do I do?"

Collins moved forward and motioned to Cram. "The two of you need to hold her down. It all needs to go into the wound, and the body needs to be still to let it run its course. She will struggle." He still thought Athen was a woman, and Ruby was disinclined to change that supposition. He rolled up his sleeve. "I understand the process is quite painful."

Ruby said, "You understand? You haven't done this before?"

Cram interrupted. "Get up there, hold the arms, and

put your knees onto the shoulders, Ferret," he ordered. Ruby clambered onto the flat, upturned hull and did as she was told.

Cram gripped Athen's legs and then lifted his eyes to Ruby's. Eyes full of fear.

Collins unstoppered the little bottle and held the liquid above the wound. It glittered in the half-light. "Ready?"

Cram muttered something about his mam and then nodded.

Collins turned to Ruby. "Ready?"

No. "Yes," she said.

He flicked a little lever on the side of the bottle. Gray powder passed down into the green liquid from a tiny compartment, and the whole thing flashed deep blue. "All right," he said, and held his hand hard down on the back next to the wound.

Collins poured the stuff in. Athen whimpered, then screamed into the fabric, and then began bucking like a sea serpent. His head struck Ruby full in the face, and she saw stars. She held on, though, and sucked some blood from her split lip. Finally Athen came to rest, pulling air in ragged gasps.

The midshipman was looking at her across Athen's back, face ashen. His hair was mussed, and his shirt was torn at the neck. He nodded. "Now we need to do the other side." Ruby cursed inside.

The first thing she saw as they turned Athen over was the bloody wound. It was smaller on this side and more precise.

The second thing Ruby saw was that Athen was not a boy. Athen was a girl, with an upper half to prove it.

Ruby's savior, sheathed in sweat, far too pale and gritting her teeth, whispered, "Athena Boyle, pleased to meet you."

Then she fainted into the pile of crimson lace.

She looked like a princess while she slept. Mind you, not one of those flouncy, chittering creatures who faint and sigh and run screaming from the dragon. This was a warrior princess, who would stand and fight and slay the beast with a broken ax head, salvaged at the last moment from the hoard. Ruby traced the air just above the line of her jaw. What had seemed delicate on Lord Athen was solid and muscular for a girl and set in resolve even as she slept.

They had put her back in the breeches and shirt of her gentleman's clothes, salvaged from Cram's bag, and covered her with her coat for warmth. The ruined dress lay at the foot of the boat like a pile of finishing rags, stained with red paint. After Athen—she corrected herself—after *Athena* had fainted, a strange silence had descended. They'd poured the remaining putty in the wound, and the patient had remained mercifully unconscious.

As soon as it was done, the tall midshipman had made his way to the other room like an arrow from a bow, muttering something about propriety, and leaving Ruby and Cram to dress their patient. It had been awkward.

Cram had artfully arranged the wide belt, tricorne, and dueling sword on a nearby workbench. He was over in the corner of the warehouse workshop, alternately banging, grinding, or sawing something. He had left his post by the upturned boat with a frown as soon as Ruby had pulled a chair across the wood-strewn floor and crunched down next to Athena.

She had never seen Athena Boyle's hands. They were more delicate than those of most boys Ruby had met, but they had seen work, even through the gloves that now lay beside the coat like a pair of masquerade masks. There was a thick callus in the valley between the thumb and forefinger—from years of fencing, Ruby guessed—and there was a ropy strength to the wrist that Ruby most certainly did not have.

Athena was heroic.

And she was a liar.

Just then Athena opened her eyes. She seemed mildly surprised to see Ruby and quirked the same infuriating smirk that had cut Ruby so deeply that first moment in the carriage.

Ruby rapped her on the nose with a tight roll of paper.

"Ow."

"That did not hurt."

"It did. It most certainly did."

"Well deserved then."

"I had thought you would have slunk back into the gutters by now?"

Ruby ignored the question and unrolled the paper, holding it above Athena's eyes. It was the baker's letter, the one her father had nicked for her back on the *Thrift*.

"What does it mean?" She cut off the girl before she could speak. "Speak truth to me, Athena Boyle. You are a liar and a cheat, and so am I, but we are in this storm together and sinking fast. No half-truths and no unspoken words, neither."

"You are welcome."

Ruby ground her teeth. "Thank you for saving my life. You are a hero. When I am queen of Andalusia, I will throw you a parade. What is this letter?"

Athena tracked a speck of sawdust as it floated through the half-light. "It is mine. May I have it back, please?"

"Did you not hear me?" She continued to watch the speck, so Ruby tried a different line. "This letter has power. You used it to strong-arm my father, and he may be many things, but he is not easily bullied. What is it?"

"And in association, who am I? Is that not the true question?"

"The letter calls you a baker and a grocer. You are neither."

"Do you know the dry weight of a pound of flax? I do. In fact—"

"What is this letter? Tell me!"

Cram, across the room, chose that moment to begin hammering the dents out of his butter churn.

"He likes you, you know." Athena braced an elbow on the bottom of the boat and slowly levered herself up to sitting.

Ruby helped, steadying her back. "Careful."

"The wound is packed and clean, and the putty will hold everything steady, until the flesh replaces it." She probed gingerly under the coat. "The middy did his job well. It pains me, but it is only pain. I am fit as a fox fur, as they say."

"Fiddle."

"What?"

"Fit as a *fiddle*. Did you grow up in a castle or something?"

"Technically Boyle Hall is a holdfast. He does like you, you know."

"Cram? I almost got you killed. He's just waiting for his chance to lay me out with that churn."

"Whatever you may think, the three of us are bound. And in enemy territory. Cram over there and this wounded counterfeit fop are your allies. Your crew."

"Fine then. Crewmates don't keep secrets. What is the letter? And who are you, Athena Boyle?"

Athena pushed her coat away and made to get up but then winced and thought better of it. "Pray hand me my waistcoat? I feel naked without it." The vest was embroidered in a pattern of peacocks, and Ruby helped guide Athena's arms through the holes.

"You are correct, of course. I fear you may not like or believe what you hear." Athena began to button the intricate buttons. "I will have you know that I am breaking an oath to do this. I do not take oaths lightly, but I see that you will know or you will be gone again. My family, the Boyles, belongs to an ancient organization."

"Not another ancient organization," Ruby moaned. "I have read *Bastionado*, and I like a good yarn as much as the next girl, but if you think for one moment—"

"It is an organization, and it is ancient, and I am telling you what you wish to know. Or, I am attempting to." Athena did not look up from her buttoning. "Shall I continue?"

Ruby waved. "Well. Speak."

"An ancient organization, then, and one that has weighed and measured the actions of princes of the church, kings, even nations. It has pitted itself against the great and the cruel, all in the name of keeping the world balanced."

"What is this famous company called?"

"The Worshipful Order of Grocers."

Cram was sawing at something across the room.

"Excuse me?"

"The Worshipful Order of Grocers. You are laughing."

"I am." Ruby could not help herself. "Not the most

impressive name for a secret society."

Athena sighed. "That is the point. We do not stand out. We blend in. Our task is to keep the great powers in balance. The order began as a merchants' collective. Governing the spice trade, fairness, and the like. Our symbol is a pepper mill. Well, our second symbol."

"What is the first?"

"A camel."

"A camel on a pepper mill? Terrifying. Not to mention difficult."

"Ruby, please."

"Does the camel have a hat? With a feather on it?"

"Do you want to hear this?"

"Sorry."

Athena pulled an arm into her greatcoat. "That letter is a badge, if you will. The bearer can use it to obtain help from other members of the order in dire circumstances."

"That is not what it says. It says you have recipes."

"Should it say, 'The bearer of this letter is on a secret mission, possibly against the crown; please provide illegal aid'? It is code."

"But you used it on my father."

Athena shivered and pulled the greatcoat up to her neck like a blanket.

"Is he a member of this bakers' circle?" Ruby asked.

"Grocers. The term includes practitioners of the baking arts, as well as distillers of strong spirits."

"You did not answer my question."

"No, I did not." Athena agreed. "But I have answered your first question and broken three of the prime ingredients of the master recipe in the process." Her eyelids flickered. "I would prefer you did not mention this to the people we are going to see."

Ruby stood up. The assumption of authority was just as infuriating in the girl as it had been in the boy. "I never said I would go see anyone. I have more questions."

"Ruby, we are in dire straits, and my patience is exhausted." She called over to Cram, "Pack our things, Cram. We should leave nothing here for trackers or gearbeasts to trace. The dress, too. I must rest, but then we shall be gone." She turned to Ruby. "Thank you for the help with my wound. Within a few hours Cram and

I will depart to see some people who may help us rescue your father. I would prefer it if you left with us, especially since you seem to have no other recourse. But I will not attempt to hold you against your will. If you wish to sulk here like a peevish child, perhaps Grundwidge Fen will be more helpful the second time around."

With that she lay back down and covered her eyes with her hat. Within moments she was asleep.

It was quiet.

Ruby picked up a piece of gravel from the floor and threw it as hard as she could against the hull of an unfinished barge. It rang like a drum. A child? A child? This jumped-up grocery clerk had no right to name her such. She was a pirate, a rogue, and a fighter. And she was as helpless as a newborn.

She threw another rock at the barge. It missed and weakly clattered into the shadows behind. Athena did not stir. Ruby headed into the front room to gather her things. And think.

CHAPTER 21

Cloathes will never make a Gentleman.

—Cloverdale Farnsworth

Athena Boyle. Ruby could not believe it. Half of her wanted to run back into the warehouse and guard her even if the roof fell down. The other half wanted to weep. Still another half headed out the door and kept running until she hit the West Indies, another half slammed the brig door closed and threw away the key, and yet another was dancing an odd little jig. That was far too many halfs for one Ruby, and they were tugging her apart.

So she did as Gwath had taught her. She grabbed up all the feelings and distractions, rolled them up in her mind, and then locked them away in the iron chest she kept in the bottom of her belly. It was her secret hold, just like her cubby on the *Thrift*. She stalked over to the midshipman, Collins, who sat at an old table beneath the light filtering through one of the boarded-up windows. He had pulled a few tools from a fancy leather roll-up and was fiddling with something. In a flash of memory Ruby saw it sitting on Grundwidge Fen's shelves. Was their savior also a thief? She couldn't decide if that made her feel better or worse.

He was absorbed in his task and did not turn. He was a tall lad, perhaps Athena's age, skinny as a rope. Jamaican? Algerian? All the extra flesh left at birth had been funneled into a huge, pointed nose and equally large hands. One hand cradled a stylus of some sort, and his fingers were scarred and burned gray, red, and even lime green in numerous places, and the nails were bitten to the quick. A set of linen gloves were tucked into his belt next to his clocklock pistol. What was it with these boys and these gloves? But then Athen—Athena was not a boy. Anyway.

Ruby cleared her throat.

He turned as if he had been burned, stood, and slid his project behind his back.

She held up her hands. "Stand easy, Captain Courageous. No cause for alarums and bucket brigades."

He relaxed somewhat and chewed on his lip. Gwath had said to her once that silence was a tool. He was observing her as well. Intently. Like an insect pinned under glass. She did not like the sensation.

She crossed her arms and leaned against a rough wooden support. "What is your name?"

He chewed his lip more forcefully, "Henry Collins. Er, Midshipman Henry Collins, posted to His Majesty's Ship *Percival*."

"Why did you help us, Henry Collins?"

He scratched at his ear. "Um, well, I saw that you were in danger, and I"—he cleared his throat, repeatedly—"I could not stand by and watch innocents be hurt or killed."

Ruby stared at him. Did he think she was stupid?

"Do you think I am stupid?" she said.

"No!" he blurted out. Then, after a moment: "No."

"The scars on your hands mark you as a tinker of some sort."

His hands found their way behind his back. "I work with metal and the furnaces on my ship, nothing more."

Ruby rolled her eyes. "And the goo and melting walls back there at Fen's? How do you explain that?"

"Certain parts of a midshipman's education involve basic instruction in the chemystral arts," he said.

"Basic?" She laughed. "You made a great cake the size of an entire room and then poofed away a thick timber wall."

He blushed.

"You will not be able to go back to the navy. Most likely you are an outlaw. They will hang you from a topmast if they catch you."

She waited.

Collins cleared his throat again. Finally he offered a strangled "You see, I saw you in this strange dream I had, and—"

"Oh, scuttle this." Ruby snaked his pistol right out of his belt. She aimed it at his nose. "You will forgive me if I have grown suspicious of new friends unexpectedly entering my life." She drew back the hammer. "Why did you help us, Henry Collins?"

He looked down the barrel of the gun and, oddly, relaxed. He stilled the lip chewing and ear scratching and raised his hands.

"You will not believe me," he said.

"I have seen many strange things in the past week or two," she replied. "Do not assume that there is anything that I will or will not believe. Your coolness in the face of a weapon does serve you well."

"It is not loaded. I do not trust guns." He unfolded up to his full height, and his head brushed a crossbeam. He was easily as tall as Gwath, almost six and a half feet, though he had far less weight. "Will you believe me when I tell you that I am part of a secret society and indeed part of an even more secret brotherhood within it whose task it is to monitor that same secret society?"

She tried to interrupt, but he pressed on.

"Will you believe me when I tell you that your father, whom you call Wayland Teach, once had a different name and was at one time a member of our company? Will you believe me when I tell you that you, Ruby Teach, may carry with you a secret for which nations will wrestle and fall?"

Ruby looked at him.

"Barnacles," she said.

Collins folded back into himself and rested his forearms on his bony knees. "I told you you would not believe me."

"What secret?"

Collins chewed his lip. "That I don't know."

She raised her arms in her torn-up boy's getup. "Look at me. Tell me, please, where I'm hiding this secret." Collins did not respond. "And of course, now it's a 'great secret.' 'Nations will fall.' A bigger man than you once told me that if the mark will not trust your little lie, make it a big one. That is quite the fairy story."

He smiled. For a moment the nose, hands, and eyes no longer belonged to a looming buffoon but to an ancient hermit or to a secret minister to some clockwork lord of Tripoli.

"Look to your own crew, Ruby Teach."

"What do you mean?"

"For one, this Athen Boyle is more than he appears."

He was funny. "Thanks for the tip."

"Well then." They looked at each other.

Ruby handed him back his gun with an exaggerated flourish, and he surprised her with an equally overdramatic bow.

"Have I satisfied your suspicions?" He tucked his pistol back into his belt.

"No, but what use is an unloaded pistol?" She craned her head to get a better look at the thing on the table. It was a child's top, covered with engravings. "Why are you working on a fancy spinner?"

"For our protection." He made room next to him on the bench. She didn't sit but looked over his shoulder. He shrugged. "I have never seen one of these outside of a book."

"A spinner?"

He chuckled. "It is a miasmic ward." When Ruby just looked at him, he continued. "It is a special kind of top. The spinning is actually a mediating device for disseminating a chemystral reaction in a measured and unified manner."

"The top helps it put out the same amount of something?"

He smiled again, impressed. "Correct."

Ruby knitted her brows together. "Just because I was born on a boat doesn't mean—"

"I am sorry." They sat in silence, and he turned his attention back to the artifice. It was made of bronze and about the size of a hand. The body of the top was etched all around with thick clouds, masking a range of mountains hiding behind.

"Let's give the peaks a spin," Ruby said, and reached for the toy. Henry's hand darted out, covering her own. It was warm and dry, like paper. "Please don't," he said, and then pulled his hand back just as quickly. "This is a very delicate mechanism. I mean, I am sure you would be delicate with—"

"I won't touch it." She sat on her hands.

"Thank you." He blushed. He took the calipers and explored a two-pronged peak, right where the mountains met. They swung open, like the lid of a box. "Ah." He produced a silver-inlaid snuffbox from his jacket and used the calipers to tease a small cube of wet blue clay out of it.

"Fancy." Ruby reached for the snuffbox.

He closed it and slid it back in his jacket. "Yes."

"Can I see it?"

"It was my father's."

"So that means no?"

"It has some small reagents in it that can be quite volatile."

"So that means no?"

"Yes."

Collins set the little cube inside the cavity of the top and then closed the chest plate back over it. With a tiny click, the highlands became whole again. He cupped his hands in his lap and turned to Ruby. "All right. Now you can spin it."

She raised her eyebrows. "What if I don't want to spin it anymore?"

"Then whoever is following you will find us."

"This child's toy will protect us?"

"One of the Tinkers working with the Reeve discovered that you are marked in some chemystral fashion. This will mask our scent, if you will."

"Our *scent*?"

Henry nodded, chewing his lip.

Anything to throw that scarred bloodhound off their trail. "I'm ready," she said.

Two little wires with tiny handles wound out of the top. On his command she was to pull them apart to start it spinning. He stared into the peaks for a good while. Ruby felt something shift: The air? Her blood? A premonition?

"Begin," he said without looking at her.

She gave a good tug to both wires, and the thing started spinning with a low hum.

She was watching his eyes; otherwise, she would have missed it. He crinkled them, just slightly, and there was an accompanying *pfft* from the top. A plane of deep purple smoke emerged from the clouds and crept outward in all directions.

She took a step back, but Henry said, "It's all right. It won't hurt you."

The circle of purple smoke expanded toward both of them like water and then up *over* each of them, like the finest cloth. You could see through it, but everything was tinged lavender. It moved on in a circle for a few more feet, slowed, and then stopped, hanging in the air, about five feet past them in every direction. It was like nothing she had ever seen.

She whistled. And then she inhaled. It smelled like feet.

The midshipman was frowning.

"What?" Ruby prodded him. The smoke shroud moved with her. "It worked, didn't it?"

"Only a very little bit," he said.

"What was it supposed to do?" Ruby asked. "Make a smoke pony?"

"Fill up this room and the next, masking all of us. It

would have hidden us from any chemystral locaters for a few days."

"How long will this last?"

He looked at the top. "As long as that spins. My best guess? A few hours at most. I will go tell your servant."

She made to follow him out of the circle. He stopped her.

"You need to stay there. You are the one being followed."

"What?"

"You are the one they are searching for. Lady Boyle and the servant and me, no one is looking for us. The man my leftenant mentioned, Rool?"

Ice ran up Ruby's back. "I know him," she said.

"He is a Reeve, yes? They are the hands of the king, empowered to bring justice as they see it, without constraint and with great chemystral and martial power. Each one is an army, and he is their captain. And they are looking for you, Ruby. You know that, but you do not seem to hear it. Please stay there."

And he went into the boat warehouse, leaving her

sitting on the table, surrounded by a platter of smoke, with no other company than a smug little spinner.

She wanted to push it over.

But she didn't.

CHAPTER 22

Choose One (1):
  Artificer: I wish to further explore the creation of alloyed engines and artifacts, which are the physical expression of the Tinker's craft.
  Dynamist: I wish to further explore the creation of chemystral cells and reservoirs, which are used to power engines and artifacts.
  Scrutinist: I wish to further explore the mysteries of chemystral science and extend the boundaries of our understanding of the Tinker's craft.
                    —Form 1017-B, Declaration of Advanced Study

Athena Boyle was still sleeping. Or so they said. Cram and Collins had been in and out of the warehouse several times, but Ruby was still trapped in the little pond of purple vapor. The top, perched cheerfully next to her, had begun to wobble slightly, back and forth. She hated waiting. She wanted to do something. She had no idea what to do. Ruby also had no idea how a parcel of smoke and a stupid brass trinket could mask her from Wisdom

Rool, but she'd hop on one foot and sing "God Save
the King" if it had a chance of keeping that man away
from her.

"What is this place?" Cram was leaning against one
of the thick beams, and then he slid down into a heap.

She pushed the broken sign toward him through the
sawdust with a stick: LIAMS BROTHERS, FERRYMEN AND RIVER
TRANSPORT.

"What does it say?" Cram asked.

"You don't have letters?"

"Never saw much use." He shrugged. "The language
of metal is on its way in. I can flash my sums like a Boston
banker. My mam used to say—"

"The sign says this is a place where people made
boats and sold transport across the Schuylkill River."

Cram kenned it straightaway. He snorted. "And if
some grand master pulls up a big stone wall through your
back porch and over your head, it makes it a heavy task
to get to the water."

Ruby nodded. "And most of the water ran out of the
river when they drew the Lid out of the ground. You can

walk through it or jump over it in most places."

The midshipman came in from the other room, rolling down his sleeves, fresh from checking on Athena.

Ruby poked Cram with her stick. "How long have you known?"

"Ow. Easy, Ferret. Not longish. Just after you left the big house. She, well, I still knew him as 'he,' though truly I might speak of 'he' as 'she' now that we be past the point of no return"—he reached for the next thought— "however—"

Collins looked up from his waistcoat buttons. "You did not know she was in disguise?"

"Did you?" Ruby asked.

"Well, no. But I thought that—"

"Just because we are together does not mean we know all there is to know about one another," she parroted back to him.

"But they came to save you. That is not a trifling thing."

That hit her, but she forged on. "You saved our lives. Do we know all there is to know about you?"

He scratched his ear. "Most definitely not."

She turned back to the servant. "How did you find out?"

"I—"

"Why did you not tell me?"

"Let me finish, Ferret."

She stuck her finger through the plane of smoke and wiggled it. A little hole opened in the current, and the oily vapor flowed back into it. "All right."

Cram squirmed. "My master. My mistress"—he thought for a moment—"my *employer,* was in a right state after you skarpered out. Bangin' on walls with the hilt of the sword, cursing at me like some ancient sailor, and then sulking in a corner. Stared at a pocket watch for the longest time. Then my . . . employer snaps the ticker closed and strides into the big bedroom at the top of the stairs. Calls me up there, and I am to help . . . this person get into yon flouncy gown, which had been discovered in the wardrobe. There was a pile of buckles and sashes and ties in the most private of places, and in cranking that demon of a dress down, I became once and for all certain that she is indeed a lady." He blushed a deep crimson in the half-light.

"So why did you dress up like Madame Froofenhaus and her butler?"

"That Rool fella was searching for a gentleman and his servant—"

Collins broke in. "She was looking at a timepiece, you say? While trying to discover Ruby?"

Cram's eyes narrowed. "Yes, sir."

"May I see it?"

They narrowed more. "I do not think that be a good idea, sir."

Collins said, "It could be important."

"Be that as it are, sir." Cram held on to his bag like an orphan child with a sweet cake. "Her things are trusted to me, and just because you helped us with that potion, and thank ye for that"—he firmed his backbone—"I do not think I should let ye root around in her frillies like it were a Sunday market day."

The top wobbled.

"You are loyal. That is to be commended. However,

your loyalty may be clouding your judgment," Collins said.

Cram bridled. "And what do you know about loyalty, ya great beanpole? These are her things, not yourn. I ain't going to say it again."

"I think you should reconsider." Collins stood up. All the way up. "I must see that watch."

Cram fingered his butter churn, and the rat turned into a wolf. "You come and take it."

Ruby stood on the table, ready to jump in between them, pool of smoke be damned.

"Why do you want to see my watch?" The voice came from the doorway into the workshop. It was Athena Boyle, pale and leaning against the doorframe, with dueling sword drawn.

Collins blanched. "Lady, is it wise for you to be standing?"

She smiled. "Sir, I think it is far past time, from the look of things. Besides, I promised Ruby that we would be off." She levered herself from leaning to standing. She still looked very weak. "Now. My savior, Midshipman

Collins, is it?" He nodded. "Midshipman Collins, why is my charge surrounded by a highly sophisticated chemystral ward?"

Ruby bristled. "Hang on. When did I become 'your charge'?"

"It is my task to protect you, Ruby, and to guide you to safety."

"Is it also your task to acquire more holes than a ruined fishnet and bleed out at the drop of a hat?"

"That has been an unexpected part of the assignment, I must admit. People seem to acquire a great many holes when they spend time with you."

Cram chimed in. "Truer words, Ferret. Barked my shins more in the past week with you than ever I have till now."

"You would not be saying that, neither of you, if I could come out of this smoke."

The servant nodded. "Most like that's true."

"Please. You are distracting me from my inquiry. Mister Collins?"

He pulled on his ear. "Yes, Lady Boyle?"

"Lord Athen."

"As you wish."

"Why do you want to see my watch?"

Henry Collins said, "Thought, grant us grace."

Athena made a face, as if she had just swallowed something bitter. She responded, "Grace, protect us all."

Just then the top fell over, and the smoke around Ruby vanished like mist at midday.

All was motion. Collins hurried over to the boarded-up window and eased a board open so that he could see out into the street. "Pack your things if you please. We need to remove all hints of our presence from this room." He turned to Athena. "Have you any blue vitriol in that bag of yours?"

She snorted. "Do you mistake me for the queen of Sheba, sir?"

He ignored the question. "We have to go. Now. Can you walk?"

"If need be," she said. Her words were jaunty, but Ruby could see that she was struggling.

Collins tucked the top into his leather satchel. "With

the passing of the ward, Miss Teach will be visible again, and they will begin closing the net."

"Cram, hurry and gather the remains of the dress from the workroom. We can leave no trace for their trackers." Cram held the bag close to his chest, eyeing Collins on his way out.

Athena Boyle smiled out of the side of her mouth. "The midshipman is correct. Time to fly."

CHAPTER 23

CHATSBOTTOM: *Where is my carriage, Farnsworth?*
FARNSWORTH: *It is somewhat Exploded, milord.*
CHATSBOTTOM: *Exploded, you say?*
FARNSWORTH: *But Mr. Thunderfatch will no longer trouble your lordship.*
CHATSBOTTOM: *Quite right. Good chap.*
—Marion Coatesworth-Hay, *The Tinker's Dram*, Act III, sc. iv

Heroes rarely thought about baggage. Cram was discovering that to be a universal truth. Another universal truth: Lace was heavy as cornmeal when there was enough of it.

The gearbeasts had picked up their scent, and he was falling behind. The professor, the ferret, and his lady were carrying exactly nothing among them, while he was toting Lady Athena's Bag of Wonder, the Dress of Doom, his Churn of Smiting, and his own cumbersome kit. He wasn't a complainer. He could hear Mam in his head: "Moaners never get the pie, boy, and more, they always end up scrubbing the pan." But there were these steps, see. Four hundred and fifty-two so far. They were cut into what Ferret called the Lid, but it was more a wall here. The Lid stretched above them somewhere in the gloom, too far away to think on.

Leg, leg, leg. Keep moving the legs. *Leg, leg,* and he could have kissed the stair maker. The next step was a wide landing.

"Wait," Lady Athena gasped. The professor was breathing heavy as well.

"We cannot keep up the stairs. If they catch us, we are all done. The gearbeasts will not tire, and we are in no shape for a fight."

The professor gasped. "I can get us to safety."

"As can I." She was looking at her watch again. It was gold and well worn. She was holding it out in front of her now, arm pointing at a weathered metal door set into the stone wall. The lever was secured with a solid-looking padlock. "Ruby, can you open this?"

The girl stared back down the stairway.

"Ruby?" Athena repeated, louder and more urgent.

Ferret snorted. "Can you flounce about in a party dress? Out of my way." She pulled a ring of picks out of her coat and made for the door.

"Wait." The professor was two steps up. "Where are you going? You need to come with me. That leads outside the city."

Athena clapped the watch closed and waved it at him. "That is fortunate because we need to go outside the city."

"No! There is nothing but wilderness out there. We need a trusted refuge," Collins said.

Below them in the dark, like faraway beetles, the faint clack of metal claws sounded on stone.

Cram got up on one knee. "Hear that?"

Collins nodded. "They are coming for us now. We must keep moving."

"We are moving." Athena peered down the steps, unsheathing her sword. "You or I can secure the door from the other side. They will not be able to follow us."

"And then we will be farther away from help and near to the wilds, unable to return to the city." He stepped down onto the landing. "Miss Teach! I can take you to friends that can protect you and keep you safe. We can help you find your father."

In the half-light Ferret looked young, and scared. She fiddled with the picks. "I thought you were together, with your secret phrases."

Athena shrugged. "I thought so, too. Mayhap we were wrong. I am taking you to my people, Ruby, and they are somewhere through that door."

"And mine are up the stairs," Collins insisted.

"And there be shadows coming up them stairs fast," Cram said from his perch on the edge of the landing. He could see them now, shapes holding on to the leashes. Then the barking sounded, like a hound's but tinged with iron.

"Ruby!" Athena's voice cut through the half-light. "You must choose."

"Agreed," Collins said. "I will follow you wherever."

She looked between them for a moment. Collins's face was stern. Athena Boyle smiled.

Cram thought he could smell something burning, like a kettle that was too hot.

"The door," Ruby said, and the heavy lock was open in a flash.

Athena ripped it open. Light shone through and blinded Cram. He hadn't seen sunlight for days. There was an old stone landing beyond with trees far below. "Go! Go!" Athena cried. "Keep running, we'll catch up!"

Ruby ran through and down the stairs, Cram fast on her heels. His legs were like water, though, and he tripped on the raised metal lip of the door. He turned as he fell to the other side so he landed on his back, protecting Athena's bag.

That was how he saw his mistress tear through next and then, whirling, kick Henry Collins hard in the chest.

The kick knocked him back through the doorway and onto the landing inside.

Athena yelled, as if he were slow behind, "Collins, come on!"

The professor was quick and got back onto his feet, but he was not quick enough. As he was lunging forward, he caught Cram's eye, wrenched a brass key out of his pocket, put it to his lips, and whispered something.

"The Friendly Dollop spice shop. Tell her." Cram heard it clear as day, as if the bloke were standing next to him.

Athena slammed the heavy metal door closed and threw the lever.

She turned, eyes wide, face flushed. "My bag, Cram. Quickly!" The order startled him, and he passed her the bag. She pulled out a ceramic flask and slammed it on the lever. The metal melted and fused in seconds.

Without a word, Athena Boyle handed Cram the bag and followed Ruby down the stairs.

What had he just seen?

A glimpse into the affairs of his betters.

He put it out of his mind. He tried not to think about what might be happening on the other side of the door.

"Cram!" Ferret was calling to him from the bottom of the stairs, half eaten up by tall grass. Beyond her were a little stream and, by Science, the sky. Halfway down the stone steps, Lady Athena had turned back to look up at him, waiting. She had not sheathed her sword. For better or worse, he had made his choice. The heroes still needed their things. Cram shouldered the bag, adjusted the dress on one shoulder, tucked his churn under his other arm, and followed.

CHAPTER 24

Aequilibrium in omnibus
(balance in all things).
　　　—Motto, Worshipful Order of Grocers

"By all odds that should not be standing," Ruby whispered. They were peering over a low hill at a rickety collection of random scraps of wood, held together by twine, tar, and a huge helping of faith. It sat in a tiny clearing in the woods just over the weak trickle that used to be the Schuylkill River. The wind picked up slightly, and Ruby was certain that the stiff breeze would be the end for the shack then and there, but the thing stayed upright, defying all logic.

Athena looked less confident than she sounded. "Cram," she said, "this is the Archer smokehouse, correct?"

"That be what the old woman told me," Cram said through a mouthful of pie. They had decided that he was the one of the three that could risk being seen, and he had been making liberal use of Athena's coin to purchase food from the locals of the Dregs. He called it softening up the natives. "This smoked trout come from that smokehouse, or so she said. Tasty," he added. He hefted a jug of cider he had liberated as well. "No word on where this come from." He took another swig. "Also tasty."

Ruby scanned the horizon. The forest loomed to the west, a solid mass of brown and green. Back behind them the wall of Philadelphi rose high above the trees, with the buildings of UpTown perched above like ravens. Nestled between, the Dregs was a collection of hog robbers, scratch farmers, ne'er-do-wells, and other folks who were too poor to even have a home in the city. Gwath and she had never spent much time in the neighborhood, mostly because it was bad business to steal from people with no money.

"We need to get inside that shack," Ruby said. Athena's finery stood out here like a peacock on a dung heap. More than that, whatever mark Athena and Collins had been moaning about was still on her, and that boded no good. Unless they could find another way to mask it or remove it, the gear hounds and men and Wisdom Rool would be on them again soon enough. It still hurt that the young alchemyst had abandoned them. She had liked Collins, and she thought he had liked her. And he had *saved* them. And then he had just left when he didn't get his way.

Gwath Maxim Nine: "Keep to the Crew." That meant the two people at her side. How they had come together did not matter. They were hers now.

Athena grunted softly and brushed at her side as she stood. Ruby could not help admiring her grit. That wound must hurt more than she let on. She flexed her own wrist inside its splint. Every time she moved it, some sharp edge ground up against another one. They were taking on water, and the pumps were failing.

In the end they just walked straight up to the door. Athena with her hand on her hilt, Ruby clutching a chunk of rock, and Cram following, churn at the ready.

Someone was snoring inside. Loudly.

Athena glanced back, face lit up. Ruby nodded that she was ready. Athena knocked.

The snoring stopped.

A ruckus followed. Shifting wood and some sort of clanking. Then the click of a clocklock. Then another.

"Who is it?" The voice from the other side of the door scraped like a saw on heavy stone.

Cram and Ruby looked to Athena. Athena tucked a strand of hair behind her ear, opened her mouth, and then shut it.

"Say something!" Ruby hissed at her.

"I do not know what to say. It is possible there is a password," she whispered back.

"But you have it, yes?"

"Not really."

"What?"

BLAM. The wall near the door exploded outward,

leaving a hole the size of a head at waist level. The shot had also disintegrated most of the cider jug. It ended right below where Cram was holding on to the neck.

"That came from Maisie." A voice rumbled out of the shack. "I have another thunder gun in here: Loretta. She is bigger than her sister, and irritable to boot. Now. Who is it?"

Athena cleared her throat. "My name, sir, is Athen Boyle. I come visiting with two servants. We are selling spices."

There was no response.

"*Spices*, I say."

Cram crouched to the ground with his hands wound around his head. He looked like a frog. Ruby thought being a frog might be nice in the next life.

"Open the door. Let me get a look at you," the voice said.

"Thank you, sir." Athena took a step back and slowly opened the door.

The shack was crowded and dark. It was filled with hanging racks of fish and meat. A narrow alley led through the center of the racks, and at the other end of the alley was a massive, cushioned, elegant easy chair. The man sitting in it had a bald head, fenced by a riot of greasy brown hair, and a suspicious squint. There were two fowling pieces on stands in front of the chair. One sizable barrel was smoking and resting up at the ceiling, and the other was pointed straight at them.

"We do not have much call for spices out here, popinjay," he said. "I do not see many merchants leaving the pretty city for our little corner of dunghill. What are you doing in my smoke shack?"

Athena scanned the interior of the shack, and she seemed put out or confused. "There is no one else here?"

"Just me and the jerky. Who were you expecting? Cotton Mather? Gov'nor Spotswood and the Knights of the Golden Horseshoe?"

"Possibly, possibly." She looked down at her shoes, and her tension went away.

Ruby followed her gaze to a mound in the center of the dirt floor of the shack, only a touch higher than the rest of it.

Athena took a step forward, and the bell of the long
gun followed her.

"May I?" she asked, pointing toward the mound.

The man followed her gaze, and then he grunted.
Eloquently.

"Robby help me, please." Ruby knelt and followed
Athena's lead, clearing the dirt away to reveal an
ironbound trapdoor. It was dark, varnished wood, inlaid
with an intricate carving of a pepper mill. At the edge
facing them were three keyholes, one small and narrow,
the center big and rounded, and the third keyhole shaped
like a square.

"Cram, my bag if you please?" Athena looked up
at the big man, asking permission. He nodded slightly,
amused. Cram reached into his large sack and pulled
out the smaller oilskin bag from inside. Athena retrieved
some powder from a sealed envelope and sprinkled it
into a crystal bulb full of silver liquid. She upended the
bulb to pour out the liquid, but when it landed in her
hand, the fluid settled and hardened into a large silvered
key.

"My, my," said the man, who did not look impressed in the least.

It was an easy match. Ruby's practiced eye told her that the key was a sweet ringer for the center hole.

Athena placed the key on the plate next to the lock, and it did match perfectly. She looked up at Ruby. A dare? Ruby nodded her head. Athena's eyes crinkled. Turning back to the trapdoor, she took the key and fitted it smoothly into the smaller, narrow hole at the top. The key *lessened* as it contacted the lock. It fitted like a glove, and when she turned it, the sound of gears unlocking filled the smoke shack. Ruby tried to not look surprised.

"Fermat's Lock." The man nodded in approval. "Glad to see they still send some of you prepared. Course, I'm not surprised. Big admirer of your father."

Athena glanced out of the corners of her eyes at Ruby and Cram. She cleared her throat. "Thank you."

"Name's Abel. Abel Ward. Go on down, Journeyman Boyle. We have been expecting yewse. And your guest." He gave Ruby a queer look.

He reached behind the chair and handed Athena a battered tinker's lamp. "You should be fine with this. The password is 'gypsum.' The gatekeeper will take your iron and your flasks. Watch your p's and q's with that one. New, jumpy, and still very, um, official."

The trap led down a wooden ladder to a dirt landing and a hallway. It twisted several times and got a bit cooler. Ruby wondered if they had doubled back on the river, but the air was dry as parchment against her skin. Something about the passage felt strange, but she could not figure it. Then Cram spoke up.

"So silky," he said. Ruby looked down. The walls and floor were earth, but everything had been smoothed down, like pitch in a seam. It was cold and hard, like stone.

"Like the chapter house, but less fancy," Cram said. At Ruby's look, he said, "That carriage I drove in Boston, 'twere owned by the Tinkers. The Boston chapter house was full of walls like this, but most had carvings and swirlies and things."

The carriage. It brought her up short. Was that truly just a few days ago? She felt a little dizzy. So many things had happened. So many people that she might never see again.

In the dark, behind her, Cram whispered, "I miss my mam."

Her stomach got heavy. She had taken his life that day, as true as Wisdom Rool had taken hers. "I am sorry for what happened," Ruby said. It felt small. "I'll make it right by you, I promise."

He looked at her funny, as if she had grown another head. "My thanks, Ferret." He brushed past her and then turned back. "Don't think that'll make me not call you Ferret. Ferret."

"I won't," she said.

"Keep up, shirkers," Athena said from up ahead. After opening the lock, she had been moving more easily, as if she had shed a weight. "You both should know that the place we are going runs on rules and discipline. Speak only when spoken to. I have a certain position among these people and can speak for us all. It will go better if you allow me to do so."

At the bottom the corridor turned sharply to the right, and the hall beyond glowed with a harsh orange light. Athena rounded the corner and then came to a halt. Ruby could not see past her.

A voice like nails pulled across slate crept around the corner. "Password."

Athena's mouth was a line.

"What is it?" Ruby asked.

"That voice," Athena said. Then louder: "I know your speech, sir, but I cannot place you."

Ruby sidestepped around the bend, and a scent of metal washed over her. The corridor was blocked off, floor to ceiling, by a massive bronze door. Light emerged from the eyes of a great carved animal head, roaring jaws wide open. In the glare of the eyes, she could not quite recognize the animal. Was it a lion? A dragon?

Cram came up behind her. "That there's a roaring camel."

Ruby blew out her breath. "Oh, please. More camels? Really?"

Athena grimaced. "It is an important symbol of the order."

"Not very fierce, though, is it? When I think of fierce,

I think of predators—you know, lion, wolf. Even a guard dog."

"Most certain not a camel, though," Cram said.

"You stay out of this," Athena shot at him. "Ruby Teach, have you ever been spit at by a camel?"

"Spit at?"

"Yes."

"Why would I let one spit on me?"

Cram coughed. It might have been a snicker.

"They are fierce and terrible. Do not make that face. They are."

The voice rang out impatiently from behind the metal door. "Do you hear me? The password and your iron right now, or I will flood that hallway with phlogistic particulates, and you can continue your debate of natural history as little piles of sulfuric ash."

"Gypsum," Athena said.

"Very well." A large drawer slid out of a cunning panel in the door. "Now your iron, big and small. Also any reagents or catalysts."

"Must we?" Athena called. "I am a journeyman

of the order, and we are allowed to carry our arms in London."

The voice snorted, nasal as a rhinoceros. "Does this look like London to you, you mollycoddle!"

Athena narrowed her eyes at the door. "Your lack of respect will be dealt with. Do you know who my father is?"

"I do. And I know who you are, Lord Athen Boyle, and if you wish to challenge me, you may, but to do that, you must enter this gate, and to do that, you must. Put. Your iron. In the drawer."

They complied. Athena's sword and Cram's bags. Ruby missed her knives. After, a clacking of gears sounded, and a breeze pushed against her face. The door opened outward until the camel's nose touched the smooth wall of the corridor. Athena strode through, with her gloves in her hand, primed to challenge the rude brigand on the other side. She stopped chest to face with a short hawk of a girl, hair pulled back tight as ship cables.

"Greta Van Huffridge," Athena sputtered.

Ruby had never heard her sputter.

CHAPTER 25

9th. Over Strident Objection from a Minority, Abigail Booker allowed to deliver her findings re: experimentation with Igneous Fluid. Cause: one part brilliant scholarship, another part Mlle. Booker's Ferocious Thumping of Mr. Smathers, compounded by her threats of further physical exertions if not allowed to speak. Excellent talk.

—Minutes of the Alembic Coffeehouse, UnderTown,
March 4, 1718

"Do you wish to slap me, sir? To challenge me to a duel?" said Greta Van Huffridge. She thrust her chin upward at Athena like a spear. Ruby's neck muscles tightened in sympathy. The girl could not have been taller than five feet. She was fifteen or sixteen but was dressed like a woman thrice her years, in a salmon pink mantua, patterned all over with hideous butterflies.

Cram whispered behind her, "If she didn't kill us

with fire from behind that door, she certain could have blinded us with that dress."

Athena covered her surprise with a bow. "Miss Van Huffridge," she said, "I am so pleased to remake your acquaintance."

"You are nothing of the kind," she spit. "Get your people inside this door so that I may close it and we may proceed with this charade." She seized the crank of a large brass wheel and began spinning it for all that it was worth. Gears engaged, and the door crept back toward them. It was as thick as Ruby's arm was long and closed with a thud and the heavy sound of locks engaging.

Greta grabbed an engraved horn hanging from a tube that passed into the earthen wall and yelled into it, "I require a replacement on the Dregs door, IF YOU PLEASE." She hurled it back into its hook and pinned the three of them with a stare. Her nostrils flared. "We will wait here until my relief comes. Touch nothing." She pulled herself back onto a stool, turned her back to them, and began making entries in a large book perched on a shelf desk that hung out of the back of the door.

"Miss Van Huffridge"—Athena raised both her hands in surrender—"I beg you to not let what happened between us in London color our relationship here."

The pen tore through a number of pages. "Nothing happened between us in London, sir. Nothing."

Before Athena could respond, Ruby said, "How well do you know each other?"

Greta Van Huffridge turned to a clean page and attacked the book with renewed gusto. "Please inform your baggage that I speak only to persons of a certain merit or social standing and that he occupies neither one nor the other."

Ruby felt her face redden. "If you come down off that stool, I'll show you how well I can hear. I'll box your ears and create a pleasing ringing sound for your ladyship."

Athena put herself between the two. "Robby, she is baiting you."

"Oh, yes, I know." Her hands itched. "And I mean to use her as bait on the nearest fishhook I can find."

"I mean, violence is forbidden here. If you attack her, you risk the ire of the order."

"I don't care about your stupid order. What about you? You were just going to slap her in the face and challenge her to a duel."

Athena grabbed her shoulder. "She is a girl. If she were a boy I would have presented her with my glove, and we would have settled our disagreement outside the confines of this house."

There was something else she was not saying. Then Ruby saw it. "Ah," she said.

Athena flexed her fingers. "Yes. As two gentlemen we would have been presented with a certain latitude. That is an advantage men have in polite society."

It hit Ruby like a bucket of water. They did not know that Athena was a girl. None of them. "I see. Fine. Very well. Lord Athen."

No one spoke until a boy, his hair burned off one side of his head, came to relieve Greta. He sat on the stool and immediately began writing in the huge tome on the desk.

Their prissy guardian pulled a number of levers on the side of the door near the wall. The wide metal drawer, presumably laden with their weapons, popped out of it. Cleverly attached wheels hinged down and turned it into a rolling cart. The tiny girl set off down the hallway, pushing the cart in front of her at a brisk clip. They had no choice but to follow. The passage continued on into an oblong room that had several other hallways entering it from different directions.

Its only furniture was a rough wooden table in front of another carved bronze door. Behind the table sat two hard men, both wearing masks. They were cloth affairs that covered the nose and eyes. They were indigo, and each was inscribed with a drawing. One bore an ax, and the other a flame. A nasty-looking ax lay in front of its namesake, and several envelopes, ceramic vials, and an iron box in front of the flame. Greta stopped at the opening of the room and said, "Greetings, Sir Ax."

He grumbled, "With whom do you pass?"

"I pass with Bishop's Yellow."

A swollen boil on his nose peeked out from under the mask. He nodded and said, "Come forward." The two men examined the contents of the rolling case carefully.

Flame, skinny with a heavy beard, whistled when he pulled Athena's sword out of its sheath. He cataloged the items and then put them in a large locked chest set into the floor beside the table. His deep voice surprised Ruby. "These will be returned to you upon your exit."

Ax looked Ruby up and down and prodded at her left coat pocket with the long haft of his weapon. "What's in there?" She counted to five before she moved her hand. It would not be good for them to see her shaking. She slipped a finger through the loop and fished her picks out into the light. He shrugged. "We take only weapons, but use those inside, and you'll get more than a whipping."

He wrote Athena a receipt. Flame opened the iron box and produced a stained wood carving shaped like the snout of a pig. It was the size of a fist and chased all over with pewter swirls.

"What is that?" Ruby whispered to Athena.

"It is an olfactor," the man said as he poured a drop of orange liquid into one of the nostrils of the carving. "Stand very still, if you please," he murmured. He slowly passed the hog snout over Athena and then Cram, front and back, top to bottom. Ruby was next. When the snout passed over her right shoulder, the pewter swirls changed to black.

Flame held his hand very still. "Ax," he murmured. The big man lifted the heavy ax as if it were a hatchet. It glinted in the dim light. A pistol appeared in his other hand.

Ruby applied Gwath Maxim Eleven: "If They Are Twitchy, Do Not Twitch."

Flame cocked his head. "Boy," he said, "is there something you wish to tell us?"

"I don't understand," Ruby said.

He moved the olfactor away, and the pattern carved into the pig snout returned to its original pewter gray. When he passed it back close to her shoulder, the gray turned black once again. "We use this to detect chemystral markers that might lead others to our door." His eyes were cold behind his mask. "You bearing breadcrumbs, little Hansel?"

Her stomach dropped through the floor. The mark Henry had told her about. "Um, yes." The two men tensed. "But I don't know where it is."

Ax's knuckles were white. "You give it to us, now, boy, or we'll take it."

Athena spoke up. "I may be able to help."

"You had best, journeyman." Ax adjusted his grip. "This runt is here under your ward."

Athena ignored the big man. "May I come forward?" Flame nodded. Athena moved next to Ruby. Her hair smelled like hay. "Robby, would you mind taking off your coat, please?" Ruby did as she was told. Without a moment's hesitation, Athena peeled the little trail of green goo off the back of her shirt, the goo that had splashed on Ruby as she escaped down the trap at the town house. "I wager that this is the object of your inquiry." She held it out to Flame, but he refused and motioned for her to set it on the table instead. He passed the olfactor over the little pile of rubbery stuff, and the color indeed flashed black. Ruby was thunderstruck.

"Explain," the bearded man murmured.

"This boy here was my quarry, and he is a slippery one. I had to mark him, so I could find him if he bolted."

Ruby dug her toes into her boots. It was the only way she could stay quiet. *Athena* had marked her? Not Rool?

Flame nodded. "I see. You know it is part of the compact that you should reveal any chemystral flares before entering another chapter house." It was not a question.

Athena shrugged. "I did not. My apologies." She said it as if she had bumped into him in a coffeehouse. "In my part of the world it is not a requirement, rather only a courtesy."

"So you show us no courtesy?" Ax slammed his weapon onto the wooden table. Athena shrugged again. "You are in our part of the world, you jumped-up dandy. We scratch and scrabble for what we get this side of the water, and if you got no courtesy, you got no respect. I'll wager that—"

"Thank you for your cooperation, journeyman," Flame interrupted.

"Thank you for your vigilance, sir." Athena nodded him a bow.

Flame avoided Athena's eyes and pulled a medallion

out of the thicket of his beard. He touched it to a carving of a willow on the door. It swung silently open. He motioned over his shoulder and said, "Welcome to the Warren."

The door closed silently behind them. The corridor beyond was like the ones before it, smooth and featureless. Ruby's heart was battering at her chest, and the scar below her eye was throbbing. Athena had marked her. Twice. The first time in the carriage was for amusement, surely. But now this.

Yet the marker must have been how Athena and Cram had found her. She might have been trapped in a cell or hung from a hook in Wisdom Rool's study or worse. She owed Athena for that. But Ruby thought that Athena had revealed everything to her. The thought of still more secrets jabbed at her, an ugly thistle in her side.

At the same time, she could not help catching the looks that Greta was giving Athena. She was a fierce mooncalf, to be sure, and whatever had "not happened" in London had ended in Miss Van Huffridge's hating Athena, but like an angry puppy. A worm gnawed at

Ruby's chest whenever she caught the looks and sighs and mooning.

Athena treated Ruby just as Greta had said. She was baggage. Valuable baggage, to be sure, but goods to be handled and delivered. Wherever this passage was leading, she was not certain she wanted to discover where it ended.

Athena seemed comfortable with all these doors and guards, but Ruby could not help wondering if the measures were to keep people in, not out. Gwath Maxim Number Twenty-two said, "Always Look for the Chimney," but as far as she could see, there was no chimney. It was tight as a drum. An ant would have trouble breaking into this place.

Greta led them briskly past laboratories, workrooms, and people. They clipped past a classroom where a boy who might have been from China was reciting to a small group of other children while a woman watched, her blue badger mask bright against dark, African features. Most were dressed more like her and Cram than Athena and Greta: roughspun woolens and mended elbows. All the adults, every one, wore a mask.

Everyone they passed in the hall was busy, and

everyone was carrying some sort of contraption: tools, a tray of ceramic bottles, a disassembled set of gears that looked as if they were made of glass.

Greta led them to a small side passage, which angled off from a shadowy corner between two tinker's lamps. It felt older than the rest of the complex. Cobwebs hung in the corners. Angry voices bounced down the hallway from the door at the end. Ruby stepped more quietly and strained to hear. Gwath Maxim Number Six: "Pay Attention to the Private, not the Public."

"We cannot take this on!" one voice insisted. It was a woman. Her voice cut timber.

Another woman responded, higher, a glass hammer. "We have our role to play. We are sworn to it."

"I swore my obedience to the order, not to Godfrey Boyle. This is a dangerous game to play. We are exposed," said a man's voice.

"Yes, exactly." This was the first woman again.

Greta pushed open the door at the end of the passage, into a cozy room dominated by a large oak table. Around it sat five people, all masked.

The room went silent. Even in their masks, two of the people hid their faces: One turned away from the door, and one grabbed a book and held it over his features with a beefy hand.

One of the women spoke. She had plain brown hair and a plain brown frock, and her mask bore a burning fireplace. "What is the meaning of this?" It was the glass hammer.

Greta Van Huffridge offered a stiff curtsy. "I beg your pardon, Madame Hearth. Our orders are to bring these as soon as we find them."

The woman made a face. "Bring them, yes, Van Huffridge, but to the door, not into the study. The Penta's business is not for your ears."

One of the men, who was looking away, added, "Or your eyes." He obviously did not want to be seen, but Ruby had caught dark green eyes and a tiny hammer under his right eye before he had turned his back.

The girl paled and cast her eyes to the floor. "Pate was not at the door. I thought you would want to see these right away."

Hearth shook her head once. "The liberties you take will catch up with you. You are not in Van Huffridge House, but in the Warren. Go out, all of you, and return when I call you."

Athena spoke up, "Madame . . ."

The woman's eyes were dark and cold inside the fireplace. "Boyle means no more here than Van Huffridge, young sir. If you are a journeyman, do not question a master's orders. The hall."

They left, closing the door after them. They waited in the hall for three minutes, no more. A voice called them back in.

The woman called Madame Hearth was there, but no sign of the other four. Ruby pulled her fingernails out of her palm, and a little thought blossomed: Gwath Maxim Number Sixteen: "The Way In Is the Way Out."

CHAPTER 26

A Most Clever, Strange, and Dangerous
WAIF
A Young Girl Answering to Aruba Teach, also Ruby Teach
Of dark complexion, small stature and with features foxlike
(as drawn below)
Wanted for Crimes against the Crown
READY MONEY REWARD FOR HARD NEWS
Inquire at Berth No. 5, Benzene Yards Wharf, His Majesty's Ship *Grail*

—Wanted poster

The ornate chemystral samovar was shaped like a bookshelf, with pipes and levers cleverly concealed in metal books that pulled in and out of the shelves. However many dials, levers, and rotating panels there were, the tea that came out of it was a bitter blend of angry dirt and sad foliage.

Madame Hearth was perched in the highest backed

of the wooden chairs surrounding the table. She had not offered them seats but had her man, a bald fellow called Pate, pour tea. He had returned on the heels of their second entrance, out of breath. His mask had no image on it.

They drank tea in silence before their interviewer placed her cup precisely in the center of its saucer. "Welcome to the Warren." She had not acknowledged Cram's existence, nor had he received any tea. Ruby envied him. "Thank you for completing your mission, journeyman." She nodded to Athena. "I would have a private word with your companion. A bed has been prepared for you in the men's dormitory. You may retire there if you wish. The library and workrooms are also available to you as befits your station. Master Bale can aid you with your wounds. He is two doors down the hall to the right."

"Madame Hearth, this was not an uneventful journey. There are several circumstances of which I should inform you. Surely you wish to hear of them as soon as possible?"

"My wishes are my own, boy. And for the moment I require your exit."

"Thank you." Athena turned and, in passing, looked Ruby a warning. "We will await you in the library." And then she left, Cram in tow.

The Van Huffridge girl had found a bookshelf in the corner and was ogling it with deep concentration. "You too, miss," Madame Hearth insisted.

The girl grimaced, curtsied, and then left, giving Ruby her own long stare as she passed. The little spider would be trouble; she could feel it. The door closed, and they were alone. The man called Pate refilled her teacup, cradling it in his beefy hand.

"You will be wondering at your surroundings. This is the Warren, the halls of a part of our order called the Bluestockings. We teach science, alchemy, and chemystral artifice to those who cannot claim it in the light of day: women, foreigners, Africans, indentures. We wear our masks to make all equal. There is no class here, no station. Only hard work and merit. You may call me Madame Hearth. And you are Aruba Teach."

No one called her Aruba.

"How do you know my name?"

"The order has been looking out for you since you were born. It stands to reason that we have gathered a tidy package of information concerning you and your father, do you not agree?"

This woman, never once mentioned by her father, or Gwath, or any of the crew, had been watching over her since she had been born? Ridiculous. Ruby resisted pointing out to her that they had recently been doing a very poor job of it.

"You will be staying with us for some time, but as a sign of good faith I will answer you ten questions in this interview. Use them wisely. In return, you will answer my questions. Have we an agreement?"

Ruby's breath quickened. Finally some news. "How do you know my father?"

Sip. Clink. "He was once a member of our order and then left us to protect something for us and mask the fact that you were alive."

"Why? He took me away from . . . this? On purpose?"

"Exactly."

Sip. Clink.

Barnacles. This was an exchange, and she was throwing about the little she had to work with, applying no mind or care or strategy. "That was four questions."

"Indeed."

Ruby gathered her wits. She needed time to understand the rules. "I would ask for more tea if it were not seen as a question."

Dribble. Clink.

"Where is my father?" Ruby asked.

"As far as we can tell, your father and his crew were taken to the Benzene Yards, the Tinkers' stronghold near the river. He is being held there by the Royal Navy and the Reeve. A daunting set of jailors." She gave the teacup to Pate, who refilled it. "My turn, I fear. What do you know of your mother?"

"Nothing." For her entire life, the crew had not said ten words about her mother, though they had hinted at something dire. Her father would not speak of it. They had even fought about it. It was the only time she had ever seen him angry. He had thrown a mug across his cabin and ordered her out. Later that night, eyes red, he had woken her to give her the button she wore around her neck. He begged her not to speak of it again and swore that he would tell her when it was the proper time.

The proper time. She'd had more than a bellyful of the proper time. People of a certain age—Gwath, her father, this woman: they hoarded knowledge. They kept it locked away and just out of reach, until they needed to use it. Ruby dug her toes into the floor.

"What manner of man is Godfrey Boyle?"

Clank. The teacup chipped the saucer. "Where did you hear that name?"

Ruby took a sip of the tea. It tasted the way tin tailings smelled, but it gave her a moment. "Lord Athen mentioned him."

Madame Hearth plucked at her mask, settling it over her ear. "Ruthless, brilliant, tireless."

There was a whiff of something here. The way Hearth had answered. She was unsettled.

Ruby bluffed. "Why did Godfrey Boyle send Lord Athen to look for me?"

"Sir Godfrey Boyle sent his only son to find you when

he discovered"—she raised her spoon like a flag—"that someone had informed the Reeve of your and your father's whereabouts and that they were actively looking for you." She lowered her spoon and began stirring the tea.

"Godfrey Boyle, Athen Boyle, you, the Bluestockings. Who are you?" Ruby asked.

"We are the Worshipful Order of Grocers." Hearth spoke the name with deep reverence. "It is a common name, but a great responsibility. Our task is to keep balance in the world."

"Why do you need me to keep balance in the world?"

Hearth clapped her hands. The gloves flapped faintly, like birds in the morning. "The first perceptive question."

"Well?" Ruby said.

"We seek a recipe. Your mother gave you the key, somehow, before . . . she left. Or so they tell us."

"A recipe. And a key. Like a fairy story. Like Perseus, who killed the Gorgon." Ruby took care to keep the question out of the statement.

"Clever girl. You do possess a kind of low cunning. Unfortunately, since it was not phrased as a question, I will not answer it." Madame Hearth toyed with the handle of her teacup. "Would you like to sit down?"

Ruby sat without speaking. Madame Hearth came around the table and perched a hip on the corner near her. She leaned over. The paint on the flames of the hearth was flaking.

"Aruba, it is not my intention to alarm you. However, it is also far from my intention to coddle you. You must understand some hard truths. You are running from very powerful people, and you need protection. We can offer you this protection and indeed an education. Your mother was an accomplished chemystral practitioner, did you know that?"

Ruby shook her head.

"She was a grand master of the chemystral arts. We can help you become one—if you have it in you. You are intelligent and passionate. This is easy to see. Those are two powerful facets that will give you an advantage. A third is your lineage."

She tapped a book on the table beside her. It was plain and weatherbeaten, bound by leather and secured by a brass lock with a button-shaped keyhole. "This journal was your mother's, and it can be yours if you earn it. It is a chain that traces back thousands of years. We can restore your true family to you."

Ruby could not take her eyes from the journal. A storm raged inside her, and she struggled to stay above water and appear calm. "I have a family."

"Scalawags. Rapscallions. The dregs of the earth."

"Will you help me find my father?"

Madame Hearth offered a warm smile. "Soon, perhaps. Our position here is too precarious to make an open assault at this time, but when the opportunity is right, after you have found some skill with chemystry, perhaps we will be able to take him back. When the time is right, we will absolutely rise up and tear down the walls of the Tinkers and the merchant lords of England and reunite you with your father."

The emptiest of promises. Ruby fought to keep the red rage from her face. She hated not knowing what was happening. Ever since she was a little girl, the worst thing her father could do was to not tell her where they were bound or how long they would be berthed in port.

She was done with not knowing.

CHAPTER 27

*I will not comment upon our Affections. They are one part
Unreason, one part Madness, and no parts Science.*
—Conrado Flacian, recording secretary,
Andalu Philosophical Society

Pate showed Ruby down the hallway back into the
newer passages. They twisted and turned, but the tangle
inside her knotted even tighter. Her father, the recipe, her
mother. Could they be this connected?

Madame Hearth had released her from the interview
into what passed for night in this strange place. The
tinker's lamps, many of them curiously shaped or
oddly colored, glowed at half strength, and the shadows

raced ahead and then behind them as they passed. The workrooms had emptied of students, alembics and burners waiting patiently in formation for the next morning. In one room the woman in the badger mask stood at a chalk slate, hunting through a forest of equations. Ruby's warden, for that is what he was, hurried her on.

She turned to him. "I need to find the library." He hesitated and then nodded and led her down a side passage.

The library was a small, plain affair, with rough wood furniture. There were several orderly bookshelves and a large workbench, stocked with a set of tools. It was empty, save for Athena and Cram. Both were passed out asleep, she facedown in a leather-bound tome, and he sprawled out on the bench as if it were a bed. They seemed like a crew. Together. It made Ruby smile, and it also made her feel strangely shy.

"Hello," she said. Athena straightened quickly, stood, and bowed. Cram woke with a squeak and a jerk and fell from the workbench onto the floor. When he saw that it was Ruby and that he was safe, he waved, curled up on the sealed earth floor like a kitchen dog, and closed his eyes again.

Ruby sat down across from Athena, who rubbed the sleep from her eyes. Pate planted himself next to a bookshelf, a vigilant urn. Athena smiled. "Hello, Miss Teach. I trust your interview passed pleasantly."

"Pleasant as milady's tea," she joked.

Athena only smiled.

It was hard, with Pate there, to see her. She was wearing her Lord Athen mask with more purpose.

"Madame Hearth seems an intelligent and driven woman." Athena offered Pate a nod of the head, which he returned. "You are in good hands and will be safe here."

"And I have you two to thank for that, I know. You got me here," Ruby said.

She had much to report, but Pate was listening. The next words were tricky, dancing out of reach. "What are you reading?"

Athena said, "*Arts Martial and Practice*, Ezekiel Pelham."

Ruby laughed. "Aha, a fencing tome. Good. You need the practice."

"I'm sure a lady would not be interested."

Her stiff courtesy hit Ruby like the north wind. "There are no ladies here."

"I disagree, miss."

Ruby stood up. "Do you? Sir?"

"Yes?" Athena waited politely, the picture of a perfect gentleman. "My apologies. Have I offended you in some way?"

This was all going wrong. Athena was speaking to her like a distant acquaintance and not as she should. Ruby cast about for something to say, anything. "No. No. Tomorrow I am to begin my instruction in chemystry. I would be grateful for any advice. Will you be breaking your fast?"

"Alas, apprentices are not permitted to pass time socially with journeymen." The gray eyes were clear. Empty nothing stared out from behind them.

"I—I see."

"But I am certain we will see each other from time to

time. I will await word from London as to where they wish me to proceed next." The words were faint, drowned out by the thunder in Ruby's ears. Athena was leaving. She was leaving Ruby here. Now that she had delivered the baggage, the ruse was revealed. It was all one big sharp: the bravery, the respect, the protection. The crew.

"Of course." She drew herself up as tall as she could. "Mr. Pate, I am sleepy." The man nodded and led her out. Athena did not call after her. Ruby would not turn around.

They came to a featureless door with a brass handle in the shape of an outthrust hand, atop an old-fashioned keyhole. Pate opened it with one of many keys he wore on a chain around his waist and then held it open for her, offering her a smart bow.

"My cell?" Ruby asked.

He smiled and shook his head. "Young ladies' chambers," he said. His voice was very deep.

"Oh," Ruby said. That was perhaps worse than a cell, but still she stepped forward. Soft rugs covered the cold earth floor, and the light was a bit brighter. Pate did not follow her in but stood in the doorway. It was warm and cozy and smelled of hyacinth.

"The door at the end is locked and not to be opened," he whispered. "Young gentlemen's chambers. Yours is the third room on the right." And he closed the door, and a lock clicked from the other side. The hallway was empty.

It was the first moment she had been alone since breaking into Fen's place.

She leaned her shoulder and face into the cool, smooth wall, because she could not stand upright anymore.

She would not cry. She would not scream.

There were things that she must do.

She slipped off her boots and dug her toes into the wonderful thick weave of the rug. The tinker's lamps had been turned down for the evening, but she could still read scripted nameplates hanging next to each of the doors. Apparently the secrecy was for people who came and went, not for the students who lived there.

Pettifell. Wainwright. The door was closed most of the way, but she could hear snoring through it.

Baker. Cooper. The top had green painted vines

tracing the letters, and the bottom had an inscrutable notation scratched into the wood below the name.

Van Huffridge. And then: Teach. The paint was still wet.

Greta Van Huffridge was seated on a high stool in a spoiled pea green nightdress, picking her teeth and reading from another massive tome. Next to her was a mountain of fluffy pillows that might have contained a bed. On the other side of the room sat a plain desk and a serviceable bed, with woolen blankets and two feather pillows. There was also a wardrobe and a nightstand.

To Ruby's surprise, the tiny girl hopped off the stool and presented her a curtsy with a grim smile. "I am afraid we have gotten off on the wrong foot, Miss Teach. May I call you Ruby?"

"What?" Ruby asked. "Oh, yes." She cleared her throat. If she were to do this, then she would do it right. "Miss Van Huffridge," she added.

"Greta, please." She popped back up onto the stool and stared down at Ruby. Her back was very straight. "If we are to live together, we must put aside formalities. I apologize for my rudeness earlier, but I did not know that you had achieved merit in the order. I would never had behaved that way if I had known that you had standing."

"Thank you. Um, apology accepted." It was news to her that she had standing, whatever that was. But she would not let Greta Van Huffridge know otherwise. Another high stool sat next to her desk, which was stocked with an inkwell, paper, a letter opener, and even a simple mechanical pen. She did not know if she was to sit at it or stand at attention or curtsy over and over while making flowery girl conversation. She sat on the bed instead. That was probably safe.

They stared at each other. Greta was a fine-boned sparrow, with a narrow chin and a keen eye. Ruby supposed she might be fetching. She wondered what her new roommate was discovering on her part. Slouchy. Unkempt. Scarred. The cut under her eye was burning.

"I am happy to have another girl here. The other four are slow. They think only of gossip and boys. I hope you can keep up."

"I shall do my best," Ruby responded.

"And I hope your best will be sufficient," Greta enunciated. She continued her scrutinization.

"Do the Bluestockings normally just take people in like this?"

"No." The examination moved away from her face down her arms and legs.

"Why not?"

"It is a forbidden thing, against English law to teach chemystry to women, the landless and other peoples. Even in Philadelphi, one cannot do such things and avoid punishment. My father is a man of no small means, and even he could not have me taught publicly. He spent two years searching for the order before one of his men found this place." She turned a page in her book. "They are cautious, here, and positioned against both England and the Tinkers of Pennswood Colony."

Ruby couldn't sit on the bed anymore, so she stood. "You know Lord Athen Boyle."

"He and his serving man will have gone to bed with the rest of the residents. Madame Hearth keeps a tight curfew and early-morning hours. We will wake at the stroke of six." She pointed to a clock on the shelf. An angel's sword pointed to one o'clock. "Only five hours from now." She marked the book and closed it, then placed herself in bed. "We will then break our fasts in the dining hall with the boys, and after, I shall introduce you to your instructors. I am to be your guide in the process. I am the most advanced student here, so it is naturally my place."

"Thank you," Ruby said. "Will Lord Athen be about?" She tried to sound casual.

"Lord Athen Boyle is a journeyman sentinel of the order and most likely will be on his way on another mission soon enough. Sentinels rarely stay in-house for very long, and I suspect he misses his sword and wishes to reclaim it. That one will be on his way sooner rather than later, I wager."

"You still retain your opinion of him?"

"Oh, indeed." She yawned.

"And why is that?"

She huffed. "I thought we had an understanding of sorts. He did not. Let us leave it at that. He is a cad of the first order. He does no honor to his rather illustrious name, I am not afraid to tell you."

"I see." Ruby opened the wardrobe. "What are these?" She was quite speechless.

"Proper garments, I expect. I have not snooped. I am no busybody. I gather Pate can find somewhere to dispose of your rags." It was indeed a set of clothing for her: three very nice dresses and a nightdress, like those a young lady would wear. An actual young lady. They had provided everything that might help a young girl feel at home. There was even a small stuffed pony on the pillow.

She curled up in the wool blankets of her bed and listened to the sounds of Greta falling asleep. It was so quiet. She pulled the blanket over her head. She was hidden, cradled in the earth. She was safe, if just for a little while, from the dangerous people who were stalking her, and from those who pretended to be other than they were. This could be a place to heal, to grow strong, to start up right again, to learn the chemystral arts and become a master of alchemy. It was deeply comforting.

But it was not for her.

She counted to two hundred and then slipped out of bed. After she had eased her Robby clothes back on, it was a tricky thing to use the sheets to tie Greta down to her bed without waking her. Near the end she did wake up and almost cried out. Luckily Ruby had kept the pony ready to pop in her mouth.

CHAPTER 28

A pistol of Clocklock Artfulness (fig. 2). This requires your Cooperation of imprimis, a talented smith, and secundus, an artificer (Tinker) of no mean skill. The resulting weapon will fire three balls within the Count of Four, and is Exceeding Deadly. When these factors are considered, the high price of such a Piece will not seem Extravagant.
— Catalog, Ruben's Fine Arms and Armaments, UpTown

Gwath Maxim Number Nineteen: "Underestimate Them, and You Overestimate Yourself." She could hear him in her head as if he were next to her as she stared at the door out of the girls' dormitory. The handle was the same outstretched hand, but there was no keyhole on this side. She could pick a lock of hair if she had to, but no keyhole meant no picking, and no picking meant explaining to Greta Van Huffridge that tying her down to her bed and gagging her was simply a little-known gesture of sailor's friendship.

The door to the boys' dormitory did have a keyhole.

She slipped the lock and eased the door open into another half-lit hallway, this time of polished wood. After inching the door closed behind her, she reset the lock. She wanted no trail markers behind her. She doubted Hearth would show any lenience if she caught her attempting to escape. If Ax and Flame found her, it would be worse.

It was a longer hallway than the girls', and a door loomed at the end. There were nameplates here, too, but she ignored them as she passed. The smooth grain under her feet felt familiar. For a moment she was back in her father's cabin, buffing the finish until she could see the shadow of her face in it. But these people did not care about her, not a one of them. Madame Hearth had said as much. Even Athena had shown her true colors. Ruby was only a stupid piece in some kind of stupid game, and they had no hesitation about sacrificing her father now that they had her.

A shape materialized out of the dark in front of the

last door on the right. She stopped short.

It was an animal of some sort, curled up asleep, perhaps guarding its master's door. It moaned and whined in its slumber. It didn't have the terrifying metallic whine of the gearbeasts, but still, if it woke up and started yowling or barking, she was done and dusted!

She wished that they had left her a late supper; the beast might have taken a gift of food and let her pass. She readied her shoes in one hand and a sharp metal lockpick in the other. Providence, it was *big*. It had to weigh a hundred pounds at least. The pick seemed tiny in her hand, a sad replacement for her knives. She clung to the far wall as she moved past. The thing stirred in its sleep. She froze. It yawned, blinked its eyes, and muttered, "Mam?"

She should have known.

Cram rubbed the sleep from his eyes, which went wide in the dim light of the corridor.

Ruby put her finger to her lips to ask him, *Please, keep quiet.*

She feared it was too late, that he'd call the alarm and

wake Athena, and they would give her a cell instead of a bedroom.

Cram did not call the alarm. Instead, he waved his hand theatrically around him, up and down the hall and pointed at her: *Why are you in the boys' hallway?*

She pointed past him at the door he was guarding, which could only be Athena's: *Why is she here?*

That caught Cram by surprise, and he turned his head, looking back at the door. He turned back and shrugged: *Doesn't matter.* He repeated: *What are you doing here?*

Ruby mulled trying to lie to Cram in the middle of a hall full of potentially hostile student chemysts. So she told the truth. She pointed to herself and then made the two-fingers running sign down the hall and out: *I'm escaping.*

This set Cram off. He launched into a jerky dance of silent, energetic gesture. Ruby thought she might have caught a few bits of it. Hugging for "safe." Holding his palm to the door and himself and out to her, maybe "together" or "crew." Then he mimed kicking something, perhaps a door? And swimming. And then a long series that might have had something to do with his mother or a donkey. The overall feeling was: *Don't.*

She shrugged: *I must.*

He went still. Ruby cursed inside. He was going to sound the alarm. She couldn't blame him. He was Athena's man through and through. She caught herself thinking: If he opens his mouth, I may have to stick this pick in his throat. Can I do that? To Cram? But he did not yell, or bang on the door, or run down the hallway drumming on his butter churn. Instead, he motioned her to come closer. Something in the bend of his hand made her trust him. She moved forward, and he whispered into her ear, "The Friendly Dollop."

She put her mouth to his ear and whispered back, "What?"

"It be a spice shop in UpTown. Henry Collins tasked me to give you the name, before he, um, left us."

Time was burning.

She made to stand. He stood with her. "Ferret."

"I have to go," she said.

"A word or a note to Lady Boyle?"

Ruby shook her head. "She closed that door."

"No, I can open it just fine. See here."

"Cram, don't touch that. That's not—"

"Ah, I see what you meant there."

The big door at the end of the hall was right next to Athena's. It was not even locked. Apparently the boys were more trusted than the girls.

Ruby looked over her shoulder, and Cram was standing there, watching her, his hand on his butter churn like some kind of guard in a castle somewhere. He waved.

She returned the wave, opened the door, and stepped through it.

The hallways were shadowed and empty, half lit by a fortune of mismatched tinker's lamps set in sconces on the wall. No one was about. The peace of the place was startling. It reminded her of her hidey-hole back on the *Thrift*. She stood still for a moment and listened to the nothing in the air around her. It felt clean and quiet and simple.

It was an easy matter to trace her footsteps through the empty hallway back to the little side passage outside Madame Hearth's office. The door at the end was closed. She tried the doorknob, but it was locked. No matter. The keyhole was the mouth of a cleverly carved imp's face, and it looked simple.

As soon as her pick entered the hole, she knew she was in trouble. The innards were sluggish. It reminded her of the glue of a chemystral lock, but it was more sticky. *Never pick a chemystral lock.* She tried to pull the pick from the hole, but it was stuck fast. She pulled harder. Suddenly the imp's arms lashed forward, and its hands clamped down over her wrist. The wrought-iron fingers dug into the splint and sent bolts of pain up her arm. She swallowed a yell, but that did not matter in the least. As soon as the imp had hold of her arm, it opened its mouth wide and a blast of sound came out of the keyhole mouth.

"THIEF! THIEF HERE! THIEF!" It sounded like a lion's roar in the close passageway. Ruby pulled harder at her wrist, and it moved just slightly inside the splint.

Sears of fire ripped about inside her arm.

"THIEF! THIEF HERE! THIEF!" Then the imp began to weep. Red tears welled up in its eyes, trickling down its arms. Ruby grabbed her elbow with her other hand and pulled harder. The tears flowed from the imp's claws onto her shirt and burned a hole through it. She had no idea what the substance was, but she was certain she could not let it touch her skin.

"THIEF! THIEF HERE! THIEF!" She put one foot on the door and then lifted up her other to plant it on the other side. The red stuff was eating through the wood of the splint now. She pulled with all her might, and her arm slipped through at the last moment. She fell to the ground hard. Her shirt was shredded, and the splint was a mess, but thankfully her skin looked intact. The remains of her pick had liquefied, and the rest of the ring clattered to the floor. Cries echoed down one of the hallways. They would be on her in seconds.

The little imp's arms were still clutching at her. She grabbed her thickest iron tension wrench, and her wrist twanged with pain. She jammed the wrench into the arms and the neck of the little artifice, pinning them against the door. The thing squeaked in surprise, the tears from its eyes running backward down the door. A drop of acid landed on the joint of her thumb and burned a hole down into it. She stifled a yell. One handed, she stuck her alloyed glass pick back in the keyhole. The tumblers started to move, but then the pick inched forward. It was melting. Fifteen seconds later her finest pick was a stub, but she was through.

The room was cozy as when Ruby had left it, and quiet. The weathered journal still lay on the table next to Madame Hearth's chair. The clasp with its circular eye stared at her. She took it without thinking. It belonged to her. She also swiped a fat little pocketbook lying on the mantel. If Hearth wanted her to have "low cunning," then she would have it.

The first time she had been in this room, five people had been here, some sort of council. When she had reentered, minutes later, only one was left. So where had they gone? She stood very still.

A breath of cool air touched her skin. It did not come

from the vent. It came from an armoire in the corner.

Could it be that easy?

The closet was made of rosewood and carved with scenes of family and home. She opened it. It was empty, and the draft was more pronounced. A more cautious or suspicious person might have put in a series of false shelves or backs or even simply hung some stupid dresses, but there was no reason to hide the door from this side. There was a small handle on the back wall, and it opened easily. A chill breeze hit Ruby in the face, and a steep tunnel rose up away into the dark.

She stepped through the door and closed it. On the tunnel side it was covered with stone, and it closed with a click, presenting a seamless rock face. The air smelled crisp and clean, and Ruby ran up the slope of the tunnel toward freedom.

CHAPTER 29

Providence gives, the where we start.
Science asks and shines a light.
Fortune shocks, an unseen road.
Spirit fires and burns life bright.

—Children's rhyme, Conrado Flacian,
Pilars Cuatro, 1688

The thought of Bluestockings behind in the distant dark spurred her on, through the steep tunnel to a square room at the bottom of a flight of stairs. She had taken the Bluestockings for a strange band of hayseeds on the edge of the city, but if they had access to something like this, their influence might be wider than she imagined. She had dropped a line in the water, and she had hooked a whale. Well, Madame Hearth and her bookworms could get in line. The Reeve, the Royal Navy, the Tinkers, Grundwidge Fen, and who knew who else was already hunting her. The endless stairway finally ended at another hidden door.

The door led into a tiny courtyard with odd walls, one of those unused orphaned spaces that no one knew what to do with. A cloudy winter sky hung above, and fresh snow dusted the alley beyond. She had climbed all the way through the Lid into UpTown.

She headed down the alley, and it opened onto the posh cobbles of Bluestone Square, where the rich and powerful lived their lives and kept their pets. People who lived in the square were still abed, waiting for their servants to awaken them gently with fresh chocolate and savories. The hawkers were already out in the bright early-morning flurries. The smell of roasting pine nuts lured Ruby and her tight stomach toward a chemystral meat cart, and there they were, two redcoats breaking their fast on sizzling raccoon shanks. She could not turn her face away in time. One of the uniformed men looked from her, down at a piece of paper, and back at her. The other was nodding and already jogging toward her.

Ruby ran.

The crown had not stopped looking for her.

She finally lost the first two redcoats by wiggling through a gap in two row houses that was too narrow for them to follow. But by then the alarm had been raised, and in this neighborhood she stuck out like a wasp in a jar of butterflies.

Every time she evaded some, more popped up around the next corner.

She cut through a market tent full of sunflowers and wriggled under its back. She lost three more by squeezing past two close-set buildings. On the other side of the alley, the close walks echoed with the metallic snuffling of gearbeasts and the sharp cries of their handlers. She kept them out of sight, but they gained on her turn after turn after turn after turn.

Her legs were stone and her chest was fire as she rounded a corner into a narrow lane. It was strangely quiet, that odd slice of peace that you could happen upon sometimes in this city. Well-scrubbed cobblestones. On one side was a tidy set of brick row houses screened shyly behind bare maple trees in tiny stone courts. On the other was a tall, dark iron fence, the spikes so closely set together that they would be impossible to slip through, interrupted by a stout gate halfway to the corner. At the end of the lane lay another market square, where she could escape from the gearbeasts in the sheer press of the crowd. But at the entrance to the square, a familiar hulking shape sat on the corner of a low stone fence, eating an apple as if he had been waiting there for her for a good, long time.

Wisdom Rool bit into the apple. The rope scars even traveled across his clean-shaven mouth.

"Ruby Teach, you have led us a merry chase."

Behind her a man and a woman, clad in black like Rool, pulled up, breathing steadily, cutting off her escape. There was a gearbeast with them. Though their howls had haunted her sleep since the *Thrift*, Ruby had never seen one up close. It was built like a hunting hound, lean and agile, but without skin. You could see down to its metal bones and hinges, all a deep dark blue. Spinning wheels and pumping pistons wrestled in its wide chest, and the *tocktocktocktocktock* Ruby had heard in the ship's hold cut through the cold morning air. Its three-inch claws raked at the street, opening little furrows in the cobbles. The whole thing was metal, except for the sockets, which held the wild, staring, mad eyes of a once-living dog.

She could not help backing away and pulling at the door set into the iron fence. It did not budge. Its lock was black, sturdy, and well made.

"Locked, is it?" Rool was still sitting on the little stone wall, and he motioned her pursuers to stay where they were. His eyebrows arched. "Can you pick a lock before we can get to you? My wager is no. Not that one at least. And do not waste your breath calling for help. This is a street of law-abiding folk who have no quarrel with officers of the crown plucking up some young roustabout."

They remained like that, unmoving, until he finished

the fruit, core and all. She tried to control her ragged breath and cast about for an exit that was not there.

Rool wiped his hands on a handkerchief, which he tucked back into the pocket of his plain black vest. "Quite a pickle, don't you think?"

Ruby did not answer.

"Beasts behind you, Wisdom before you. Which will you choose?" He stood, and his voice was gravel. "I can take you to your father, you know. We are less than a quarter mile from the Benzene Wharf."

"Is he all right?"

He nodded. "Wayland Teach is safe."

"Why did you take him?"

Rool shrugged. "We were searching for you. The *Thrift* was merely the place where you happened to be."

"Why me? What am I to you?"

He chuckled. "You are *of use* to me, Ruby Teach. But there are better places for this conversation, perhaps with some food and drink in you. You look terrible, you know." He wrinkled his nose. "And the smell! Where have you been hiding?" How could he smell her? He was a good forty paces away. Before she could answer, he raised his hand. "That was impolite of me. A girl must have her secrets, and I shall not pry."

"Where is Gwath?"

His lips turned up slightly. "A man must have his secrets as well. If you come along, I am full willing to trade."

Ruby leaned into the handle of the gate to hold herself up. Was he alive after all? Did they have him in a cage somewhere? Or was he at the bottom of the Delaware River?

"Come with me, and all will be revealed. You have many questions, do you not?"

She was so tired. She thought of her hidey-hole in the hold of the *Thrift* and the safety there. All she wanted was to curl up in the corner against the dark wood, losing herself in the quiet, harmless sounds of a calm day on the water.

Rool was planted on the cobbles: a statue of a fierce general from a forgotten war. "Why not just give in?"

It may have been the way he said it. Or perhaps it

was the faintest whiff of triumph lurking behind the question. Whatever it was, it irked her. And that was enough to help her say what she needed to say.

She pulled her shoulder blades down her back and found her balance, standing straight as the wall of iron spikes behind her. "You may have me trapped, sir. With your men and your walls and your iron dogs. And you may take me, as you say. But I will not go willingly. I will not give in."

Something flared in Wisdom Rool's eyes just then—respect?—but she was distracted by an unexpected, wonderful, and faint-as-a-feather click. The latch of the gate had just, inexplicably, unlocked.

Wisdom Rool said, "So be it," and took a step forward.

Ruby did not waste her breath on prayers or curses. She hauled on the door. The heavy thing pulled open, and she dashed into an orderly garden and jerked the door closed behind her. A man stood in the doorway across the garden, and she sprinted toward him. Outside the fence the other reeves were yelling and the gearbeast was yowling with strange rage.

The man in front of her was tall with long white hair, dressed in plain dark wool. He motioned her inside, saying, "We grant thee refuge, but I fear what may happen if thou stay. Keep moving. Down the hall, straight as an arrow, through the big room, up the stairs to the round window, and then onto the rooftops. Safe passage to thee."

She hesitated. Behind him, through the narrow gaps in the iron fence, tall as trees, she saw Wisdom Rool *leap* to the top, grabbing the sharpened spikes. He held himself there, peering over into the court, blood from his hands painting the dark iron of the spikes. He was breathing heavily. "You gravely mistake, Elder," he said to the man. "That girl is mine, and you risk much by sheltering her."

"She is not willing, Reeve." The man remained still. "And we offer shelter to ones who would not be taken." He turned to her. "Go, girl. We can hold him for a time." Rool vaulted over the fence into the air, and Ruby ran like her feet were on fire.

The hallway was straight and walled with plain blond wood, and it opened into a much larger room, like a feasting hall, completely empty save a circle of chairs in its center. People sat in many of them. The same dark, simple clothing, most sitting motionless, though she paid them little mind. Her whole self was consumed with getting to the archway at the other end and the stairs beyond. She cut an arc around the circle, and halfway across Ruby realized she could not hear her footsteps. She heard no sound whatsoever. Not even the din of her tearing each breath from the air. And the men and women in the circle did not move, even to look her way.

So she ran through silence across the hall certain that Rool would catch her. She crossed the archway back into a world where footsteps and lungs were loud, and at the base of the stairs she risked a glance over her shoulder.

The men and women in the circle had not moved, but halfway across the room Wisdom Rool was frozen in midair, mid stride, captured in quiet. A drop of blood from his hand sat in the air halfway to the floor, like a fly in amber. His eyes were alive on her, and rage lit them.

Ruby bowed to him and then to the room. Then she took the stairs two at a time, three floors up to a pretty round window that opened onto the roof. She skittered away across the rooftops, high above the hunters and gearbeasts scouring the streets below.

CHAPTER 30

Aubrey Smallows
Journeyman Candidate
Boston Chapter

Dear Mr. Smallows:

After extensive consideration, the Board of Inquiry has found that you have engaged in gravimetric and calescent "experimentation" that is Unseemly and Reflects Poorly on yourself and this institution. You have endangered the reputation and lives of your fellow students and the faculty. You are hereby summarily expelled and must vacate the premises forthwith.

All journals, logbooks, and experimental apparatus must be surrendered to the bearer of this letter, the Master-at-Arms.

So ordered, this 16th day of November, 1718
Foreman Ambrosius Jecked, MCS, GmSS

The scullery maid's frock was loose around her hips. But a nice warm wrap and a bonnet to boot were also hanging there on the line, courtesy of Providence. After

Ruby slid into the servants' quarters through the attic, it was a simple thing to pop into a pantry for a quick change and a cloth bag for her things. She left a few pence on the pantry shelf because someone was getting in trouble for this. A wicker basket found its way into her hands on the way out the back door, and the butler even gave her a "hello, new girl" nod as she passed. Gwath Maxim Seventeen: "The Help Is Invisible to Everyone but the Help."

She had traveled the rooftops to the other side of the city until she thought she could risk the streets again. In Crucible Square, the market heart of UpTown, it took her a scant five minutes before a beefy chemcandle dealer looked up from his bubbling pots to give her directions to the Friendly Dollop.

The one-story shop crouched at the end of an alley, nestled between two huge bakeries. The smoke in the air tasted like bread. The whole building was hardly wider than the subtly carved door, covered with scales holding heaping mounds of spices. She had to push hard on the heavy door to get inside. The smells hit her. Sage and thyme, parsley and marjoram fought for pride of place, but they were quickly swept away by scents more foreign: cinnamon and clove and other wonderful odors that she could not even put names to. It smelled like the galley in the *Thrift,* except without the sweat or the pitch.

A grin crept onto her face, and she could not banish it.

"First time?" An old, weathered albatross of a woman perched on a stool behind the counter. "We most likely have what you desire." She waved cheerily at the surrounding walls, which were completely covered by tiny drawers, most not more than the width of Ruby's palm. The drawers crept up into the shadows, all the way to the ceiling twenty feet above. Ladders attached to tracks were scattered around the room. Each one had a little pail for carrying spice hanging from its side. It was a jewel box of a room. Spices, especially from far-off places, could be incredibly expensive, or so Gwath was always telling her. No wonder the heavy door and the locks on the inside. This was an exquisitely crafted vault.

"This is your first time," the woman repeated, and

she crinkled her eyes at Ruby. She was not big, not small, but whip thin. She rolled, barefoot and poised, out from behind the counter like she knew her business. This was someone who could do a lot more with her body than just climb up and down ladders.

Her smooth head made her eyes look bigger. "Might you close the door, please, miss?" She wiggled her toes. "My poor dogs cannot bark at the world as they used to do. They need a nice, cozy house." It *was* warm in there. There were no windows save the little one in the door, but the air was surprisingly fresh. Ruby grinned again despite herself as she put her hand between two of three stout locks and closed the door, trapping the glorious smells in with them. When she turned back around, the old woman was holding out a wooden scoop, which held a pinch of deep red powder. "That is for you," she said. Her eyes were lit and inviting. "I am never wrong."

"For me?" Ruby asked. "I could not. I am certain that everything in this store is far beyond my means." She curtsied. "My thanks, though."

The woman chuckled again. "Your means? Girl, I am

not selling. I am giving. Would you refuse a gift freely given?"

"I would not, but my mistress—"

"Hospitality is very important." She waggled the scoop, but nothing spilled. "If you partake of a woman's board, then you are safe, sworn to guest right. If you do not eat—" She shrugged eloquently. The hand holding the scoop was calloused and ancient, but those patches were in the same places that Ruby had earned hers, and not by sorting sage.

This was a test.

Ruby held out her hand, and the woman poured the little touch of spice into it as if it were gold dust. Ruby licked it. It rolled dark fire across her tongue. The flavor was hot and rich and danced from the front to the back of her mouth and back again. Her eyes watered, and she saw stars for a moment. She managed to gasp, "Thank you." A nod told her she had passed the test, whatever it was.

But there was no welcome, no change in mood. Ruby stalled. "What do you call that?"

The crow's-feet around the woman's eyes were deep. "It is powdered rocoto, a pepper from far to the south." The powder went back into its drawer, which sealed with a faint pop. She stepped back behind the counter. "Now then, how may we serve you today? Shopping for your mistress, you said?"

"Well, in a manner of speaking," Ruby said. This was the tender spot. "She wishes to have Cook make an extra special dish for my lord, and a dear friend recommended yours above all other shops."

"Our clientele are very loyal." She cleaned the scoop with a mixture from a small vial next to her. The whole feel of this was strange. The room felt *aware*, as if it were watching her. Something was going to happen. Ruby cleared her mind and paid attention. She caught the woman looking at her out of the corner of her eye, and the glance flayed her open. "Who is our champion then? Sending us new spice buyers when times are hard?"

"His name is Henry Collins." She almost missed it. The woman's hands on the brush tensed for just a moment. This was the proper place.

"Who?" the woman said.

"Henry Collins," Ruby repeated. "Tall? Almost weedy? He is a good friend to my lady's family and recommended she send someone here to sample the spices."

The woman's voice was neither warmer nor colder, merely curious, but waves of caution rolled from her. "And what is your name, miss?"

"Rebecca. Rebecca Tunstall." She improvised.

"Well, Rebecca"—she smiled—"I am sorry, but the name rings no bells. Oh, well. We are still delighted your employer is giving us her custom. What does she wish to purchase?"

"Saffron," Ruby said, to buy more time. There was no secret handshake, no checking at the door for listeners before settling down to secret business. What was she missing?

"I'm sorry, we are out. Fagle's Spices, perhaps? Three blocks over, not quite the selection." Her face was still friendly, but there was no inner warmth. Her eyes were flint.

"Could I leave a note?" She sounded stupid, but she did not know what else to say.

The old woman began cleaning up her counter with a significant look, arranging sealed bottles of beautiful smells. "We are closing now, and I must ask you to leave. Or should I summon a constable?"

That danced on her spine. "No. No, thank you." Waves were crashing in her ears as she made toward the door and the street. Through the little window in the door she saw it was snowing again. There was a click and a creak, and the floor disappeared under her feet. And then the snowing and the door and all the little drawers were moving upward very quickly, and she fell through into darkness below.

CHAPTER 31

November 3, 1705
   *All Reports of the Events occurring on or around the Island
H., including any references to Marise Fermat or the man now
called 'Wayland Teach,' or their offspring, are to be excised from
the Society's records. So ordered.*
                                    —Invisible College Exec. Order 502
                                    Signatory: Godfrey Boyle, MCS, GmLS

Ruby held her hand in front of her face again. She still
could not see it. She tried to keep calm and remember
Gwath Maxim Number Twenty-three, which reminded
you that "Sight Is for the Lazy."

She had put that maxim to use while she waited for
whoever owned the cage to introduce themselves. The
bars were not bars, but a small crosswork of metal.
Sharp metal; she sucked the blood from her index finger.

The pen was square, as wide as twice her outstretched arms on all sides. No keyholes. She wasn't even sure there was a door. The floor of the cage was bouncy, like a sail packed tight with cotton, but it had resisted all her attempts to cut it or puncture it. The air was cool. It smelled like stone, so she was in a basement, most likely carved out of the Lid itself.

The cage was unfurnished, except for a small built-in seat in the corner. When she raised the top of the seat and the smell came out, she realized what the seat was for. It was foul, but she was struck by a more important thought: If inmates were using a privy, chances are they spent more than a few minutes in this cage. Ruby didn't like that one bit.

In fact, she liked absolutely nothing about her present predicament, and she was beginning to wonder if there was anything left in the world that she did like. Certainly not kidnappers, trapdoors, secret societies, or gearbeasts. Or people who betrayed you. The box inside her, where she put all those distracting thoughts and feelings, down at the bottom of her belly, began to quiver. She had always thought of it as an iron-banded, triple-locked strongbox, sturdy and reliable. But all manner of terrible things were seeping through the hinges: fear, doubt, loneliness. She clamped her arms around her waist, clenched shut her eyes, and willed them back into the box. After a few minutes she stopped breathing heavily, and she didn't want to scream anymore. The box was still there, though, wriggling, just on the other side of her belly button.

The room was deeply quiet, and the air was still. She had called out a few times, and her voice had not come back to her. Whatever was beyond did not reflect sound.

So she counted seconds, as you were supposed to do. A cell this dark and this quiet was meant to disorient and weaken, and one of the few weapons at her disposal was to keep a hard leash on time. Gwath had always insisted on this point and would make her start all over again if while walking a wall or copying a letter, she could not accurately report how long she had been at it. He had scoffed at watches and chronoms. Timepieces were for the weak.

The only true measure of time, he said, was the beating of your heart. There was never a maxim for that, though.

At 572 heartbeats, a slot in the darkness outside the cage opened, and light tore in. She held her hand up to her eyes. The cage was an island in the center of a completely empty round room. There was not a stick of furniture to be found save a tall cabinet in the corner. Bare stone walls reached up into the dark. The voice did not come from the slot. It came from everywhere. It was old, male, and spoke with a French accent.

"Who are you?" It was a deep voice and crept into her bones from above, below, and all sides.

"My name is Rebecca Tunstall. Why are you doing this to me?" She allowed a hint of panic to creep in, and a trace of tears. Under the circumstances, it would have been harder to keep the panic out.

"Why do you think?"

"I don't know! Did I do something wrong? If I did, I'm very sorry!" The important thing was to stay with your first mask. Don't let it drop. If she changed to another character, then there would be no reason to believe that she was not lying again. "I didn't mean it. Please don't be angry with me."

"Why did you lie?"

That put things in a whole new light. What did the voice mean? Lying about who she was? About Henry Collins? "I am not certain I understand. I spoke no lie. Can you tell me what you mean?"

Silence. The slot slammed shut. She heard faint voices on the other side of that wall. One might have been the woman from the shop. They were arguing. That was something at least.

Seven hundred thirty.

Four thousand forty-one.

She used the privy. The faint breeze and deep silence emerging from it told her that it was probably a long drop from here, maybe down through one of the support pillars of the Lid. The thing was built out of stone, anyway, and so narrow that even she could not fit herself into it. No escape there.

Was her father in a place like this?

Was Gwath on the bottom of the sea?

≈≈≈

Nine thousand four hundred eight.

"Hello?" She wanted to stay silent, to show her strength, but doubt kept at her. Would Rebecca Tunstall have been so staunch? Should she have been weeping and wailing since falling into this accursed pit?

"Hello? Out there?"

There was no answer.

"Please! I'm very thirsty!" She was. She was bone dry, and her tongue was chalk. More than that, though, she was late. She had wasted far too much time with Athena and the Bluestockings, and the only cake she had for her trouble was the full knowledge that they were all laggards and shirkers. They cared not a whit for her father or the crew, only for what they could craft her into. She dug her fingernails into her hand. This was supposed to have been the place where she finally got help! She had no time for sitting around in odd little corners of UpTown. Her father was in danger, and somehow this, this *shopkeeper* had smelled her out the way a first mate weeds out a soft-footed sailor.

The slot opened again.

"Who are you?"

Ruby cleared her throat. "May I have some water?"

There was no answer. To hell with it.

"My name is Aruba Teach."

After a moment the voice replied, "The Royal Navy is looking for someone named Aruba Teach. There are handbills and such about."

"That is me. And yes, the navy is looking for me, and the Reeve, and toss in every bravo, princock, and bracket face from here to Chester for good measure. You've won the prize. You have me. I cannot wait around in this cage for the rest of my life."

"Why not?"

"I have things to do."

The voice did not sound amused. "What brought you to this place, Aruba Teach? Why would a fugitive from justice seek refuge in *une épicerie*, a spice shop, of all places?"

She saw no reason to lie. If the truth was what this old voice wanted, she would give it to him. "A young man named Henry Collins helped me escape from capture. He was dressed as a midshipman but turned on his fellows when they were going to stuff me in a sack." It felt good to finally stop lying.

"Stuff you in a sack?"

"They didn't want me to run again, I suppose."

"Where is this famous savior now?"

"Henry?"

"As you say."

She chewed her lip. He was supposed to be here. He had asked her to come here.

"He is not here now?"

"I asked you where he was."

Stranger and stranger. Henry had sent her here. He had called it a refuge. If they did not know where he was, he might be in danger. A chill passed across her shoulders. What if these men were not Henry's friends? What if the Reeve had found out this hidey-hole and had put its own men in to catch stray flies like her?

"Where is this Henry Collins? I will not ask you again."

It was true. It was true. It all made sense now. She had fallen into a nest of reeves, and it would only be a matter of time before Wisdom Rool came and took her and locked her in some strange tower for all of her life. Well, she would not give up her friends. Henry *was* her friend, she realized. Perhaps her only friend, along with Cram. And Athena? Ruby should have said good-bye.

"You are Reeve, aren't you?"

"Very nice. Question the questioner. Someone has taught you well. Perhaps these reeves of which you speak. But I am not one easily distracted."

"Someone has taught you well, too. You did not answer my question." She was free. She could play this game, and play it to the hilt. It would all end up the same anyway.

"Miss Teach, or so you call yourself." What did *that* mean? "I am in a predicament. Your grit is evident. You sit in that cage as if it were a throne room. Most begin pouring out their secrets after only half an hour."

"This bouncy floor is quite comfortable. You should make it a harder place if you want people to talk."

"You see? This is *précisement* of which I am speaking. You have some sand, young woman. *Très, très féroce.*"

"You can't sweet-talk me into telling you what you want to know either."

"Oh, with this I am beginning to come to terms." From behind her, in the walls came the sound of ratchets and gears all at once. It was loud. "So, I must resort, as much as it pains me, to other means." Illuminated in the half-light of the slot, the massive ornate cabinet began to shudder. Heat hit her like a wave. Pipes ran into it from several places in the wall, and steam rose from its top. It reminded her, in an odd way, of Madame Hearth's samovar. It was much larger, though, and the door on its front was opening.

Inside was a man shape made of shining rods and tubes that flowed red and orange. With a deep, spinning sort of sound, and it stood. The copper liquid moved like water in a busy creek, and the mechanical flexed its metal hands. It turned toward her. Its face was a featureless smooth mask, cast from the same clear metal.

"His name is Agrippa. He is, alas, one of my failed experiments." The man-shaped thing stepped out of its cabinet, and the stone on the floor blackened and sizzled.

It smelled like burning hair. The voice tsked. "I do regret it, a miracle of liquefied copper and magnesium, pulsing to and from a synthetic braincase. He has a rudimentary awareness and will follow my commands. An example: Agrippa, move into the cage."

The metal man began walking forward toward the cage and toward Ruby. The heat was fierce, and she scrambled back, putting her shoulders against the wall. When Agrippa reached the latticework, it did not stop. The body cracked like ice or glass, and the tiny pieces crawled through the gaps in the cage, to come back together on the other side.

It stood before her. The orange and red streams of liquefied metal fused and separated in rhythm, like a pulse. At another time it might have been beautiful. Now it was simply terrifying.

"Astonishing, isn't he? I was very proud of him, but he has a difficult flaw. Though he will follow my commands, he has from birth displayed a pronounced dislike of humans. He takes joy in hurting them." The thing stared at her. She could feel it looking, even if it did not have any eyes. Menace rolled from it in waves.

The voice was iron as it continued. "I will ask you one more time. If you do not answer to my satisfaction, I will ask again, but this time Agrippa will help me. If you refuse then, I will close this slat, go have a cup of tea, and we will remove your ashes when he is done playing with you. Where is the one you call Henry Collins?"

"I tell you, I do not know."

The voice sighed. "Very well. Agrippa, please ask Miss Teach about Henry Collins."

Her eyes clouded as the thing moved forward, with steam or with tears she did not know. As it reached out its hand, flames ran across the fingers and palm.

She thought of her father. She thought of Gwath. She thought of Athena. She would miss them.

And then the world went dark.

CHAPTER 32

You gravely mistake our nature. We are neither witches nor warlocks. We are men and women of science who eat with you, study with you, pray with you. If the purges continue, however, then we are no longer your countrymen, and we will have no choice in our own defense but to seize our liberty. This country will suffer.
—Pierre de Fermat, testimony to
Académie de Philosophie, Paris, 1653

The faintest of sounds fluttered about the edges of her sleep. Scratching, a mouse or . . . no. Paper. Fingers moving across paper, then wrapping around the corner of a page, then turning it. Again and again.

Her body did not feel burned. She pressed her palm down with the lightest of force, and it pushed back against a cushioned floor. She was still in the cage.

She opened her eyes.

Tinker's light poured blue through the iron latticework, painting crosshatched shadows on her hand. In the space beyond, an ancient man in a ridiculous sleeping cap hunched in a great chair, long legs folded every which way and peeking out of a lush dressing gown. Her things were piled neatly next to the chair on a small table: the bag, her picks, the journal, the wallet. Her mother's button was still on its rawhide around her neck. He was paging through her copy of *Bastionado* in the light of the tall, thin lamp behind him.

"I have always felt the villain does not get a fair shake in this one." His was the voice from beyond the door, deep and French. "He was trying to do what he thought was right, you know."

"Kidnapping the hero's love to a prison tower on their wedding day?"

"According to the hero. The true Duc de Nantes always said that he and Mirabelle loved each other with secret fire."

Ruby snorted.

"So did Mirabelle."

She snorted again.

He glanced up from the book, and his gaze pinned her to the floor. His eyes were quicksilver spheres, without a hint of white. "She did not?"

"No," she said.

"How do you know?" he asked.

"How do *you* know? Are you a historian?"

"No." He smiled.

"How do you know then?"

"I have a special connection to that period."

"What special connection? Did you steal her diary like you stole my book?" She turned her head onto the other ear, and the automaton cabinet sat there unopened and quiet, just as before.

The old man continued. "You do not agree that the villain told the truth as he knew it or you do not agree that Mirabelle loved him?" He flipped through the book, troubled, as if he were searching for evidence.

Ruby levered herself upright with both hands. "That is my favorite book, and I believe you are wrong, but I will not argue with you because more important things are at hand. Sir," she added belatedly.

"Indeed, more important things!" He agreed. "For example, are you being followed by intrepid chemystral mice?"

"Mice? No." The man was mad. "Are you mad?"

He waved the question away. "I am Fermat." He stared at her with his silver eyes. Or he might have been looking out of the corner of them at the side wall, for all she knew.

"Why didn't you have that thing burn me?"

He smiled.

"I don't think it's funny," Ruby said. "It was here, in this cage with me. I blacked out. But there is not a mark on me. Was it all a bluff?"

He shook his head with care, as if it might topple from his gaunt neck.

"Then what?" Anger burned the cobwebs aside, and she was fully awake. "Do with me as you will, but stop playing with me! And stop looking through my things. They are mine." It was absurd to make demands from the inside of a birdcage, but the contents of that bag were all she had in the world of her former life.

He nodded and closed the book. "My apologies. It was certainly impolite, but I wanted to discover more about you, and you were inaccessible."

"I would not have passed out if you had not released a demon from the lower depths upon me."

"Agrippa is hardly a demon from the lower depths. Beware of hyperbole, *chérie*. Did I say 'passed out'?"

"What?"

"Did I say 'passed out'?"

"No, you did not. Why does it matter?" He was playing word games again, and she wanted to burst through the cage and shake him by his bony shoulders.

"It matters a great deal." He closed the book and placed it with care on the pile of her things. "You did not pass out, Ruby Teach, for I judge you may be Aruba Teach, indeed, though we thought you were lying, an agent of sorts. You did not pass out." He made a pulling motion with his hands, like kneading dough. "You *changed*."

"Changed."

"*Virez* à *barrique*, yes? Into a barrel."

"What?"

"A barrel. They are used for storing liquids, grains—"

"Well, yes," she said.

"Mostly cylindrical."

"I know what a barrel is!"

"Very well."

It was difficult to breathe. She had to hold herself up with both hands.

"You seem shocked, which one could understand. But you accept the news more readily than another might," he said.

Cram had said that Gwath had somehow been a barrel. She could not imagine this old man knew Cram or had heard from him. "How could that be?"

He leaned forward. "Directly to the question, I see. I approve. I see two possibilities. One, that you are some sort of barrel automaton engineered to look and act like a human girl. Is this the case?"

She did not know whether to laugh or cry. "I don't think so."

"Very well. I agree it is unlikely. The second possibility is that you are the direct descendant of a Changer."

Ruby felt the capital letter. "A Changer?"

"As the word, so the action. Changers alter their shapes, like molding clay or carving stone."

"Into barrels?"

"Not just, girl. The most skilled can craft themselves into replicas of objects like a door or an armoire."

"Or a barrel."

"Yes, or a barrel, though I suggest you avoid fixating there."

"It happens to be at the front of my mind, for reasons you might well understand."

"Touché. Shall I continue along this line then?" She nodded, pulling herself into sitting. "Master Changers also adopt the seeming of other people: blacker hair, lighter skin, sharper face. Some even can move about and take the shape of beasts."

Gwath. He was talking about Gwath. She flushed. But was he also talking about her? "How do they do it?"

The old man clacked his teeth in agreement. "Yes. To

capacity. The ability to change is a family affair. It passes from parent to child, though it also is finicky. It skips generations; perhaps a great-uncle may be one, and no one else in the family except a favorite niece."

Family. Was Gwath related to her somehow? Her father had never said anything about that. A secret brother to her mother? Or to her father? But this was missing the point.

"I did this?" He nodded. "I . . . *changed* . . . into a thing?"

She placed herself in the middle of the cage and flexed her hands. She turned back to Fermat. "How do I do it?"

He shrugged. "I do not know. It is amazing, yes? If we ever advance past our current state of relationship"—he waved his hand at the cage—"there are a few rare texts in particular to which I might point you."

She ignored him and centered her breath, as Gwath had taught her. The old man's voice receded into the distance. She focused on her heartbeat. Though she was not sure what she was looking for, deep in her spine she felt something move. A spot or a nubbin. A feeling more than anything else.

There were barrels all over the *Thrift*. Nail barrels and flour barrels and barrels of pickled fish. She summoned a clear picture into her head, threw all her focus onto that weird place in the small of her back, and, for lack of a better word for it, *nudged*.

She opened her eyes. The old man was staring at her. His whiteless eyes were wide. "Did it work?" he asked.

"Does it look like it did?"

"No, not really. I still see a young girl in a cage. Was that what you were trying for?"

"No!"

He shrugged. "Well, then. I do not know much about Changers, but I do know that their first shifting experiences can be in response to some imminent danger. Perhaps I should release Agrippa again?"

She shuddered. "No, thank you."

He tapped the arm of the chair with the tip of his finger. "Those other things we must discuss?"

"Like what?"

"How you came to be in my spice shop?"

She shook her head. The ground had shifted, and now she had something he wanted. She was willing to trade. "Where do Changers come from?"

"The west. The people there tell stories of them."

His answers made things more confusing, not less. "But what does that have to do with me?"

He clicked his teeth. "Perhaps you come from the west. Your parents?"

"Father from Bristol, mother from France, somewhere."

"She claimed to be from Le Mans, I believe." She gaped, and he waggled his eyebrows at her.

"You know my mother?"

"And Wayland Teach as well, little intruder."

Barnacled barnacles. Did everyone in the world know her parents? "Then why am I still in this cage?"

He shrugged. "Your parents and I did not part on the best of terms, I fear."

She found herself kneeling at the iron bars, staring through at Fermat. "If you knew my parents, why did you ask if they came from the west?"

He shrugged again, more quickly and more dismissively. "Marise was a private girl and an even more private woman. She clad herself in secrets. When I knew her, our whole life together was built on them. I would not presume that what she had told me was the fact of the matter."

He clacked his teeth and rose, taking care to keep his wobbly head on the top of his neck. The old man shuffled toward the door. "Our exchange of information does not appear to be equal at this moment. You need time to sit with all of this, I think. I will return."

Suddenly the rest of her world came rushing back: Wisdom Rool, Athena, her father still missing. She was in a cage, by damn. "Wait! There is no time!"

He fiddled with the iron door without turning. "I agree, but I cannot honor reckless decision making, and you are not being forthcoming with me. I will return anon, Mademoiselle Teach. Change is like a rich meal. It needs silence to digest fully."

What could she say to get him to stay? What could

she do? There was something here, some piece of the fabric of her life. She was holding it in her hand, but it was slipping through the fingers like so much cinnamon from one of the drawers upstairs.

"I never knew her." The words snuck out of her mouth, like a dirty fly. Fermat looked back at her, quicksilver eyes glittering. "She left when I was very young." And then she told him the other story, the one that started with that perfect morning in Boston and ended with her caged in a basement with an old man who asked no more questions and said nothing as she sobbed the long truth out to him.

CHAPTER 33

*. . . with regard to Rebellious Sentiment in our colony, I fear you
have only yourself to blame. The conditions in UnderTown are
savage, at best, and many who live here have not found the Fresh
Start that was promised them in your leaflets.*

*With regard to your suggestion, I shall not offer my resignation, and
if I am removed from my post, I wager Some Consequence may occur.*

I hope you will act in temperance.

—Letter from Robert McKinnon, governor, Pennswood Colony, to
Everett Baldwin, Master Tinker, Benzene Yards, November 4, 1718

At some point in her story, Fermat knocked twice on the
door, and the leathery old woman, the one from the spice
shop upstairs, brought a key into the room. She opened
the cage, wrapped Ruby in a warm blanket, and carried
her down a narrow stone staircase. Fermat followed,
and the woman—her name was Nasira—clucked and
hummed into her hair as you might to a madwoman
or a three-month-old puppy. The humming crept down

Ruby's spine and sparked a warm glow in her chest, and she felt safe. It was the most natural thing in the world. Was this what grandparents felt like?

They took her down one flight of stone stairs into a little bedroom, just a bit larger than the bed and a single chair. Fermat eased himself into the chair, and Nasira helped her up into the bed, clothes and all. She drew a wonderfully soft quilt up to her neck. It was embroidered with elk and swans.

Fermat stared at her for a long time. What had happened to make his eyes silver? "Rest now. We will speak when you wake."

And she did sleep. Even before Fermat reached the door.

When she awoke, it was wonderfully quiet. She lay there for a good while, and the only sounds were her breath and the faint rustle of her hair against the pillow when she moved her head. Her arm no longer hurt. The acid-eaten, filthy dressing had been changed, and her arm was wrapped tightly with white linen and smelled vaguely of garlic. It was sore, but she was thrilled she could move the fingers and flex the wrist.

Blackberry tea and mushroom soup, still hot, lay on the bedside table, and spiced nuts in a little wooden bowl carved with strange, beautiful numbers and symbols. She inhaled the lot.

In the corner there was a deep bronze tub, filled with steaming water, two fresh towels, and a bar of soap that looked like honeycomb and smelled like almonds. The water was just hot enough. It *stayed* warm, by means of some clever tinker's device. It was silver and slid along the rim of the tub. Each side was carved with a head: a woman with flames for hair and a man with ice in his beard. She scrubbed, splashed, and dunked herself within an inch of her life. If she did not need to save her father, it might be fine to stay there forever. By the time she finished, the water in the tub was deep gray and had a thick film on its top. It was like scrubbing off an old skin that she never wanted back again.

Two sets of clean clothing were set out on the chair: a smart checked frock and men's clothing as well—a white shirt and gray breeches, vest, and coat. The breeches fitted as well as or better than her stolen maid's dress, and Robby Thatch had never been so sharp. There were boots. A ribbon was laid out as well, and she used it to tie her hair into a tight queue. She sat on the edge of the bed for a few minutes, but no one arrived, so she moved through the door. She was on a small landing, and the narrow stair spiraled up and also down, out of sight. She went down.

The circular stairs were many, but the stairwell was well lighted with tinker's lamps built into clever little shelves, which illuminated the carving-covered walls. Whatever this place was, it was much more than a spice shop and ruffian trap. And she, who had spent time in Philadelphi on and off all her life, had never heard of it. Every inch of the seamless granite was covered with enigmatic, flowing inscriptions. They were numbers, and letters, and odd squiggles and lines. As she followed the steps, deep into the ground—perhaps even past the floor of UnderTown by now—Ruby could not help thinking that she was in some kind of wizard's tower, except in reverse. She passed two more landings, with a locked door on each of them. On the next landing an archway opened into a very tall library. It was a circle, much like the cage room, except this was filled all the way around with shelves of books and scrolls, creeping up into the darkness. She had never seen so many books. She had never known so many books existed.

Fermat craned over a long, scarred worktable in its center. It was a huge slab of raised black marble, far too large to have ever gotten through the door. He said, "Have a look at this," and waved her over without a glance away from the table. It was covered in strange instruments and all manner of powders and crystals, rocks and liquids, tiny tools and measuring cups.

Ruby said, "I wanted to thank you for the bed and for—"

"Yes yes yes." He raised the mast of his index finger. "You are welcome, and now we are friends that once were enemies. I will ask Nasira to make you more of her favorite tea and perhaps bring you another snuggly blanket later. But that is not why we are here, and as you have told me on several occasions, you have little time."

The thing he could not take his eyes off was her mother's journal. "The clasp is a sophisticated chemystral device. Pick the lock, and the journal will be destroyed. Fire, or acid, or some such. Very dramatic. Can you help me understand this?"

Ruby nodded. "I think I can." The ivory button around her neck fitted perfectly into the clasp, and it opened silently.

They stared at each other for a moment.

Fermat inclined his head to Ruby. "It is yours, of course."

She did not know what to expect, but it certainly was not page after page of tightly packed symbols and equations. "Do you know what these mean?" she asked.

"Gibberish," he said from over her shoulder. "These look like chemystral formulae, but they do not add up." He shook his head. "Marise was never a trusting sort."

"So, a cipher?" Ruby asked.

"Indeed, Ruby Teach, indeed."

"Do you have the key?"

He paged through the web of symbols. "No. No, I

do not. And if it is possible to decipher, I think it would take weeks, if not months. Your mother was . . . very clever." He ran his finger along the binding. "You know who might be helpful with this? My apprentice, Hermes. Ah, you know him as Henry Collins."

"Hermes?"

"Yes, Hermes Cestus. Henry Collins is a false name we dreamed up for him as part of his disguise. He has a gift for ciphers, and this sort of puzzle bores me to tears."

She stopped herself from wondering what his tears looked like. "Why a false name?"

"Oh, you know, infiltrating the Royal Navy, vengeance for a father terribly wronged, standard sort of thing."

"Vengeance? For what?" Ruby asked.

"That is not my secret to give. You'd have to ask him, I'm afraid. Very private boy. Quite serious, you know. Promising chemyst. It was he who discovered news of your father in a mousey automaton tossed in a rubbage bin outside the Benzene Yards."

Her pulse quickened. "My father? How is he?"

"Our last news is from a few days ago, but he was all

right, though somewhat the worse for wear."

"Can you help me rescue him?"

He frowned. "I cannot. I will try to help you understand your predicament, but I cannot leave this place, on pain of my life. And then I would be of very little help to you."

Ruby picked up a platinum stylus. "What about Nasira? Or Hermes? Has he returned?"

"Please be careful with that," Fermat said. "No, Nasira is as bound to this place as I am. And Hermes has not returned. I am worried for him."

She placed the tool down carefully, so as not to throw it.

And so there it was. The clothes were nice, and the bath was wonderful, and the food, and the comfort, but this was merely one more place where there was no help for her. "I see," Ruby said. "I must be on my way then." She picked up the journal and turned to go.

Fermat chuckled. Then he stopped chuckling. "*Attend*. Wait. You are truly leaving? So quickly? Where will you go?"

Ruby said over her shoulder, "I don't know. But I have to get him back."

"Very well," Fermat said with a sigh. "If you must. Please don't forget that gearbeasts bite and chemystry is very dangerous and reeves can do amazing things with their bodies—"

"I won't," Ruby said. "Farewell."

It was a dramatic exit.

Except the door wouldn't open.

It was no longer even a door. The handle was still there, but the seams around the stone door had melded seamlessly into the wall. Anger boiled up from her new boots. Fermat was leaning against a bookshelf, paging through a musty old book. "Open it," Ruby growled.

"Open what?"

"Open the door, you old coot!" Ruby yelled.

He fluffed up like a startled grouse. "But it is a wall," he said.

"Well, make it back into a door and let me go!"

"I will make it back into a door and let you go." Fermat said.

"Good."

"If you pass but one small test for me."

Ruby could not believe his gall. Her father was dying somewhere, and he wanted to *teach* her something. "Very well," she said. "Get on with it."

The old man clacked his teeth. "What do you see?" He pointed to one side of the worktable, to a padlock fully the size of Ruby's head. The shackle shone in the blue light of the tinker's lamps. Its loop was as thick as her wrist.

"What kind of mad, huge chest is this for?" she asked.

He rotated the tip of the finger until it pointed straight down at the lock. "What do you see?"

Ruby's fingers tingled, as they always had when Gwath started a lesson. Perhaps he was testing her reason. Perhaps he was testing her resolve. Whatever he was testing, he was absolutely as annoying as Gwath had ever been, and she felt something stir inside her that she had not felt in weeks: the fervent and absolute desire to wipe a smug smile from a mentor's face.

"It is apparently made from some sort of metal."

He nodded. "Why do you say 'apparently'?"

She rolled her eyes. "Because I have not tested it for metallic properties, and I will draw no premature conclusions."

His mouth made an O, which she took as permission to continue.

"May I touch it?" He nodded again. She passed her fingers over the dark, mottled surface. It felt sturdy. The scratches around the sizable keyhole indicated that it had endured numerous attempts at picking. The size of the mechanism meant it would be heavy on the inside as well, and her picks would have as much luck with this thing as a paring knife with a crocodile. The joins were very fine around where the loop of the shackle rejoined the body of the lock. Too fine, while the seam where the halves of the thing came together was far too rough for such otherwise fine worksmanship.

"It is not a lock," she said.

His eyebrows crept into his nightcap. "Why do you say that?"

"It is not a lock," she said, "because it is a chest."

And she pushed the block that held the keyhole. It moved smoothly, there was a click, and the too-rough seam opened up, revealing a velvet-lined interior. A sealed letter sat inside.

Fermat yawned.

"I bore you?" she said.

"I asked you what you saw. I did not ask you to open the box."

"Opening the box naturally follows from solving the puzzle, does it not?" This *was* some sort of test. She broke the seal on the letter and opened it. Two short sentences were written on the page, in a neat, cramped hand: "I am a serpent. And you are dead."

Blood rushed to her face.

"Of course it follows, *chérie*." Fermat chuckled. "The best bait for a quick mind is to present an obvious solution to a seemingly difficult problem."

"So I need to be more careful." She refolded the paper and put it back in the lock-chest. "Lesson learned, ready for another thank-you."

"No, girl," Fermat snapped. "The lesson is not 'Take

great care.' The lesson is 'Assume not that you understand the problem.'"

She bit her lip. "And this is supposed to apply to me?"

He matched her sarcasm with his own. "Perhaps. The subject for application is currently in doubt. Let us test the hypothesis, shall we? You are rushing off to solve your problem." He produced a slate from under a pile of tiny springs. "But what is your problem?" Every inch the attentive student, he poised a piece of chalk over the slate.

Ruby had had enough. "All right, all right! I did your fool test! Don't yammer at me like I am your four-year-old pupil."

"I am not instructing. By the way, you failed the first test, so I am generously giving you another. I have asked you a question, and by refusing to answer, you are being an impolite guest." He tapped the slate three times. "What is your problem?"

She could have bashed her head on the table. "Fine. My problem is that I am trapped inside the upside-down tower of a madman."

He chuckled. "Clever, but symptomatic. The madman's tower is only a stop along the way." He moved his head about on his impossibly long neck like a tulip in the breeze. "What is your problem?"

"I need to rescue my father."

"Good! Why?"

"What do you mean, 'Why?' He is my father!"

He nodded. "Yes, but why is he in danger in the first place?"

"Because Wisdom Rool was pursuing us."

"Why?"

"He says I have something he wants."

"Good, good." He chalked, ARUBA TEACH HAS _____. "What is it? I have seen the contents of your bag. They are not very impressive. Was he searching for your copy of *Bastionado*, do you think?"

"No."

"Perhaps that?" He pointed to Ruby's mother's journal.

She ran her finger along the binding. "But I did not have this on the *Thrift*."

"I see. Anything else?"

"No." This was frustrating.

"Well, then?" He pulled a set of red-tinged spectacles from the sleeve of his robe and stared at her for a good long while.

Ruby looked at the lock. But it was not a lock. It was something else. Ah. She reached out her hand to Fermat. "May I?"

He stared. "Please."

She took the chalk and used the rag next to the slate to erase the word "has." In its place she wrote: ARUBA TEACH IS _____.

She handed the chalk back, and he clacked his teeth. "Good. Now we begin."

CHAPTER 34

Dr. MAGRABO'S CARNIVAL OF WONDERS

*The Great Bavillia, she Communicates with
the Immortals of the Spheres!
Myrtle, an Artifice Sheep with powers of Speech and Arithmetic!
The Nameless Brothers, Bearers of Talents Both Strange and Terrible!*

*Samples of Dr. Magrabo's Elemental Elixir, FREE!
Spinner's Square, Shambles, Promptly at Dusk. 5p, young ones gratis.*
—Poster

It went against every feeling in her body, but Ruby agreed that she would wait.

Upon the conclusion that Aruba Teach did not carry but in fact *was* something valuable, Fermat had transformed into a gleeful young boy. He produced sheaves of papers, pens, inkpots, rulers, divining rods, and a chest's worth of simple and complex measuring apparatuses. Some were gooey, some made noises, a few looked never used, and many were so old that she feared they might fall apart at any moment. In the hours that followed, he used them all. What was worse, she could never just sit in a chair quietly. "Excitation of fluids" required that she stand on one leg, "conservation of energy" required that she curl up inside a series of smaller and smaller cabinets, and "isolation of humors" meant hanging upside down from the chandelier.

Early on, when he was dipping strips of linen in an iron jar full of yellow goo that smelled like a diseased cow and sparkled in the lamplight, she asked him again when she could leave. He spared her the briefest of glances from his quicksilver eyes and said, "You may not leave until we know what you are. You need power. And power will come from knowing what this secret is. And that knowing can only be discovered here."

The passing of each moment ate at Ruby as he picked, poked, and prodded. The aged wonder looked to have the endurance and maniacal focus of a puppy with a brand-new stick.

"Ow," she said when he tightened the clamps yet again.

"What is wrong?" he asked.

"They are too tight," she replied, reaching up to try to pull it from her head. He slapped her hand away.

"Too tight?" he asked. She tried to nod. "Are you certain?" he asked.

"Yes!" she cried. "Yes, yes, yes! This thing is too tight. Everything you have put on me smells of pig iron or dead fish, and this was not part of my plan."

"What plan?" he asked.

"To . . . rescue . . . my . . . father." She kicked at the chair with each word.

"That again? You would travel alone to the Benzene Yards, the great stronghold of Tinker strength, and onto the behemoth His Majesty's Ship *Grail*? Sashay past their automatons, their human guards, their gearbeasts, and a whole chestful of sensitive traps, devices, and anti-theft shearsaws?"

"Yes. Shearsaws?"

"Indeed. Alone?"

"Yes, if you will not go with me. Or Nasira."

"I have told you, I cannot go with you, and I am sure you have never even seen the devastating effects of a shearsaw. Nasira cannot leave. She has sworn a holy oath to protect me. And Hermes"—worry crossed his face— "Hermes is still missing. I fear what may have happened to him after leaving you on the stairs."

She still could not understand why he had left them. "If he had not helped us, we were done and dusted. I hope he's all right."

"I hope so, too. Open." She opened her mouth, and he placed a smoky glass tube in it. It was rough on her tongue and tasted like licorice. He watched it carefully.

"Why not come with me?" she muttered around the tube. "Surely you are the greatest Tinker who has ever lived. You could bring down the walls of the Benzene Yards with a wave of your hands and a puff of your breath."

"Possibly," he clacked. "Open wider. No, not tall, wide. The edges of your mouth. Good." He removed the tube and began to swirl it in a cloudy glass beaker.

It changed to a pale blue. "You flatter well. Even if that were true, I am not lying when I say I cannot leave this place." He stuck her with a sharp metal point tied to a glass bulb, and the ampule began to fill with blood.

"Ow!"

"Show me your strength. A pinprick is no great suffering."

"It is when you operate the pin. Why can't you leave?"

"How old do you think I am?"

She whistled. "At least seventy." She added, "You move about well, but your hands and neck tell the tale." The backs of his hands were a riot of wrinkles and spots, and the wattle of his neck waggled like a flag in a strong breeze when he laughed.

"Ha! A well-founded supposition but slightly on the low end."

"Seventy-five?"

"Guess again."

"Truly?"

"I am one hundred seventeen years old." He tapped a few drops of the blood onto a powder-covered plate, which he then covered with a brass bowl.

"Oh, come on." Ruby squinted at his hands. "And what does that have to do with not being able to leave?"

"No, *vraiment*. I was born on August seventeenth, in the Year of Our Lord 1601, and I tell you this because the only reason I am able to stay alive is woven into this tower." He waved vaguely around him, up into the rafters.

"How? How is it woven in?"

He smiled sadly. "Science costs, *chérie*."

"Well, that is sad and mysterious, and I appreciate your hospitality, I do, but I need to go."

"I am sorry, but I cannot let you leave unaccompanied."

"I am sorry, but I am thirteen and you are one hundred seventeen, and you could not stop me from making a cup of tea."

"Do you truly believe this?"

She sighed. Aside from Nasira, who was strong as an ox and agile as a wolf, there was something about this place and this man that *seethed* power. She did not want to get on the wrong side of that, and besides, she had grown to like the old madman and could not bear the thought of defying him. Plus, he was right. She needed to understand what she carried. It felt, in an odd way, as if he had saved her life. Not just the "being alive" part. It felt as if he had saved the part of her that helped her feel alive. She could not cross him.

She shrugged. "No. No, I think I do not believe that."

"Good." He pried her nostrils open and looked up into her nose with a magnifying glass, then began writing down his observations. "And I, for my part, am sorry that I cannot let you leave. I had hoped that Hermes would return, so that he could accompany you, but that seems less and less likely. We are at an impasse." He removed the bowl from the plate.

The powder was completely gone.

In its place was a tiny statue, red as blood and a riot of curves and curlicues. "Now this. This is interesting," he breathed.

That was when the raven squawked three times. The beautiful slate carving perched on a shelf next to the archway into the library. Its eyes looked almost alive.

Fermat put down his pen and turned to the raven statue, then back to her. "Did you hear that?"

Before she could respond, the statue squawked again, three times.

Without a never-you-mind, Fermat began unlatching and releasing the catches on her web of calipers, compasses, scales, and rulers.

"What does that mean?" Ruby asked. She tried to help him take off the metal calipers, but he kept slapping her hands away.

"It means," he said as he grabbed a jeweled compass and a ten-sided lens from the far end of the worktable, "that we have guests."

"Not the raven, the blood." Ruby said. "Why is that interesting?"

"I will tell you, but this matter is even more urgent." As he hurried out the archway and up the stairs, he threw over his shoulder, "Come on then."

Ruby went.

The old man stopped next to the large metal door that led into the room with the cage and Agrippa. He opened up a wooden cabinet set into the wall at eye level and peered into it.

"Why not use the slot?" Ruby whispered.

"That is for when I want guests to know that I am looking at them. This offers a much more complete and private view." He clicked his teeth twice and then pulled back from the cabinet. "I do not know who this is. Do you know who this is?"

The cabinet contained two disks of smoked crystal, mounted into the stone of the wall. She put her eyes to them and could see into the room as if it were midday. There were two shapes in the cage: One was groaning, and the other was not moving.

"You can focus more closely if you squint." She did, and it seemed as if she were right next to the cage. She had to reach out and catch herself at the sensation. It was impossible to mistake that the two uninvited guests were none other than Cram and Athena.

CHAPTER 35

Cargo: None.

Passengers: 1 gentleman/fop, of England, bound for Philadelphi, 1 servant, attached to previous. I did not allow passage to donkey.

Should be fair weather and smooth sailing.

—Captain's log (secret cabinet), *Thrift*, October 22, 1718

The boy was heavy.

When the trapdoor had opened, Athena had tried to spin in the air to protect her blade from whatever impact awaited below but had been foiled by the flailing and screaming of her manservant. Cram's valor and loyalty had been proven often enough on this trying catastrophe of a journey, but his first reflex was always a pure and deep fountain of cowardice. He tried to climb Athena up out of the hole like a ladder, letting loose a fierce yodeling that would put the finest Switz mountaineers to shame. Somehow the twirling, entangled mass of them had landed with her underneath. The impact had knocked her unconscious. When she awakened, her first thought was: The boy was heavy.

Truly, for someone who looked as if he had been raised on a diet of birch bark and bad advice, Cram had serious weight. "Off, Cram," she muttered. By Science, her ribs were sore.

He groaned, but that was all.

"Off." She pushed him, and he rolled into something that jangled. A cage then. She swallowed a curse. She had stumbled into a simple trap like the most unsharpened of apprentices. And all for the sake of this maddening girl.

The walls of the cage were sharp. Her gloves took the worst of it, but one angry barb pierced all the way through to skin. "Barnacles," she hissed. And then she swore never to say "barnacles" again. The scrollwork was close set and strong. There was empty blackness beyond the cage. The air was fresh as well, no mean feat in an underground cell. The Worshipful Order's extensive briefing about Philadelphi had not mentioned a place like this. Someone had crafted this stronghold with uncommon skill, grace, and secrecy. If it was not the Bluestockings or the Tinkers, that left only one suspect on this side of the Atlantic.

Her father had told her bedtime stories about Pierre de Fermat. They had never helped her sleep.

Metal screeched against stone, and a panel opened in the dark, searing light into the room. She protected her eyes. Cram groaned and pulled his tattered waistcoat over his face. The intricate cage clarified into the light, rising up high to the ceiling. Her blade was unharmed after the fall. She loosened it in its scabbard. Small comfort. Whatever sort of man kept people in decorative cages and summoned secret towers into pure stone, she would try to be ready to meet him.

Courage was exhausting. But it helped keep the fear out. She lay on the cushion and stretched back, crossing her legs. "How can I help you?" she called. "I would have my man here welcome you into our home, but we seem to be unable to reach the door."

"Why have you come here?" The voice came from everywhere and was edged, metallic, foreign.

"If you please, might we freshen up a bit? Is it close to teatime? I fear my pocket watch was crushed to bits in the fall."

"Why have you come here?" it repeated.

"I am seeking a girl called Aruba Teach. She was sent here by a friend. We are friends of hers." She hoped that was all mostly true. It was a desperate gamble to come here in the first place, especially since she had kicked Henry Collins down a stairwell into a crowd of reeves and gearbeasts. She was not proud of that moment, but Athena had a duty to the Grocers and to her father. Regret was not useful here. Nor was sympathy. Ruby seemed to be a very important piece in this high-stakes game, and she had to recapture her.

The voice returned. "Why do you seek this girl?"

She was tired of lying, and there was no tactical advantage here in antagonizing her captors. "She is important."

"To whom?"

"To a great many people."

"Why is she important?"

"I do not know." Athena said it through her teeth. There was something about Ruby that was crucial to the order, but her "superiors" on this side of the Atlantic would tell her nothing of why, and her father had been silent on the matter. It chafed at her.

"If you do not know, then why do you seek her?"

"Because those are my orders." And because she was terrified for Ruby.

Silence.

"Anyone you brought with you?"

"No. I came here by myself."

"There is a young man beside you in the cage, no?"

"He is my servant!" Cram was still motionless in the half-light from the door, but Athena could see that his breathing was changed. The clever devil was playing possum. It was only food or the promise of food that made him stupid. Otherwise, he was quite a cunning companion. She made a mental note to feed him sparingly if they ever got out of this alive. "This is ridiculous! Is Ruby Teach here or no? Is she safe or no? If she is not, I swear to you I will pull this tower down around your ears!"

"You lie. Ruby Teach is nothing to you."

"No man gives me the lie. Come out from your hiding place, coward, and let us settle this!"

"Ooooh, coward is it?" The voice laughed and then went cold. "If you tell me why you truly seek this Ruby Teach, you shall see me."

Sweat broke out on the back of her neck. The truth of it was there was no reason, no plan, no logic in the least for her actions. Ruby's disappearance had shocked everyone. The Warren had been raised in the early morning and turned upside down by Hearth, Pate, and the others. They had questioned her, and not gently, but she had been able to say truthfully that she had no idea where or how Ruby had gone.

As soon as she had pried the news out of Cram that he knew where Ruby was headed, they had collected their things and left, without even a by-your-leave to Madame

Hearth. The thought of Ruby alone, in the hands of Wisdom Rool or worse, filled her with rage and fear, and she knew only that it could not stand.

What Athena *said* was: "It is my duty to protect her."

"So you swear? Duty, and nothing more?"

"So I swear, by Spirit and by Bacon's idols."

And the door opened. And there was Ruby, standing there in the light in a smart suit of clothes with her hair pulled back in a tight queue. And Athena could breathe again.

But Ruby's eyes were cold. "I know for a fact that you are a cracking good liar, *Lord Athen*. But we have no choice but to test your truth. If your duty is to protect me, I hope you've learned a few tricks since the last time because you brought quite a few friends spice shopping with you."

CHAPTER 36

I care not for the quality of thy tools or thy currency. Find thee
a valiant heart, and thy task is done.

—Elias Fell, Philadelphi Meetinghouse

"Enough." Athena Boyle rummaged in the pockets of her coat.

"We must hurry," Fermat said, over his shoulder. The tinker's lamp he held cast his features in ghost light. This deep down the stairs there were no sconces, and Ruby thought the stones looked older or thicker, somehow, than those above.

"I agree that we must hurry, but we are traveling in the

wrong direction," Athena said, pulling the Worshipful Order of Grocers letter from her waistcoat. "The Bluestockings followed us, and they have surrounded your shop, but they are our friends in this. I see no quarrel here. In fact"—she grinned—"this strikes me as a meeting of long-lost allies." She presented the letter with a flourish.

Fermat held it up to the tinker's lamp and scanned it. Ruby wanted to snatch the thing, crumple it up, and eat it. She ransacked her mind for some sort of defense, some stratagem to trip up the unstoppable force of the letter. Her father had obeyed it. The watchmen of the Warren had respected it. If Fermat was indeed part of the Grocers, no matter how charming or wise or on her side he seemed to be, he would be forced to help Athena haul Ruby back up the stairs, out of the spice shop, and into the waiting arms of Madame Hearth. Fermat glanced up from the letter, and Ruby braced herself.

He chuckled.

"Boyle." He snorted and choked for a good long time. "You are here on behalf of *Grand Master* Godfrey

Boyle?" The way he said "grand master" sounded like the way her father called backriver bargemen "sailors." Fermat held the lamp up to Athena's face. His quicksilver eyes widened. "Oho! Even more wonderful, you *are* a Boyle. Are you not, mademoiselle?"

Athena glanced away at the wall. "I am his daughter."

Fermat truly began to laugh now, deep, hearty guffaws that shook his body and threatened to dislodge his nightcap. "You have been traveling with her?" He pointed to Ruby.

"Yes, that is correct. I am charged with her protection."

"Oh, I imagine that is the case." Fermat wiped his eyes.

"What do you mean?"

"Master Boyle and Wayland Teach have a remarkable history together, and I shall be fascinated to see how it plays out between the two of you." He waggled the lamp to and fro, lighting first Ruby's face, then Athena's.

"What kind of history?" Ruby cut in.

"Yes, as she said. What kind?" Athena added.

"It is far too long a story to interrupt our need at the moment. I will say that they were rivals over the affections of a young lady." His silver eyes darkened. "However, at this moment you have presented me with this letter, yes?"

"Yes."

"And what is your demand, so that we may be perfectly correct in our interaction?"

"My man and I"—she clapped Cram on the shoulder—"will take Ruby, and you will release us back into the street, into the company of the Bluestockings with whom I came."

"What?" It was Ruby's turn to sputter. "You said that—"

"I said that I did not think they followed me and that I did not think that I had brought them here." Athena interrupted. "All of those things are true. However, it is still my duty to return you to a place of safety, and the only safe place for you that I know on this side of the Atlantic Ocean is the Warren."

"This place is safe!" Ruby insisted.

"Not anymore." Cram chimed in.

"Well, it is still somewhat secure." Fermat chuckled. "It would take Madame Hearth and her companions a good long time to penetrate our defenses here, especially since they must operate without being detected. Still, any fortress can be breached. It was the tower's privacy that kept it safe."

Ruby launched herself at Athena, but Cram caught her and tried to wrestle her back. "Easy, Ferret."

"Let go!"

Athena looked sad, not triumphant. "I will tie you if you resist, Ruby."

"You liar! You said you would protect me!"

"And so I shall, but you may also need to be protected from yourself."

"Quiet!" Fermat barked, and they all stopped moving. "Ruby Teach, do you wish to return above with Athena Boyle?"

"No! No, I do not."

He turned to Athena. "I must respond to your letter, must I not?"

Athena hesitated, then said, "Yes, you must."

"Then here is my response." The old man blinked, wrinkled flesh flickering over silver sea. "No."

Athena was flabbergasted. "No?"

"This is not a word you often hear, I am thinking," Fermat said. "The meaning of it is quite simple. It means—"

"I know what 'no' means, old fool!" Athena sputtered. Then she threatened. "Think deeply on what you do here."

Fermat's smile vanished, and his eyes shone. He handed the lamp to Cram, who took it without thinking, and he stepped in, straightening his crooked back, his neck and head looping so he was staring almost straight down at Athena. "You are clever, talented, and a child of privilege." He clacked his teeth. "You have skill, talent, wit, beauty, and some honor, and yet in the end your actions show you as little more than a bully."

Athena was silent.

"You know who I am?"

Athena whitened and nodded. "Fermat," she whispered.

"I am Fermat, and you forget yourself," he said. He turned to Ruby, who tried to remain as still as possible. "Do you know the meaning of this name?"

Ruby shook her head.

"It means that letters like this"—he held the paper between his thumb and forefinger, as if it were a particularly disgusting insect—"no longer apply to me."

Athena rallied. "But you are part of the Worshipful Order, you still—"

Fermat interrupted, without malice. "Yes, yes, I was part of the order, but no longer." He crumpled the paper up into his palm. "You are children playing with a blacksmith's forge, and you cannot even see the raging fire you may light in the house of your betters." He opened his fingers and uttered a few strange words that skittered past Ruby's ears. The crumpled flower of paper blued and then crackled into a sculpture of ice. He whispered a few more words, and Ruby felt pulses of heat coming from his hand. The ice melted very quickly and ran in rivulets between his fingers to the stone floor of the stairwell. "Your chemystry is but one step along the way, child. It is not the end of the journey."

He wiped his hand on his robe, and he was an old man again; the little stone stairwell smelled like rain.

"Well, now, that is settled. We must hurry." He turned and strode down the steps.

As the soft light receded down the stairway, Ruby set out after it without a word or a glance back. Cram's shuffling steps soon came after, and her heart lifted. A few moments later another set of footsteps followed, and she could not say whether she was happy or sad.

They traveled far into the earth, all fixed in their own thoughts. Ruby was certain they must be deep under the level of the ground. The steps terminated in a short hallway, which abruptly ended in a wall.

Fermat turned and raised his arms like a high priest. "I have brought you to a special place."

"A special place?" Ruby asked. The dead end did not exactly hold promise, but Fermat knew his business, and Ruby was learning that the old coot had a flair for the dramatic. He had missed his calling selling snake oil to country bumpkins.

"The exit," Fermat intoned, and he stalked to the far wall with one arm raised. "Is this not obvious?"

"What is obvious is that there will be some spectacular occurrence in only moments, where we shall discover that all of our preconceptions were incorrect and we shall launch onto a new journey that we could have only imagined before." Athena barely looked up.

"Indeed, young journeywoman, one should always expect mystery." He took a small leather bag out of the folds of his robe. "It is more courageous."

Athena said, "Courage is rare, it seems to me. Expecting it leads to disappointment."

"Disappointment is a part of life, my lady. We cannot control it." He turned to Ruby. "I fear, *chérie,* that here we must part ways."

"How?" Ruby said. Dread found her again.

"The Bluestockings could tap at my front door for ten years and never force their way in, but their poking and prodding will draw attention from greater powers. I must send you away before we erect more potent wards around the tower."

"More potent wards? From whom?" Athena asked.

"To protect us from the Tinkers, dear girl. And the Reeve." He ticked them off on his fingers. "The persistent and misguided Madame Hearth and her squad of dauntless educators will draw them all here. You can be sure of that."

He looked at Ruby. "Do you trust me?"

She nodded. It was Athena's turn to snort.

Fermat continued. "I can place you close to your father. I am going to open a door, an egress away from here. It will take you to a quiet place deep inside a dockyard building of the Benzene Yards, the home of the Tinkers. Henry Collins was masquerading as a young officer, and he would come and go from his room this way. We knew that your father was close to here, Henry thought somewhere in the ship just opposite this building."

Henry Collins knew about her father?

"Once you are through, the door will close, and you will be cut off from my help. You may stay here under my protection, if you wish, but doors like this one will soon be closed off, and I think it will be some time before they are open again. Once the wards are raised around the tower, I will not be able to open the portal."

Safety or danger. Comfort or family. It did not take her long to decide.

Ruby nodded. "Whatever you need to do, do it."

Athena and Cram stood as one.

"No, thank you." Ruby shook her head. "You tried to take me again. You are loyal to your Grocers. This is not your fight."

"We are coming with you. You cannot go alone," Athena said.

"How can I know you will not betray me again?

"You can't." Fear flashed in Athena's eyes. "But we are all that you have. I have sworn to protect you. Let me prove that I am a man—I am a *woman* of my word."

It was that last, and the fear that she saw, that helped Ruby decide. "All right."

Athena nodded once and asked Fermat, "Do we know what awaits us?"

Fermat shook his head. "I know that the place was quiet and hidden. However, with Henry taken, we cannot be certain it has not been discovered."

"Very well." Athena drew her sword. "I do not think this will be a long stay, whatever we find."

Cram nodded and grabbed his butter churn. "Just in case, Ferret."

Fermat looked at the three of them. Ruby had no idea what seeing through liquid metal was like, but for a moment it felt as if he were peering into her soul. Then he nodded. "Please seek news of Henry. He is dear to me."

Ruby said, "We will."

He produced a small clear lens from the innards of the bag. He held up the lens to his eye, turned his back on them to look at the wall, and uttered tangled words that cut through the air.

Ruby's ears popped. There was a sound like a dock settling, and a heaviness passed over, as if the tower had fallen on her. It did not hurt, though, and was gone as quickly as it came. In the wall was a rippling circle of stuff taller than a man. It shimmered, like heat on top of the southern sea.

"Thank you," she whispered to Fermat, and stood up on tiptoe to kiss him on the cheek.

"Aruba Teach," he whispered back. "What they seek? It is in your blood."

She came down off her toes. Her blood? "Well then, I'll have to make sure I don't lose any of it."

Then she walked forward into the portal before her fear got the better of her.

The world turned upside down.

CHAPTER 37

CHATSBOTTOM: *I fear you are shot through with clocklock balls, my sweet lad!*
FARNSWORTH: *Aye, sir, but for my armor.*
CHATSBOTTOM: *Yet you wear no breastplate nor vambrace.*
FARNSWORTH: *What need I with breastplates when I have this good, stout ham? It is thrice cured, milord.*
   —Marion Coatesworth-Hay, *The Tinker's Dram*, Act V, sc. ii

Cram swallowed a moan as his belly plopped out of his body, danced a jig in a circle around him, and then climbed back in through his spine. Wherever they were, it was dark and smelled of the sea. He shuddered.

"Are we where he said we was going?" His whisper echoed.

"Shh!" That was Ferret, he reckoned, and a moment later a sliver of soft blue lit her face. The tinker's lamp swung around to show thin slices of their surroundings. The first thing it showed was the throbbing portal they had come through, which swirled in the air a few moments and then winked out.

A pillar.

Rough wood wall.

Then on to Lady Athena. His mistress's unguarded face held a deep, angry fear before she realized that she was lit. Fast as lightning, she slipped on her old reliable smirk. Relaxed and above it all, aloof and clever. He had first seen what lay under that mask the night that Ferret had cut out from the Warren. When the alarum bells had rung, it wasn't two shakes before she flung open the door to her room, half dressed, her true face naked for all to see. A face full of terror and confusion. As soon as she saw Cram crouched there in the hall, she had shaken it off like morning dew. But he had seen it. That wee moment, and a few others like it, were what made him want to keep his mistress safe.

He sat back on his haunches. They were in a skinny space between two walls. The faint shadows of pipe ran along the ceiling, and the distant scent of burning iron reminded him of his time back in the Tinkers' chapter house in Boston. It seemed like forever ago.

Deary, he was hungry. He felt about in his bag for a likely-looking crust of bread and tore off a piece. The ripping made a tiny sound.

"Shh!" Athena and Ruby both whispered.

Good thing he did not need to do that again. He popped the crusty bread in his mouth and kenned his mistake too late. The chewing sounded like tearing down a plaster wall with a hammer.

"Sshh!"

They were making more noise than he was, he reckoned, but he stopped chewing. What else was he to do? Swallow it whole? They certain would not want him choking and rolling on the floor and banging about with a giant hunk of loaf stuck in his gullet.

Lady Athena had joined Ferret next to the wall, and they were passing their hands over the same part of it. Probably searching for some manner of secret portal. Between the two of them he trusted one would clue it out sooner or later. Now that the bread had softened it chewed better, and his mind woke up. Food and sleep. Why did heroes fear the stuff? If there was one lesson he would teach to his younguns, when he had younguns, it was "Your pa always says, 'Get your sleep and your grub settled. Then tackle the great evil on a full belly.'"

Now that he *had* at least a measure of full belly, the thought sneaked back in through the back door of his braincase. Cram had been dancing hard with the thought, ever since they had fallen down that pit in the magic spice shop.

"She needs to tell her," it insisted.

He played coy. "Tell her what?" he said to the Thought in His Head. He did make sure to use his Head Voice, so as to not call attention. The two shadows were whispering to beat the bang in each other's ears. They were pushing and pulling on every crack, bump, and wrinkle they could find.

The Thought, curse it, tromped on his gambit. "You know what Mam always said?"

"Don't you tell me what Mam always said!" The

nerve of the thing! "You'd be nothing without me!"

"Still and all," it reasoned, "you should have told the magician. He was deep scared for Henry Collins, and he deserved to know."

"It weren't the right time, and it ain't the right time now." Cram put his foot down, and it would have made more noise than the bread, but a door in the wall did indeed squeak open right where Athena and Ruby had been poking. "Now get out of my noggin. I have work to do."

It walked off a ways, but he could feel it skulking.

Ferret fiddled with the tinker's lamp, and light crept into the room beyond. It might have been a bedroom, except it had been turned inside out and ransacked. The wardrobe was splinters and parts of uniforms were scattered all over, the sea chests had had their bottoms knocked out, and the cloth ticking of two gutted mattresses lay like snow across the top of all of it.

Ferret leaned in to the two of them. "If this is what has happened to his room, then they are on to him. I fear for him."

Lady Athena swallowed.

CHAPTER 38

Carboshaeth, White Steel, Friar's Iron: There is no substance, chemystral or otherwise, that cannot be unmade.
—Frederik of Westphalia, *Alchemycal Heresies*

The hallway beyond the room was empty, and they crept down a narrow circling staircase that deposited them in a comfy little sitting room, surrounded by trim wardrobes, each with a chair in front of it. None of the armoires had doors, and freshly pressed blue uniform jackets hung in each, below a shelf that held smart midshipman's caps, in the new style with small brims and flat tops.

Athena quickly began unbuttoning her waistcoat,

eyeing several of the wardrobes for one that might suit.

Ruby whispered, "What are you doing?"

"I am acquiring a disguise, Miss Teach," she responded as she pulled on one of the narrower coats. The stitching was exquisite, and the fit as well. She popped on a hat and struck what she hoped was a rakish pose. Cram had left most of his weight in the upstairs hall from sweating it all out, and Ruby was wound tight as a Switz timepiece. Someone had to lighten the mood.

"I see a stilted fop of a boy," Ruby said. "How is that a disguise?"

Athena ignored her. They could discuss the benefits of living as a gentleman some other time. "We are about to enter into the realm of the navy, and I will tell you this much: In a fort or ship of this size, it is nigh impossible to know everyone. For the whole apparatus to work at all, the uniform must serve as recognition. We shall be officers not too high up the tree, and we shall sail clean through to our goal." She pulled the next one off its hook. "Cram, I hereby promote you to the rank of midshipman. Your mam would be very proud, I am sure." The coat's platinum buttons flashed in the lamplight. They were flash, certainly, and using a precious metal for such a mundane purpose spoke to the importance of this ship. They were sharping their way into one of the most well-funded, expertly staffed places in the empire, and she still could not believe she was taking such a deep risk. She said nothing of that, however. Instead, she said, "Ruby, choose a coat and trousers, please. We have little time."

The girl shook her head. "No. We do this my way. We sneak in as servants. Nobody notices servants."

"When servants know their way about," Athena said. "What happens when you lose our way in yon great stack of metal? Will you ask its captain where you can find the tea and crumpets? Or the first mate the way to the officers' mess? Or the restricted floors?"

Ruby bristled. "This is a ship! I have lived my whole life on ships! Have you? Before you crossed from England, I am certain that your most terrifying sea voyage was capsizing your toy boat in the tub and then crying to your governess!"

It was funny, but Athena had long learned to keep

her smile in check with Ruby. "You may think you travel into familiar territory, captain's daughter, but the *Grail* is as much like the *Thrift* as a castle is to a crofter's hut. What we need is *weight,* what we need is *authority*, and these"—she tossed Ruby a coat—"will give that to us."

Ruby snorted, but she held on to the coat and went looking for trousers.

Cram piped in, "No boots, milady." Indeed, there were no boots to be found. Though Ruby had somehow acquired a smart new pair, after days at sea, underground, and in prison Athena and Cram's boots fell on the quality scale somewhere between downright ragged and nonexistent. Two of Cram's toes were taking the air.

"Then don't let them see your feet," she said, playing jaunty, though she did not feel it.

As Cram and Ruby pulled their uniforms on, Athena cracked the doorway and was assaulted by a wave of sound. It was bustling out there. She had to put her shoulder into a small man wrestling a huge wheel of cheese or else he would have spilled into the sitting room, so great was the press of people outside the door. The little man's eyes narrowed, and he puffed up, looking for a fight, until he saw Athena's uniform. He tugged his forelock and instead turned back into the crowd, using the cheese wheel like a big round battering ram.

Most of the press were sailors or teamsters with heavy crates and barrels, even a few small wagons, pushing, pulling, cursing, and joking. The door led onto a wide balcony that led down great ramps to the wharf below. Opposite the door, across a wide bridge, a tall portal, twenty feet high, opened in a wall of black metal. The wall soared upward, and Athena had to crane her neck to see a similar bridge onto the deck high above. The collected thunder of hundreds of voices, wheels, and beasts filled the air, trapped between the dock and the ship, so that they could not have spoken to one another if they wanted.

"Come on," she mouthed, and she plunged into the herd, holding Ruby's hand.

Halfway across the bridge Ruby's grip tightened. Athena swallowed a curse. She risked a look back and followed Ruby's eyes across the water, to a dock down the wharf, where the *Thrift* floated in the *Grail*'s shadow like a newborn duckling under its great metal mother.

Men were moving on the deck. Ruby, wild eyed, mouth agape, almost pulled Athena over back the way they had come.

Athena dug in her heels and yanked Ruby in close. "What would your father say?" she said in Ruby's ear, as loud as she dared.

The dark centers of Ruby's eyes, inches from Athena's own, narrowed. She closed her lips. She nodded.

They turned and carried on.

And indeed, the two marines at the door barely batted an eye at the three midshipmen floating on the sea of grunts crossing the wide and crowded metal walkway. They were too busy trying to pry the angry little cheese man Athena had met before off the shoulders of a big sailor who was wearing said wheel on his leg like a massive cheesy anklet.

They passed through the doors without a hitch, but all three stopped when they crossed the threshold.

"Mam, that is big," Cram muttered.

The hold of the *Grail* was a cross between a cathedral and an ancient cave, lit by big, smoky chem-torches and strewn with house-size stacks of boxes, tools, and who knew what else.

Ruby muttered, "Barnacles," and then she started walking. Athena was with her step by step. She could hear Cram behind them, struggling with his bag. She could not look back, however. Now that they were clear of the press, the three midshipmen needed to be confident and secure of their position and posts. Hesitation would mark them as out of place.

So she walked straight up to two young sailors tipping a massive barrel labeled "Salt Pork" from a wagon onto the floor.

"Men," she barked.

They came to attention. "Tell me, quickly, where they hold the prisoners. I have not been this far belowdecks, but I bear urgent news for the jailer."

If they questioned her at all, it would be over. Instead, they barely gave her a glance, straining at the taut rope. "Two decks lower, sir, through that far door and down the ladders. Turn right at the engine room."

And that was that.

The bowels of the *Grail* smelled like burned bread, and the air was sodden and hot as a burning lake, but the directions were easy enough to follow. So easy, in fact, that when they turned right at the engine room, she had no idea that the passage would open up immediately into an stark, orderly space, with a desk covered with papers, a startled marine sergeant, and a row of narrow iron cells behind.

Athena exhaled. Only one cell was occupied, and there he was: the prisoner.

Henry Collins.

CHAPTER 39

Your Majesty, I beg you. Leave the Colonies be. Wake them, and Pompeii will be as a child's tantrum.

—Wilhemina Caul, lord captain of the Reeve, 1688–1702

Ruby spoke up. "Sergeant, we require your prisoner for transport."

At the same moment, Athena said, "Sergeant, I think we have taken a wrong turn. Please point us to the engine room."

The sergeant, an older man with gray hair only on the sides of his head, had an expressive face. The emotions marched across it. Confusion. Concern. Alarm.

He was very quick, and he would have made it to the speaking tube in the corner of the room if three bodies had not slammed into him simultaneously. He banged his head hard on the bulkhead and passed out cold.

A mad idea came to Ruby. What if she could change, like Gwath? She focused all her will on the sergeant, his bushy gray hair, his bulbous nose, the scar on his neck. She closed her eyes, painted a picture of him in her mind, and she *pushed* with everything she had.

She opened her eyes.

Cram was looking at her.

"Do I look like me?" she asked.

Cram squinted.

He said, "What? Yes. What?"

"Never mind." Ruby pulled the sheet from a cot in an open cell and began tearing at it, pulling strips from it, and binding the bald man's wrists and ankles. A large ring with a few keys hung from his belt. "See if you can get Henry out of there," she shot at Cram. "Hurry!" He broke himself out of a stupor, grabbed the keys, and began trying them one by one in the cell door.

Athena just stood there, like a statue, staring at Henry. "*Move*, Athena. Help me with these!" Ruby hissed. The older girl set to it with a will, staring intently at the strips she was tearing from the thin sheets.

The cell door creaked open behind her as she started on the marine's feet, and then a few moments later Cram said. "None of these fit the irons he's wearing, Ferret!"

"Blast it." She stuffed the rags into Athena's hands. "Can you finish? Can you make a strong knot?" She nodded once, already focused on her task. Athena was cool under pressure, Ruby would give her that. Ruby scrambled over the jailer and into the cell. "Help her ladyship with the knots and his gag. Tie him to something heavy . . . the desk?" Cram nodded and passed her, his face white.

Henry Collins was sitting on the floor, back against the cot, long legs splayed in front of him. The irons held his wrists close to the floor. They were big, thick things, but simple; she could pick through them like a hot knife through lard. She flashed him a quick smile. "Why, hello, Henry Collins, fancy meeting you here."

And then she knelt down and saw his foot.

She had never seen a broken leg. Sprains, sure, but never broken. It was nothing like the dancing apprentice's foot she and Gwath had made long ago, all flat and bloody and oozing. Henry's foot and ankle were swollen, purple, twisted just so, and inarguably, exactly wrong. He was a stag in a snare: trapped but defiant. "I'm sorry we lost you along the way, Hermes Cestus," she whispered through clenched teeth, and then she picked the locks, one, two, three, four.

He raised his eyebrows when she used his real name. "As am I," he said. "But I am glad you are here now, Ruby Teach."

"I'm going to keep calling you Henry." He laughed.

"Let me help you," Ruby said. He leaned forward, but as skinny as he was she could not lift him alone.

It took Ruby, Cram, and Athena two minutes to get him around the desk and to a chair by the door before they had to take a rest. They had bumped him several times, and he was unconscious from the pain and streaming sweat. His foot smelled oversweet, like spoiled peaches.

Cram massaged his own shoulder, muttering to himself.

Ruby whispered to Athena, "Can we take him? If we are slow, we may be caught. Or we may lose my father."

Athena gazed back at her for what felt like a quarter of an hour. "We must," she said. "No matter the cost."

Henry let loose a death rattle. Which turned into a chuckle. He flopped his head around to stare at Athena. "Well, let's get on with it then."

He turned to Ruby. "I know where your father is."

Sprawled over the three of them like a rag doll, Henry Collins directed them down shoulder-width back corridors and around hidden bulkheads, all the while slipping in and out of consciousness. Ruby's gut was roiling.

"Insane," she gasped through clenched teeth. Supporting Henry was like hauling five or six bags of wet flour, any one of which might at any moment fall to the floor, breaking the bag. Or, in this case, breaking the Henry, whose fragility had already been firmly established.

"You know, if anyone, and I mean, anyone sees us . . ." Athena whispered.

"Questions, running, fighting, running, capture," Ruby grunted.

"Except with this bag of bones we won't be doing much running."

Ruby nodded. "Fine. Questions, fighting, capture. Better?"

Athena said, "Well, no, not really. Mind that doorknob."

Their charge chose that moment to wake once again, hissing breath in, and he lolled his head from side to side, taking the lay of the land. "Almost there," he whispered, "around that corner and then up to the officers' quarters." He flopped his arm over Ruby's shoulder to point the way. "Careful, this leads back to the main corridors."

Cram crept up ahead while Ruby and Athena held Henry between them.

"Why did you leave us?" Ruby asked.

Athena turned to Henry as well. His eyes rolled back and forth between them for what seemed like quite a while. "Angry," he finally breathed out. "I was angry you weren't following me. I tried to get back to my home and got caught."

Cram popped his head back around the corner and waved them forward. They shuffled on.

"Capture was not what I'd hoped for, but I still have faith," Henry said, his eyes never leaving Athena. "You have to believe everyone will get what they deserve. And I believe it. I really do."

The pain must have been giving him fits. His voice was growing far too loud. "Hsst." Ruby shushed him. "Henry, please."

He nodded and stopped talking, the smile still on his face.

As they closed on the corner, a posse of smells pulled Ruby on, odors that she hadn't smelled since Gwath's galley: fresh bread, sizzling onions, an earthy, juicy waft of roast chicken. In the narrow hallway beyond, Cram was using pieces of tablecloth to secure the hands and feet of a little, blond, and very unconscious steward. The only other things in the dim passage were a rolling cart, groaning with a feast fit for royalty, and a small sliding door with a tinker's lamp perched above it. Besides the bread, onions, and chicken, the serving dishes crowded one another, piled high with pheasant, venison, buttered beets, all manner of greens, and a great peach pie.

"There's a slice missing from the pie," Ruby said. Cram shrugged and kept to his tying. "Not that I mind. Well done, Cram." He stood up and smiled, chewing all the while, mouth covered in golden crust and gooey filling. Athena kept watch as they folded Henry into the bottom rack of the cart and rolled him into a small room beyond the sliding door.

"It is a lift," Cram explained. "They have one in the Tinkers' Guild in Boston. Before he went to sleep, the porter told me this one goes all the way up to the officers' mess. He said the captain's cabin is just a few doors down the hall."

He slid the gate closed behind them and blew into a small set of whistles hanging from a nail in the corner. After a few moments, hidden gears lurched into motion, and they began rising.

Ruby poked him in the shoulder. "Thank you, Cram,"

she said. "And thank you, Henry," she said to him.

Cram shrugged and helped himself to another piece of pie.

"One question: How did you get the tablecloth off the cart?"

He winked. "That's a serving man's secret, Ferret." His face fell.

"What is it?" she asked.

He swallowed. "I been talking this out with my inner voice, and the inner voice has a question."

"What is it, Cram?" she repeated.

"When we find your pa—"

"Yes?"

"What do we do then?"

They stared at her. Athena with her sword, Cram with his churn, Henry Collins tucked under the cart.

They were looking to her because she was the leader. She was the captain. This was her mission, her father, her story, and they were ready to do what they had to.

She opened her mouth, and nothing came out. Not one blasted thing.

They stood there for a few moments, the gears whirring in the background.

Then the lift came to a stop, and a tiny bell somewhere went *ding*.

The gate and a set of sliding doors ratcheted open, and the four of them were staring into a gorgeous, well-furnished, and most definitely occupied dining room.

CHAPTER 40

Chaos is the Tinker's undoing.
　　　　　—Oswald Portwallow, *A Young Boy's Tinkercraft Primer*

A trio of viola, gravichord, and cello played a jaunty tune.

Ruby could see the center of a long dining table, covered with fine china and crystal. The rest of the room was hidden, blocked by the doorframe. The far wall was peppered with a series of windows and alloyed glass doors, which let in the brilliant light of a bluebird winter sky. The seats Ruby could see were empty save one, whose occupant was finishing off the last bites of an appetizer, what appeared to be a very succulent plate of pigeon wings.

A wing fell from the hands of Wayland Teach and landed on his plate with a soft clink. He was thinner and unarmed, and only had eyes for Ruby. When he did not leap over the table and rush to her and instead picked the pigeon wing back up and chewed at the last bits of flesh with the faintest of shakes of his head, she knew that he was not dining alone.

Athena and Cram were watching her, waiting for her play. So was Henry, his head stuck out from under the cart. Every last shred of her wanted to scamper into the room and throw her arms around her father, but Gwath Maxim Ten demanded another course: "You Must Never Lower the Mask." Instead, she picked up a platter of pickled quail eggs and rounded the corner.

The table filled the room with only a narrow passage between the empty chairs and the walls. At its foot was the trio of musicians, an old man and two women. At its head sat a captain of the Royal Navy, clad from head to toe in a midnight blue uniform, a scabbarded dueling sword in the chair next to him, red mutton chops marching down his jaw. A red iron gearbeast crouched at his feet, mad eyes staring. Two burly men, blond on the left, bald on the right, in stewards' whites, stood at attention behind him, cudgels hanging from their belts. She fixed her eyes straight ahead in what she hoped was a proper middy's deference.

"Where's Cotton?" the captain asked.

She kept her eyes on a merman carved into the wood paneling. He was floating in a flask upheld by the lion of England. "Sir?"

"Where is Steward Cotton, Mister . . ."

"Thatch, sir. Come down with a case of the rickets, sir. We had to make do." Were the eggs slipping? She could not feel her hands.

"Very well, carry on."

"Thank you, sir."

"Captain MacDevitt, how goes the search for my girl?" her father asked.

The officer made an uncomfortable sound. "You

know I can't tell you, Teach. I will say she is a wily one. You could help us, you know. She would have my protection."

"Big Bill has repeatedly and impolitely asked for my cooperation. My response will be the same."

"Alas."

Another doorway led out into an ornate smoking lounge. A possible escape route? The table felt ten miles long, but she finally arrived next to the captain. She presented her wares. He took two.

"Thank you, Thatch. Our guest as well, please."

"Sir." The gearbeast was snuffling, and it let out a low, metallic whine as she passed behind the captain to the other side. The space between the doors and the table was equally narrow. There was a balcony beyond. She risked a glance up, and the light shone through the glass doors onto Wayland Teach. He seemed more interested in the eggs than in her.

"These are excellent, Teach! Eggs of the gods!" the captain exclaimed behind her. "Your first time at table, Thatch?"

"Yes, sir."

"You're doing well."

"Thank you, sir." She could have touched her father if she wanted. He looked tired. There were bruises on his face. He leaned forward to choose two eggs with care from the platter, revealing to Ruby that his legs were clad in thick irons. Eggs served, she didn't know what else to do, so she stood at attention behind her father, staring straight ahead. Into the lift, where Athena and Cram were stationed, slack jawed, behind the food cart.

"Thatch," the captain drawled.

She snapped to, chest tight. "Yes, sir?"

"Did Cookie have anything for us besides pickled eggs?"

"Yes, sir," Ruby said. Athena, eyes wide, began whispering to Cram, who began shaking his head as if to throw it from his neck.

"Well?"

Then the cart began to move forward. By itself.

Athena somehow fell into stride behind it and rounded the corner, as if she had been pushing it all along.

She elbowed her sword hilt around into the small of her back. Henry Collins's head popped up above the line of the table. He had rolled out of the cart before it left the lift. Cram was still staring, shaking, churn clutched in a death grip across his chest.

The captain clapped his hands. "Aha! The feast appears. Mister?"

"Bayle, Captain."

"Mister Bayle. A round of everything, please. Don't spare the pie."

"Yes, sir." The cart snagged on the thick Turkish rug.

"Your first time at table as well?"

"Yes, sir." Athena wiggled the cart, but it would not unstick.

"Teach, I sometimes envy you the size of your *Thrift*," the captain said.

"Do you, Captain?"

"Indeed. *Grail* is a majestic queen, but she is enormous. And that means I sometimes cannot offer my young officers my personal supervision or even acquaintance. Bayle?"

"Yes, sir?"

"How long have you been with us?"

"Since early summer, sir."

MacDevitt nodded. "You came on at Portsmouth?"

Athena blinked. "Yes, sir."

"Then surely you have been 'round the mast long enough to tell me why is there no covering on this cart?"

"Sir, we, Cotton—"

"Moreover, no one comes on my deck with boots in such a state. Mister Bayle, you are relieved."

"Sir—"

MacDevitt gave a grim smile. "None of that. Shine those togs, and we'll have you back up here in no time. It's not as if this is your only chance. Gregor, call down to Big Bill. He can finish the service."

The blond one reached behind him for a speaking tube.

They were done. He would call down for Big Bill, whoever Big Bill was, and Midshipman "Bayle" would not know his way out the door, or they would discover Henry and Cram in the lift, or Steward Cotton down below, or even that sergeant in the brig, and then in no time at all they would all be fitted for leg irons she imagined were very similar to her father's. All the running, the hiding, the struggle, all burned up in a moment.

Except Athena Boyle had drawn her sword.

Except Athena Boyle had leaped onto the table and was sprinting full tilt down its length, extending her blade in a perfect lunge over the captain's shoulder, and pinning blond Gregor's meaty hand to the intricately carved paneling, just shy of the speaking tube.

Gregor howled. Athena's blade flicked down to hamstring him for good measure, but then she pulled back lightning quick to parry a series of swift strikes from the captain's blade. Gregor reached for her but tripped and knocked his head hard on the table.

Ruby ducked down next to the chair and slipped the locks on her father's irons. He leaped up, brandishing the chain, and caught the bald steward's club just in time to stop it from slamming into Ruby's skull. The steward lashed out with his other elbow and caught Teach a wicked blow across the face. He kicked out at

Ruby, and she threw herself down.

The red iron gearbeast was there, its claws tearing up strips of rug. She pushed herself backward on her elbows, but the beast was gaining, and then a shape smashed into it. The snapping, cursing mass rolled over and over until Cram flew out of it, slamming onto his back. The thing lay atop him on its back, his churn wedged between its jaws. It writhed like a snake, trying to twist and get its claws into him.

The venison platter lay on the floor in the ruin of the feast. She grabbed it and hurled herself, platter first, onto the flailing mass, trying to block the claws. The beast scrabbled its legs as if it were swimming, and the silver shredded like paper. Blood blossomed on her jacket.

The musicians were falling over one another on their way to a door at the foot of the table, and Ruby would have been pleased to sally off with them but instead barely dodged another deadly claw and somersaulted back from under the table.

She banged into the balcony door just in time as a blade whistled in front of her eyes. Both Athena and the captain were on the table now, spinning a web of steel. The captain was stronger, but Athena was faster. He rained down an overhand slash at her, and she barely managed a wincing parry, but before he could capitalize, she dealt out a stop thrust. She was on him in an instant, face unreadable, dealing cuts and thrusts that drove him back down the table, both of them mincing and dancing between the china plates and candelabra.

Henry Collins had somehow pushed his cart over so he could guard the other steward, knocked senseless by the table.

Her father had gotten behind the bald one and had the chain across his chest. The man had his hands up underneath the links, and Wayland Teach's thick arms quivered as the shackles inched away from the steward's throat.

The *Grail*'s captain parried a slash wide and then roared and drove his shoulder into Athena's chest. She stumbled back across the table, struggling to keep her balance, free hand stretched out behind her. Muttonchops quivering, her opponent drove on, extending into his own lunge, straight at Athena's heart. But she contorted underneath the thrust, and her hand shot up, flourishing a loop of white. It was a napkin, and the captain's blade shot through the hole in the center. Quick as a mongoose, the napkin snapped, she twisted her wrist *just so*, and the sword flew out of the captain's hands, jangling hilt first into the gravichord.

Athena placed her point on the captain's chest.

"I do miss my cloak," she said, to no one in particular.

Silence followed, with only the snapping and grunting between the gearbeast and Cram punctuating the quiet.

"Orthros, heel," the captain said, and the thing instantly stopped struggling. Cram did not let go.

Ruby turned to her father. "You were dining with the enemy?"

His face split into a grin. "You'd rather I starve? He's an honorable man and keeps a fine table."

Ruby wanted to run to him and bury herself in his arms, but considering the chain he still had wrapped around the dangerous burly man, she made do with a peck on his cheek.

"You came for me," he whispered, and all she could do was nod.

Athena dabbed the sweat from her forehead with the napkin in her free hand. "Your orders, milady?"

It took Ruby a moment to realize Athena was speaking to her.

"Is dessert out of the question?" said a familiar voice.

It was Wisdom Rool, striding in from the door to the smoking lounge.

As if by instinct, Ruby and her band disengaged, backing through the glass door onto the balcony's far corner, while the dining room flooded with sailors, marines, and reeves. There must have been twenty of them, and Captain MacDevitt ordered them to all corners of the room. The fall from the balcony to the deck below was at least as high as the crow's nest on the *Thrift*. They were trapped. All the while Rool stood just inside the doorway, taking a long pull from a cobalt tankard and staring right at her until everyone was still. He handed the mug to a marine as he passed and poked his head out the balcony door.

"Permission to come aboard?" He was waving a lacy white napkin, a tiny parley flag in his great fist.

All the rest, even her father, were looking at her. She nodded.

"Thank you." Rool dabbed at the flecks of foam on his mouth. "I have been turning Philadelphi upside down searching for you, you know." He rolled his shoulders.

"Stay back." Athena pointed her blade at him. "You shall find me more prepared than when last we met, sir."

Rool's eyebrows crawled up his forehead, "Of that I have no doubt. Sir." And he sketched the faintest of bows. "However, I must tell you that your outlook is bleak. The lift is now locked, the door only leads to a legion of foes, and that assumes you pass through me and my companions, which I think unlikely at best. Surely a student of the masters can recognize a hopeless position. You have no choice here. Put down your weapons and live, or hold on to them and die."

The words cut into Ruby. "A moment? To come to an agreement?"

"Of course." He smiled. "You have made a brave

showing here, and I am not so dishonorable that I would not allow you your good-byes." He backed across the threshold into the dining room.

They were a pitiful huddle. Athena bled from several nicks on her arms and legs. Ruby's father's nose was a broken mess, and he wouldn't stop blinking. Cram pressed a second napkin to his thigh, over an already crimson one. Henry sat against Cram's churn. It might have been the only thing holding him up.

Their eyes shone.

"We fight our way out," Athena gasped. "A tight pack to reach the door, and then Ruby slips through."

"He's lyin' about the lift, I know it!" said Cram. "Duck under the table, and—"

"Air shafts. Too small for us, but Ruby—" Henry muttered.

"Lord Athen has it right." Her father tried to focus on her. "A quick strike to distract them, you sidle past, the *Thrift* is not far—"

Or could she risk trying to change? Make the biggest wager of her life? That this great danger might finally let her take the shape of some sailor in the press of battle? And then simply walk away to safety?

But what about her friends? Each one of them had just pledged their lives to spring her out of this impossible trap.

Give their lives so she could run.

That would not happen again.

"I would never have made it here without you," Ruby said to them. "And we never would have found my father." She hugged Wayland Teach tight. What would his face look like when he found her mother's journal and its button key in his pocket? "Thank you." She caught Athena's eye. "As a crew you're not half bad."

Then she took two quick steps and jumped onto the railing, holding herself steady on the canopy above.

The fall looked suitably deadly. Her heart hammered in her chest. She teetered, dizzy from lost blood.

"Don't move," she said to her companions.

Rool was back in the doorway. "Jumping off that railing?"

She licked her lips. "Maybe."

"I thought you had more sand than that, girl. And more sense. Splattering spectacularly to the deck will not save your friends."

"I believe it may."

He cocked his head. "How so?"

"Wisdom Rool, you have, since this began, been seeking me, is that not the case?"

He nodded, once.

"And you have been chasing me all this time because of something I *am*, yes? Or something I know?"

He nodded again, slower this time.

Was her left boot slipping? Just a bit? "Well, you are very fast and intolerably strong, but I do not think even you are fast enough to grab me before I fall to my death, changing forever whatever thing that I am and removing all possibility of discovering whatever it is that I know."

"Ruby!" her father cried.

Athena called, "Ruby, you cannot think that—

"Quiet, please!" she said. And to Rool: "Am I correct?"

He lifted an eyebrow. "You might be surprised."

She shuddered. "Fair enough, but are you willing to risk that happening, even if there is only a small chance that you will fail?"

Rool measured the distance between them. "What do you propose?"

"If you let these go free, I swear to you that I will be your prisoner and that I will help you with what you seek."

There was a chorus of No's, and We Cannots, but she could not look at them. Her eyes were locked with Rool's, unreadable in his scar-crossed face.

"What if I lie?" he asked.

This was the tricky part, the heart of the wager. "You are the lord commander of the king's Reeve. You are a fearless, tireless, conscienceless monster. But I think you are an honorable one."

He nodded, a third time. "Done."

CHAPTER 41

$$\mathcal{A}(u) = \int_{\Omega} \left(1 + |\nabla u|^2\right)^{1/2} \, \mathrm{d}x_1 \ldots \mathrm{d}x_n,$$

—Marise Fermat, *Journal*

The *Grail* grew ever smaller as they sailed down the Delaware River. The carpenters had improvised a chair for Henry out of a barrel, and he propped his newly splinted leg up on a pile of rope with a stifled moan.

"Cheese, Henry Collins?" Cram asked him. "The *Grail*'s captain keeps himself a fine Cornish gervie."

"Thank you, Cram," he said.

Henry chewed on the cheese, considered his options,

and settled on "grim." Fermat's tower was under siege. His naval prospects were dashed, as were all his careful plans. The aft deck of the *Thrift* was full of pirates, rogues, and scoundrels. Grim indeed. Yet oddly, he felt safer than he had in a very long time.

At what cost?

Two tiny figures stood on the balcony where the reaper had missed their little band by a hair's breadth. One was the lord commander of the king's Reeve, and one was a good friend newly lost. Ruby Teach had saved him twice. Captain Teach had said to Ruby, "We will come for you," and Henry would do all he could to reunite Ruby with this family. He owed her.

And he owed Athena Boyle.

"Cheese, Lady Athena?" Cram asked.

"No, thank you, Cram," Athena said. Wayland Teach raised an eyebrow at the title.

She would not pretend anymore with the crew. They were Ruby's people, and Athena owed them honesty. She hoped, given the muttering and scowls that had followed her about the *Thrift*, that they would hold her friendship with Ruby in some regard, even if they did not think much of her.

For where else was she to go? The Bluestockings would not welcome her, and news of her failure, her betrayal would soon reach her father. Now that she had lost Ruby, it was her duty to try to get her back. She had to make it right, no matter the cost to the Grocers, to her family, or to her.

The smaller of the two figures on the balcony held her arm up in farewell. Athena bowed and brushed the wet from her cheeks before she straightened. Wayland Teach lifted his hand to his daughter. "You are all welcome on this ship," the captain said. "But if you stay, know that our only goal will be to bring her back."

Cram and Athena nodded. Henry Collins said, "Of course."

Cram patted Henry on the shoulder and took another bite of gervie. The cheese was brilliant, but it didn't cut his hunger. It didn't feel right, sailing away from Ferret.

That girl was part hickory, part iron, part devil, and part wildcat, but that Rool fella meant her no good, no matter his promises.

The faces around him seemed to agree. Lady Athena, the captain, Henry Collins, the crew, they were all as grim as a whiskeyless wake. He sighed. He knew what that meant: more running, more trekking, more fighting, and maybe even more dying. The cheese finished, he turned his thoughts to finding a bigger bag.

CHAPTER 42

If a gentleman Forges blindly ahead, he will most likely Pierce Himself.

—Ezekiel Pelham, *Arts Martial and Practice*

She stood at the railing and watched the figures on the deck of the *Thrift* as they sailed out of sight on the Delaware. Athena, Cram, Henry, her father, and all the crew: They were safe aboard and free once again, and every one of them on deck staring back at her. Rool had given her only a moment with her father and none with the others. Wayland Teach had whispered in her ear, in a voice that was nothing like a false pirate's, "We will come for you," and then the marines had carted the lot of them out of sight.

She held her arm aloft. Her father waved, once, the jaunty feathers of his captain's hat once again on his head. A slight figure next to him bent deep in a graceful bow.

Wisdom Rool stood next to her. "You did the right thing, Ruby Teach. Your friends would have died if you had not chosen to stay with us."

"Save me your praise, Reeve." She did not turn her gaze away from the *Thrift*.

He was right, though. They all would have died. And more, there were too many things she needed to know. What had happened to Gwath. The truth about her mother. The truth about herself. And none of those answers was on the *Thrift*. She would no longer run, and she would no longer ask others to save her.

Rool stared at the receding ship as well, his thoughts his own.

They watched until it disappeared into the early-morning light on the river. It was a clear morning, and she wondered if the horizon reached all the way to the sea. When she was certain the ship was no longer there, she tugged her brand-new black Reeve tunic once and asked, "Why did you seek me then? Why did you chase me across the sea and under the earth?"

Wisdom Rool leaned over and whispered in her ear. "Why because, Ruby Teach, there is a war coming. And we need you to win it."